Connor Clover
and The Lost Children

Helen Oghenegweke

First published in Great Britain in 2003
2nd Edition 2004

H and T Books
PO Box 3096
Norwich
NR1 4WW

ISBN 0-9545824-0-3

Typeset by Spire Origination, Norwich

Printed and bound in Great Britain by Page Bros (Norwich) Ltd

For my husband, Tim,
for sharing my dream.

Believe in the power of dreams
for they do come true.

Acknowledgements

I would like to thank Ben Butler for his enthusiasm and help, to Delia Robinson for her expert advice and most of all to my husband, Tim, for being my rock of support. I would also like to thank our three children, Olivia, Thomas and Jessica who have been the root of my inspiration.

CHAPTER ONE

A Frightening Encounter

It was a cold November morning in the small town of Wislington. Everything was peaceful except for a deep voice bellowing up the stairs of number 46 Willow Way.

'Hey, worm bag! Come down here now!'

Connor Clover woke up startled. With wide eyes like an owl he stared up at the dark ceiling. Before he could think, stretch or yawn, the voice thundered again.

'Are you deaf or something?' it hollered impatiently.

Connor sat up. His head was spinning. It took several seconds to gather his bearings. He'd just had the strangest dream.

'I'm coming!' Connor called sleepily.

He twisted awkwardly as he struggled out of bed. He put on his slippers and tied his dressing gown around his waist. Connor understood from an early age that it wasn't a good idea to keep his uncle waiting. Not unless he wanted to see him stamp his foot like a buffalo and scream down his ear.

Blind as a bat without his glasses he tripped over his dirty washing. He pulled out his glasses from the pocket of his dressing gown, where he'd left them the night before and placed them firmly on his nose. The alarm clock beside his bed told him it was only five-thirty in the morning. Connor groaned loudly and quickly left his room.

'It's the middle of the night,' he grumbled, trying to rub his headache away.

Downstairs in the hallway he caught a shadowy glimpse of himself in the mirror. It was a mystery how his blond hair defied gravity and proudly stuck up like a tuft of grass. His latest attempt at pinning it down all night, by wrapping it tightly in a damp bandage, had failed miserably. The harder he tried to flatten his hair the more it insisted on sticking up.

He entered the living room in a daze. Through a thick cloud of cigarette smoke he saw the television flashing. Connor cautiously approached the sofa, where Uncle Dorcus was sitting next to Aunt Fagan. They had been stuck in the same chair for two whole weeks.

It had all happened after a serious food fight had broken out between them. Being his usual brutish self, Uncle Dorcus had squashed a cream bun on the end of Aunt Fagan's lumpy nose. She, being just as savage had picked up a treacle pancake and thrown it over her brother covering his entire face. Losing his balance he had grasped hold of her and pulled her down on to the sofa with him. The sofa had given a loud rumble, accompanied by a splintering noise, before collapsing under their weight. Now the sofa resembled an exhausted animal, its wooden legs currently pointing horizontally along the floor.

'They don't make furniture like they used to,' Dorcus had commented, peeling the treacle pancake off his face and eating it. When he had finished, he had pulled the flattened bun off Aunt Fagan's nose and eaten that as well. She didn't mind; she had been otherwise occupied with her hand deep inside a box of popcorn, munching away like a potbelly pig with cream and jam smeared around her chin and whiskers.

The room hadn't seen daylight for a good two years, due to the preferences of Dorcus, who had taken quite a fancy to dark, dim atmospheres. This gave the room no chance to air and rid itself of the lingering stench. Aunt Fagan, who was snoring loudly with her head rolled to one side, didn't seem to mind the smell either.

Connor didn't like being in the living room for two very good reasons. The potent cigarette fumes made him feel he was slowly suffocating and the foul smell radiating from his relatives was absolutely disgusting.

His uncle yelled again before Connor had a chance to tell them he was already there.

'You good for nothing, green, warped toad. Get down here now!'

'I'm here, uncle,' Connor replied, covering his ears just in time.

'Come round here so we can see you. Just as I thought. Nothing but a waste of space,' his uncle scoffed. 'Well you took your time, didn't you, you little flea bag. Look at that clock. I want you to look at it closely and tell me what the time is!' Bloodshot eyes watched him intensely.

'Nine-thirty,' Connor replied quietly, looking down at the floor to avoid his uncle's fierce gaze. 'It must've stopped last night. It's only five-thirty in the morning.'

Connor's heart missed a beat when Aunt Fagan turned her head sharply. She narrowed her beady eyes into an evil glare, eyeing him suspiciously. She'd been awake the entire time.

'You liar! That clock is right! Explain to us why you haven't prepared our breakfasts yet, you sluggish little worm. You lazy brat! You need to be taught a lesson. If only I could get out of here I'd soon sort you out!' she spat coarsely.

She wriggled her legs desperately, huffing and puffing, but no matter how hard she tried she remained steadfast to the sofa. The only thing she achieved was a slight sweat on her forehead.

*'The clock really **has** stopped!'* Connor wanted to scream, but knowing it would only make matters worse he remained quiet. They weren't interested in the truth. They never were.

Tears stung Connor's eyes as his uncle pointed his dumpy finger at him.

'Did I ask you to tell me lies? Did I ask you to talk back? No I didn't. So shut up you little pip squeak!' Uncle Dorcus thumped the arm of the sofa so hard it disturbed the dust. Seconds later he was suffering a coughing fit and wheezing breathlessly.

'Now see what you've done to your uncle!' Aunt Fagan screeched. 'Get out of here and bring us our breakfasts!'

Closing the door behind him, Connor went straight to the kitchen. He opened the window and took a deep breath of fresh air. The only other lights to be seen were the street lamps down the road. All the neighbours in their safe little houses were still sleeping, like he should be.

The kitchen was chilly and dark. Connor switched on the light and shuffled sleepily to the cupboards. A small spider scuttled across the ceiling, retreating to a safe corner.

The upright freezer was overflowing with food and getting anything out was quite a challenge, especially since the shelves had been discarded to create more space. As soon as the door opened an accumulation of food and ice fell on to the floor.

'Fiddlesticks!' Connor cursed.

'What are you doing in there you useless toenail?' screeched the unmistakable voice of Fagan.

Connor gritted his teeth and refused to answer, knowing that if he did, he'd probably scream for hours. Unfortunately, to make matters worse, there was no more ice cream.

'Are you thick or something! You'll have to go and buy some from the shops then. Right now,' his aunt ordered, snapping her crocodile jaws.

'What? Now? It's too early!' Connor wished he hadn't spoken.

His uncle raged at him for several minutes, giving him a lesson in respecting his elders – in this particular household it was a lesson not valued by Connor.

He dressed quickly and added an extra sweatshirt. He put on his coat, scarf and woollen gloves and hurried out of the house. Shivering, he closed the door behind him and began the one mile trudge to a twenty-four hour garage. The biting cold immediately stole the warmth from his cheeks. The darkness terrified him.

Connor wanted to walk hastily along the pavement but he was too tired. He hated his life. Why couldn't things be more normal?

Despite his circumstances, Connor found himself laughing. Living with his aunt and uncle was like living with pigs and having a surname like Piggot made it seem even funnier. His aunt and uncle's diet consisted solely of sweet, sugary food and bags of crisps. They ate it in the morning, they devoured it for dinner, they scoffed it for tea and they snacked on it in the middle of the night.

But it wasn't what they ate that made them terrible people, it was how they treated him.

'He's a nuisance. You can understand why they abandoned him,' his uncle often snarled, his fat lip curling. 'He's too much bother. Too much hassle to look after. Kids are awful creatures but he's the worst. Why ever didn't they get rid of him when he was born?'

'I'll never know,' his aunt would reply just loud enough for Connor to hear.

Over the years their words never lost their impact. They stabbed deep into the core of Connor's body, twisting deeper and deeper. If only his parents hadn't abandoned him, his life would be so different now. His aunt and uncle never spoke about them, unless it was to criticise them for having a child.

A few days ago Connor had come across an old newspaper cutting, with a picture of a young couple and child. He'd found it by accident in an old suitcase at the bottom of his aunt and uncle's wardrobe when he'd been searching for his birth certificate. It was such a lovely picture it drew Connor like a moth to a burning flame.

The man in the suit had dark eyes and black spiky hair. The woman was slightly shorter than the man. Her blonde wavy hair came down to her narrow waist. Connor thought she was beautiful. The young chubby child, holding the woman's hair with clenched fists, was held between the two of them.

The headline read: *Couple Missing Presumed Dead*

The article continued:

> *Yesterday, a young couple disappeared in an aeroplane accident near the Bantree Mountains in Mexico. Rescuers have been searching in vain. So far, only the wreckage of the aeroplane has been discovered. Ryan Clover age 45 and his wife Christy Clover age 45 are feared dead. Their only child Connor Clover age 2 is currently being reunited with his mother's brother, Dorcus Piggot.*

In excitement, Connor had tipped the entire contents of the suitcase on the floor. But apart from a few blurry photographs and a pile of dust there was nothing else of interest – until he came across his birth certificate. Never knowing his true date of birth it came as quite a shock to realise his birthday was next Tuesday. Altogether, his search had proven extremely productive.

Connor was bursting with questions. When he had tried to ask about his parents:

'Why do you want to know?' Dorcus had shouted. 'They never wanted you. Can't you understand that, you little wart!'

Connor didn't bother him again.

Why his uncle still maintained he had been abandoned, Connor would never know. He put it down to basic cruelty. For now the newspaper article remained in his jeans pocket for safekeeping.

But Connor soon discovered the newspaper clipping wasn't all it appeared to be. For a start there was no such place in Mexico called the Bantree Mountains. He'd searched the atlas with a fine-tooth comb but no matter how hard he looked the place didn't exist. The library hadn't been much help either. Even the Internet didn't provide any clues. It was a complete mystery and Connor was back to square one.

It had now become a ritual to view the picture of his parents each night in bed. He was thrilled knowing he looked like his parents and bore no physical resemblance to his aunt and uncle. His mop of blond hair and blue eyes were certainly inherited from his mother whereas his oblong facial shape, large ears and nose were more like his father.

With his hands thrust deep in his pockets, Connor recollected his dream of last night. He'd dreamt of someone crying. Slowly, like a fog lifting, a woman came into view, holding a toddler. It was his mum. Connor viewed the dream as if it was a play and he was the only one in the audience.

'I can't bear this!' his mum cried. 'I can't bear to leave him. It's not right for him to grow up thinking we are dead. It's not right. He needs us!'

'It won't be forever,' his father said. 'He needs to be protected. He's the saviour for our people. We must give him a home where no one will think of looking for him. Definastine must be defeated. If we succeed then Connor will never have to face his destiny. He needs us to let him go, so he can have a chance to live.'

Connor observed his dad kissing the toddler on the forehead.

Then his mum held the little boy tighter, tears rolling down her cheeks. The toddler looked anxious and frightened. He didn't understand what was happening.

'Don't forget us,' she whispered, handing the toddler over to someone else. 'We love you.'

Then Connor saw her falling to her knees and screaming out his name. 'I love you Connor!'

'Mummy! Daddy!' The toddler held out his arms. 'I want my mummy!'

But his mum was held back by his dad as the little boy was taken away from her.

Connor yearned to believe the dream was real. He knew the toddler was meant to be him when he was little. But the newspaper article was proof it couldn't possibly be real. His parents were dead and Connor tried to think of it no more.

It wasn't long before he arrived at the garage. He filed his memories to one side and walked towards the lighted building occupied by an elderly man. Connor frowned. The man appeared to be talking to someone and making wild gestures with his hand but there was no one else in the shop.

'He's mad,' thought Connor.

A crispy frost had settled on the forecourt. Connor's footsteps crunched gently as he made a path towards the window where the old man quickly sat down and lifted a newspaper.

'Excuse me,' said Connor politely. When the old man didn't reply, he spoke again but louder: 'Excuse me.'

The old man lowered the newspaper and peered down his large nose towards Connor. Then he took off his extra large wire-framed glasses and wiped them on his sleeve.

'What can I do for you, young man?'

'I'd like a tub of ice cream, please.'

'Ice-cream?' quizzed the old man, stroking his long goatee

beard. 'At this time in the morning? You should be in bed. I hope your parents know where you are.'

'It's not for me. It's for my aunt and uncle,' Connor explained, wrapping his arms about his body.

'So they sent you out here at this time in the morning?' He shook his head and frowned. 'Some uncle and aunt you've got. And I thought I'd seen everything today.' He shoved the newspaper under the gap in the window. 'Read this. You'll be surprised what's been happening in the world.'

The old man stood up and went into the shop to get the frozen dessert. Full of curiosity Connor read the headline of the newspaper: *The Lost Children*. He read the whole article before realising it wasn't one of the usual newspapers. It was called UFO Times. The article covered the disappearance of children in the world.

The Dark Master, Definastine, has strengthened his forces. Only last month the planet Darl was destroyed unmercifully by his army and a significant relic was stolen. The consulting mirror is a very powerful tool. It can see all things past and present. By using the consulting mirror, the inhabitants of Darl were responsible for the sudden breakthrough in the whereabouts of the missing children. It seems this is what prompted Definastine to attack the defenceless planet.

Children have been vanishing for centuries from the planet Earth. On the night of a full moon more children vanish from their beds.

It has been firmly believed that the full moon holds powers beyond our comprehension and does in fact serve another purpose. It has recently become known that it holds the key to opening a dimensional gateway from Dramian into our own world and vice versa. If this is true, are any of us safe?

Many great law abiding star-spirits from other worlds have been visiting our people for thousands of years. Unfortunately this includes Definastine, the greatest destroyer of all time.

Connor stood gazing in wonder, looking mildly amused by the article.

When the old man returned, he continued talking. 'Those kids have been disappearing for years. No one knows why or where, until now!'

'You can't be serious,' laughed Connor. 'Aliens don't exist, everyone knows that.'

'Don't they?' the man grinned, revealing brown stained teeth. 'Don't be so sure. You've just seen a newspaper only meant for members of the AAA council.'

'What's that supposed to mean? Car breakdown recovery or something?' Connor stiffened when he thought he heard another sound from behind the counter. The old man started coughing and making all sorts of strange noises.

'Are you all right?' asked Connor.

'Oh, I'm fine.' The man gave a final cough. 'It stands for Alien Agents Alliance, actually.'

'Whatever,' Connor smiled. He paid the man for the ice cream. 'If you're trying to freak me out it hasn't worked. I know aliens don't exist.'

'You try telling that to the UFO fanatics,' he snorted with laughter. 'Whatever you do, don't hang around this morning. I wouldn't want you to go missing like those other kids.'

'Don't worry about me, I can look after myself.'

'Just be careful!' the man shouted as Connor trudged across the garage forecourt. 'Don't talk to strangers. Plenty of them about nowadays!'

Connor turned and waved, leaving the safety of the forecourt for the dark depths of the night.

Once Connor was out of sight a man and a dog crawled out from their hiding place beneath the counter in the shop. The man had scruffy brown hair and wore a chestnut coloured coat.

'Well, you heard what he said, Tookar,' chuckled the old man. 'You don't exist. Are you sure this is the kid the Starstone wants as a host?'

'Definitely,' Tookar replied. 'I must go after him.'

'Not now. You'll frighten him to death!' the old man declared.

'What! I think you did that all by yourself,' Tookar replied. 'Look at your teeth. What on earth did you colour them with? And telling him there are plenty of strangers about, not to mention the subject of the children going missing.'

'Forget what I said. At the end of the day he doesn't know you from Adam.'

'But I know him. Now, are you going to unlock the door or do we have to do it the hard way?'

'Don't go. He's jumpy enough.' The old man folded his arms stubbornly. 'Besides I'm not going to help you.'

The man in the oversized coat looked down at the dog. 'Now, that doesn't sound very helpful, does it, K? Well, you heard what he said. If he doesn't want to help us, perhaps some gentle persuasion will help him change his mind.'

'Now, now gentlemen,' said the old man flustering. 'I'm sure we can talk about this amicably.'

'Perhaps a gentle nip on his bottom will do the trick,' Tookar carried on.

The dog growled softly before lying down, with its head resting between its paws.

'What are you doing? I said go and bite his bottom!'

The dog tilted its head to one side and eyed Tookar impatiently. Moving its jaws in a strange motion the dog started speaking. 'Don't think for one minute I'm going to lower myself to act out a basic canine characteristic. I'm not budging!'

'Crazy dog!' Tookar muttered, rolling his eyes impatiently.

The old man flung his arms in the air. 'Oh, I'll open the door. Anything to get you two out of here. But promise me you won't scare that kid. Think before you act, please!'

Tookar raised his hand to his forehead in a salute, 'I promise.'

The darkness encompassed Connor and he shivered more with fear than from the cold. Several street lamps either flickered or weren't working and Connor cursed the council for not fixing them. A few cars with blazing headlights passed, creating monstrous shadows all around him. The trees stirred restlessly. Why did it seem to take longer getting back? Connor shrugged uneasily and decided it was probably due to his limbs freezing. He imagined the headlines in tomorrow's newspaper: *Boy Freezes Walking Home.* Connor shuddered at the thought.

Connor had never been particularly fond of the snow, especially when his aunt and uncle threw him out in the blizzard and refused to let him back in. If he closed his eyes he could still picture their faces jeering at him from the window. In those terrible times, Connor would sneak off to visit Mrs Rosebud, an elderly lady who lived two doors away with her pet dog Mrs Damson.

Connor gave a shiver. The frosted air had managed to burn through his clothes, draining his skin of any remaining warmth. Icy vines entwined his limbs, spreading up from his scrunched toes to his shivering shoulders. Right now, Connor disliked the cold as much as the dark.

The article he'd read at the garage was playing heavily on his mind. With the slightest noise he found himself jumping and turning fast. Every time there's a full moon, more children go missing. How could that be? Where have they gone? Connor glanced up and breathed a sigh of relief. The curved banana moon was far from full.

He clumsily increased his pace, as if his feet were made from two blocks of ice. In a desperate attempt to keep warm, he buried his face in his scarf. The warmth from his breath tickled his senses with pleasant sensations. Sounding like a train chugging along, Connor breathed deeper to make it warmer. At least his chin and mouth would be warm, if nothing else.

He was just congratulating himself on reaching his road when a deep voice spoke from the darkness.

'I've got something for you,' said the stranger.

Connor spun around. For a terrible moment he remained glued to the spot. A man wearing an oversized coat was standing behind him and fiddling with something in his pocket.

'Ah – here it is!' rejoiced the stranger.

Feeling vulnerable, Connor's breath quickened. He was frightened someone had followed him and he knew nothing about it. Where had the man come from? Beneath the seamless blanket of cloud overhead, the surrounding gloom continued to shroud the man's face.

A dog was standing beside the stranger waggling its tail.

'He won't bite,' said the man. 'He's a big softy really. He's a Rhodesian Ridgeback. Meant to be a guard dog but well – he's harmless.'

The camel coloured dog shifted forward, sniffing Connor, before rolling over to reveal his belly.

Connor backed away. He loved animals but he wasn't stupid enough to start playing with one. The dog jumped up and Connor flung his hands up to prevent the dog from knocking him over.

'Hey – get down!' scolded the man. 'Sorry Connor – he's just excited.'

Connor shook his head, moving further away, trying to create distance between himself and the man. His voice was quivering when he asked, 'How do you know my name?'

'Don't look so worried. I'm a friend,' he replied. 'I know your parents.'

Blood drained from Connor's face. There was no way this man could know them. His parents were dead.

Connor turned and fled. He feared for his life.

'Wait!'

But Connor didn't wait. Panic made him run so fast that he didn't pause until he reached his house. Breathing like a squeaky toy, he stumbled up his garden path and fumbled for his key. Connor decided no matter how much his uncle shouted he'd never go out in the darkness again. He was almost safe. The key went in the lock. He was about to turn it when a large hand grasped his shoulder and spun him round. Connor immediately felt another hand across his mouth.

'Shh!' the man commanded. 'I'm not going to hurt you. I've a letter for you.'

Connor continued to struggle with every ounce of effort he possessed but the man was far too strong. He tried to call for help but the large hand dampened his cries. His legs trembled in fear. And to make matters worse a horrible smell like rotten mushrooms came from the man's hand.

'If I let you go, promise not to scream. Here's the letter.' The man eventually released him and Connor screamed louder than he'd ever done in his life.

To his astonishment, the man suddenly vanished and the dog took flight down the road. Connor fell backwards in shock. His head struck the wall and darkness swiftly passed over him.

'He's waking.' A doctor was leaning over Connor with a peg on the end of his long thin nose.

Connor slowly opened his tired eyes and for a brief moment wondered where he was. He couldn't see properly. His vision was blurred. But he made out a familiar array of shadows and knew without a doubt he was in his bedroom.

'Here you are,' said a young woman, handing him his glasses.

'What happened? What are you doing here?' he asked the doctor.

'You knocked yourself out, Connor. How are you feeling?' the doctor replied.

'Horrible. My head is throbbing badly. How long have I been here?' Connor also felt sick but he didn't want to mention that. He tried to remember what had happened but little pockets of cloud robbed him of his memory.

'You've been in bed for the best part of the day. It's two-thirty in the afternoon. You knocked your head pretty bad,' the doctor told him. 'But the swelling will go down soon. Apart from that you'll live.'

'What were you doing outside at that ungodly hour?' queried the woman. Her long auburn hair fell softly forward past her shoulders and freckles covered the bridge of her nose.

'All I remember is going to the garage to buy a tub of ice cream,' Connor explained

'It was lucky for you your neighbour, Mrs Rosebud, came to your rescue. She was the one who called us. Please, excuse us for a moment.' The young woman pulled the doctor aside for a private word but Connor could hear her clearly.

'I knew it,' the woman hissed into the doctor's ear. 'He's suffering from exhaustion. Those two brutes downstairs have been abusing him. What has this poor child done to deserve this? He'll have to be placed in another home or something.'

'We don't know anything as yet, Deana,' the doctor calmly replied.

'What don't you know?' she snapped. 'He needs help. Isn't that obvious?'

Connor took an instant liking to Deana.

'Okay. I was thinking about finding a carer to come into this home but since you're here and have no sense of smell, why don't you?'

'Thank you, Raymond,' she smiled. 'You won't regret this.'

'No, I don't think I shall,' he replied.

CHAPTER TWO

The Shrouded Letter

Deana moved into the spare bedroom on Friday evening, bringing a single suitcase with her. Together, Deana and Connor cleaned the room to make it more homely. A day later and Deana had settled in.

On Sunday, arrangements had been made for a larger sofa to be delivered for Dorcus and Fagan Piggot. Several firemen had turned up at the house with special lifting equipment and cutting tools to free the two of them.

Four hours later after being washed and dressed in new clothes, Dorcus and Fagan sat on the brand new heavy-duty sofa. It was unique since it had a lifting mechanism to help raise them off the chair so they could finally walk again. The old sofa had been heavily wrapped with a plastic sheet before taken away to be destroyed.

But Dorcus and Fagan were refusing to speak to anyone. They had been through a most undignified experience and were strangely quiet for the rest of the day.

For the first time in his life Connor was feeling happy, especially with Deana. She was easy to get along with and in some ways he felt as if they'd been friends for ages. He discovered she was 22 years old and bossy at times but had his best interests at heart. She often wore her long hair swept back from her face in a ponytail, revealing freckles across her cheeks and the bridge of her nose.

But something soon began to bother him. On a few occasions when he was trying to sleep, he could hear Deana talking in her room. At first he thought she owned a mobile phone but she later confirmed she didn't. One night, curiosity got the better of him. He crept out of bed and pressed his ear to her door. He could hear another voice speaking. So he tapped on her door, only to find her alone in her room.

'You must have heard me playing my CD,' she smiled. 'I didn't realise it was so loud. I'll turn it down.'

So Connor went to bed and was plagued with dreams of a smelly man who had mushrooms growing out of his ears and a dog that wouldn't stop licking his face.

The next day was Monday and Connor eventually woke up at ten o'clock. He slowly got out of bed and opened his curtains to discover the day was grey and dreary.

Although Connor felt able to go to school, Deana insisted he took another day off.

'One more day won't make a difference,' she told him.

Connor had found himself resting properly for the first time in years. He was able to wake up late and do whatever he wanted. The doctor's diagnosis had been correct. It was only a matter of time before Connor would have collapsed due to exhaustion.

'A good rest is what you need,' the doctor had said.

This was all very well in theory but after a relaxing weekend Connor soon began to get fed up. To alleviate the boredom he decided to go for a short walk.

'Connor, wait!' Deana called from the kitchen. 'Before you go, I just want a quick word with you.'

'Sounds serious,' Connor replied. He entered the newly transformed kitchen, where cupboards were now tidy and worktops sparkled. 'You've done a good job in here, thanks.'

'That's okay. I just wanted to give you this. I found it in the pocket of your jeans yesterday.' Very carefully, Deana pulled out a newspaper cutting from her apron pocket.

'What are you doing snooping in my pockets?' said Connor quickly, snatching the paper away from her. 'Your job is to keep an eye on me and help me look after my aunt and uncle. I don't remember 'nosy' on the list.'

Deana raised up her hands in surrender. 'Hey, I'm sorry. I didn't mean to upset you and I wasn't prying. I came across it by accident. I always check the pockets when I wash jeans. Besides,

I don't regret finding it. I'm glad I did. Otherwise it would be an unidentifiable piece of paper by now.'

Connor fell silent. What a fool he was. He wanted to kick himself for judging her too harshly. She had only been trying to help.

'I'm the one who's sorry,' he grumbled, his face flushing with embarrassment.

'I just wanted you to know that I'm here if you want to talk,' she smiled awkwardly. 'I'm not here to meddle into your affairs. I'm being employed to help you out, nothing more. But if you do want a chat, you know you can trust me.'

Connor fell silent and watched as Deana made a cup of tea for herself. 'I could do with a drink as well,' he smiled, trying to bridge the awkward gap.

Pouring Connor a cold drink into a tall glass, Deana then pulled two chairs from under the table and sat down. Connor sat opposite her.

'I don't remember my parents,' Connor confessed. 'I only found this newspaper clipping a couple of weeks ago. I'd always been told they'd walked out and abandoned me, leaving me with my aunt and uncle. But now I know the truth. They won't be coming back for me because they're dead.'

'Is that what you believe?'

'What else am I meant to think?' asked Connor. 'The article explains everything. My parents are dead.'

Deana's eyes saddened. She reached her arm forward and grasped his hand. 'It must be difficult for you.'

'Not really. In a way I feel better knowing that they didn't get fed up with me and desert me. On the other hand, I'd always hoped they'd turn up at the door and say they're sorry, then take me away with them to a fantastic life somewhere else. But I've got no parents to rescue me. This is my life.' Connor slowly sipped his drink.

'Don't give up hope of a better life. You never know how things will turn out.'

Connor smiled. 'I suppose. But I've not been able to go to school much. I'm way behind the other kids. What hope is there for someone like me?'

'I know this won't seem like much to you at the moment but there are things happening in the world that involve you – I mean – I know you'll end up doing something really worthwhile with your life.'

Connor made a face. 'You seem pretty sure about that. I only wish I could find out more about my parents. I don't even know if they had a job or what they ended up doing with their lives.'

'I could help you out there. I know someone who works as an editor for a newspaper. I'll see if they can help me dig up any more information.'

'Would you?' Connor's eyes lit up. 'That would be fantastic!'

'Can I keep this clipping a bit longer?'

'Sure, but whatever you do, don't lose it. It's the only picture I have of them.' Connor stood up from the table and was about to leave the kitchen.

'Before you go, there was something else I wanted to ask you. What should I give your aunt and uncle for breakfast?'

'You might want to write this down. Twenty-four pancakes soaked in maple syrup and ice cream. A large bar of chocolate melted and poured over thirty packets of crisps. Fill two large saucepans to the brim with rich chocolate toffee cookies and five packets of marshmallows and add fifteen spoons of sugar. You'll have to deliver their breakfasts on the ironing board in the cupboard, as no normal size tray is big enough. Then just lay it across their laps.'

'Oh,' Deana replied, 'I wondered why they refused the cereal and toast I gave them yesterday.'

Connor was laughing. 'Give them what you like. You're in charge now.'

Connor hung around and peered through the door as Deana delivered two healthy bowls of cereal. Just as Connor suspected, his uncle threw the food on the floor.

'Are you trying to poison us?' he screamed.

But Deana was no soft touch. She screamed back at them, mimicking a schoolmistress as she told them off. 'There's no need to be so rude! You can forget about breakfast this morning.' She picked up the bowls from the floor and scooped as much of the cereal into the bowls as she could. 'If you're not going to eat this, you'll not be having anything else until dinner time.' Lifting her head high in the air she marched off. Dorcus ranted and raved until his throat was sore.

'She can't do that!' Fagan snarled. Dorcus was furious but couldn't complain because he'd lost his voice. 'What's she doing in our house anyway? That brat of a boy should be looking after us. Where is the useless blockhead anyway?'

Outside in the corridor Connor was trying not to laugh.

'You'd better be careful!' Connor warned her.

'I'm not having them talk to me like that!'

'I didn't mean that. If you starve them too much they might lose weight, jump off the sofa and come after you.'

'That's a horrible thought,' Deana smiled and slapped Connor's arm. 'Stop trying to scare me.'

'Hey – don't injure me. You're supposed to be looking after me!' Connor dodged her next blow.

'Go on and get out of here!' she laughed.

Connor closed the front door behind him. He stood on the doorstep breathing deeply. For the past two days he'd been cooped up inside the house. Right now fresh air was a sheer delight, like tasting ice cream, after only ever eating sprouts. He pulled his gloves out from his pocket and was putting them on when a squeaky voice called out to him.

'Hello dear!' Mrs Rosebud, the elderly neighbour, waved to him from her garden. 'Lovely day isn't it. I'm glad to see you're feeling better. You gave me quite a fright the other morning.'

'Yeah, sorry about that. Thanks for helping me,' Connor called.

'Don't mention it,' she replied. 'I'm just happy to see you up and about. But I can't stop to talk. I've got pies in the oven!' With that she hurried off into her house.

Straightening the collar on his coat, Connor noticed his gloves were covered in camel coloured hairs.

Then the strangest sensation washed over him. He started feeling dizzy. A ghostly vision of a man with a dog rose from the deepest pit of his memory.

The man said he knew his parents.

Connor began to sweat uncomfortably. Slowly he began to remember what had happened earlier that morning when he fell unconscious. The man had smelt awful, as if he'd been sleeping on the streets. A hand was covering his mouth. There had been a letter. It was all coming back now. The man knew his name. He knew where he lived.

The man had dropped a letter on the pavement. But where was the letter now?

Connor scanned the front garden. There wasn't any letter lying around, but it had been quite windy the night before and Connor suspected that if it had any chance of being in his garden then it would have been blown behind the large rosebush where most of the rubbish accumulates.

Connor wasn't feeling hopeful about finding the letter but something impelled him to look. He carefully reached his hand behind the plant but still managed to scratch himself on a menacing thorn.

'Ow!' Snatching his hand back, he gave his small injury a quick rub before proceeding to tug at the litter.

That was when he saw it. It lay slightly apart from the other rubbish, resting against the fence. He picked it up and smiled nervously when he saw it was addressed to him. But it wasn't like an ordinary letter. It shone and shimmered in a magical way. Connor thought it must be some kind of birthday card since he was going to be twelve tomorrow.

'I wonder who this is from?' he thought.

Clutching his letter excitedly he turned and went back inside his house. Standing in the hallway, Connor could hear Deana talking to someone in the kitchen. He closed the front door quietly and crept closer. Who was she speaking to? Keeping as quiet as he could, he listened intently. The discussion was sounding serious.

'So you didn't actually give the letter to Connor. Where is it now?' she demanded.

'It must still be in the garden,' a man replied. 'I looked but I couldn't find it.'

Moving closer still, Connor slipped silently against the wall.

'So what's the next plan?' Deana asked. 'And remember, I won't let you do anything to jeopardise his life.'

The man replied. 'Your parents want him back at the AAA. The council has already agreed that this is for the best. You must realise that I have his best interests at heart too, for without him, I'll never be free to leave this planet.'

'But there have been problems with security at the AAA. I don't want him going there. Not yet – not with Definastine on the loose using portals willy nilly and turning up when you least expect him to. Surely he's safer here with me, in this small dreary house.'

'Times are changing,' said the man. 'We have the best guards to help protect him there. Anyway, it's time this was delivered to Connor. The time has come. Are you any closer to telling him anything about his destiny?'

'No,' Deana whispered. 'It seems so unfair. He's had such an awful life and it's about to get worse.'

'You can't keep the truth from him. It has to happen today. Definastine is closer than ever. Connor needs to be prepared.'

'Prepared for what?' asked Connor, bursting into the kitchen. To his horror he found Deana alone. He squinted and thought he saw a shadow standing next to her but it was all too vague.

'Connor!' said Deana startled. 'I didn't know you had come back – that was a quick walk.'

He eyed her suspiciously. 'Who were you just talking to?'

She shook her head nervously and tucked a loose strand of hair behind her ear. She glanced about the room and, in a tone much too nervous and jovial, she quickly replied, 'Oh, no one.'

'Don't fob me off. I heard a man speaking in here,' he insisted.

'Well, I can't see anyone. Can you?'

'I don't know how he vanished but there was definitely a man here. What's going on? It concerns me, doesn't it?'

'No, its nothing to do with you.' She turned to the sink, picked up a tea towel and began to dry a plate that was already dry.

'Don't lie to me. I heard my name mentioned. I heard you mention Definastine. Who is he?'

'Forget about it,' she snapped.

'No, I won't!' Connor shouted back. 'Tell me!'

'You wouldn't believe me even if I told you the truth.' Her voice trailed off. Still holding the tea towel, she folded her arms across her chest before facing him. She was about to speak when her eyes fixed on the letter he was holding. 'You've found the letter.'

Connor frowned and widened his eyes as something clicked into place. 'Is this the letter you were speaking about? Tell me, I need to know.'

Deana gripped the tea towel tightly. She placed her delicate hand to her open mouth.

'Deana, I trust you,' Connor said. 'As soon as I saw you I knew you were someone to be trusted. Don't start lying to me now, please!'

'There's so much to tell you. I was hoping to shelter you from it but I was wrong. I know that now. Perhaps it would be better if you read the letter first. It should help explain some things.'

Connor quickly disappeared upstairs before she could say anything else. His face was burning with anger. Why was Deana treating him like a child? Why did she lie to him?

As Connor slammed the door to his bedroom, Deana closed her eyes and sighed heavily. There was no avoiding the truth now. She would have to tell Connor everything. She took a deep breath and a single tear trickled from her eye. She wiped it away quickly and sat down at the table. Shaking, she poured herself another cup of tea. From the back pocket of her jeans she pulled out a photograph of two adults and two children, taken ten years ago when she – the older child – had been twelve, and the younger one two. She stroked her finger across the picture and returned it to her pocket.

'He knows you're here. There's no point hiding any more. You might as well show yourself,' she said.

Suddenly the figure of a man appeared, transparent at first but growing more solid by the second.

'I think it went quite well,' he said, 'given the circumstances.'

Deana shook her head hopelessly, poured some tea into another cup and waited for Connor to come running back down the stairs.

Connor sat on his bed, holding the letter. Something strange was going on and he knew it concerned him. He stroked the envelope. It felt smooth and silky. He quickly ripped it open and threw it on the bed. He thought no more about it until it quivered and fluttered, grabbing his attention.

'What the –?'

Against all logic, Connor was suddenly faced with the impossible. Without any assistance the envelope began moving. Connor jumped up from the bed. He backed away slowly, fearing that the envelope would attack him. Very gently the two torn pieces merged together, like metal to a magnet. The transformation was only just beginning. Connor watched in suspense as the paper joined and mended itself along the torn edge where it had been ripped.

Once repaired, the envelope rested on the bed motionless. Connor's fear was swiftly replaced with curiosity. He was no longer scared, just overawed by the miracle. He carefully picked up the envelope and examined it. It had fixed itself so no visible tear could be seen and it felt surprisingly warm, as if it were alive.

He tore it several more times and watched in fascination as it repeatedly mended itself. He almost forgot about the letter inside it. Now he had witnessed this miraculous display, he wanted to show Deana straightaway. But he didn't.

Instead he picked up the strange creamy piece of paper he had discarded and noticed it felt more like fabric than paper and tickled his fingers like a feather duster.

The letter appeared to have no message. Hundreds of letters from the alphabet were dotted at random. The letter was unreadable. The words were jumbled up. A child hammering at a computer could have written what presented itself in front of him.

'Is this some sort of joke?' he whispered.

Connor threw the letter aside. Picking up the envelope, he raced downstairs to show Deana. 'Here, look at this!' he said excitedly. Ripping the envelope in half, he placed the two halves a short distance from each other on the kitchen table. And just like before, the paper quivered and mended. 'Isn't it fantastic?'

Deana smiled, not looking at all surprised. She calmly sipped her tea. 'I take it you haven't read the letter yet.'

'No, there was no message. But isn't this fantastic?' Connor's face was beaming. Amused, Deana watched him with interest.

'I remember receiving my first one. It really spooked me out. I screamed and hid in the cupboard for hours. Not even mum's chocolate mousse could entice me out.'

'You've had a letter like this before?'

'Yes. It's a shrouded letter. Only the person it is delivered to can read it.'

'I can't,' said Connor blankly. 'There's no message on the letter except some nonsense words.'

'You need to hold the letter for several seconds before you can read it.'

With a puzzled expression, Connor dashed back upstairs. He sat back on his bed, holding the letter eagerly between his hands, wishing for something to happen.

He didn't have to wait for long. Suddenly, as if by magic, the soft fabric began to tremble and the typed letters began to shuffle on the material, moving of their own accord to form different words. Connor gulped loudly and dropped it as if it were a scorpion. Immediately the letters rearranged themselves back into nonsense words.

His face crumpled in confusion and fear. Hesitating, he reached out to touch the letter and watched in fascination as the letters repeated their earlier display with a magical life force of their own, shuffling once again to form understandable words. He wanted to drop it but he didn't. Within his quivering hands, it soon became clear enough to read.

'To our beloved son, Connor,

As circumstances have changed with the failure of our mission, we needed to get in touch with you. We know you have spent your life believing we are dead but we are in fact alive.'

Connor gulped loudly and read on.

> *'What you must understand is that we love you. It broke our hearts letting you go but we had no other choice. Your life was in grave danger and still is. Please be careful, son. You have been chosen and because of that you will be hunted by a terrible evil'.*

Connor found himself laughing nervously. This letter was beginning to sound like a bad joke.

> *'We weren't allowed contact with you, until now. We were hoping to defeat Definastine so you wouldn't have to, but the prophecy has come true, and now, many lives will depend on you. Trust Tookar, for we have sent him to help you. There's never a day that goes by when we do not think of you. Try and get to the AAA as soon as possible for your own safety.*
> *We pray we'll be able to see you soon.*
>
> *Loving you forever*
> *Your*
> *Mum & Dad (Christy & Ryan).*

Connor sat motionless on the edge of his bed. He was terribly confused.

It had taken a while for the words to sink in. His parents were still alive! Could it really be true? But it didn't make sense. If they were alive it meant that the newspaper article was wrong.

He shook his head. Nothing made sense anymore. What prophecy had come true? Who was Definastine? What terrible evil was hunting him? Who was Tookar?

That strange man with his dog was dangerous, wasn't he? But surely he wouldn't be giving a warning about himself, would he?

Oh, it was so confusing. Connor screwed up the letter and threw it on the floor, but just like the envelope it ironed itself out.

Then Connor remembered why the male voice in the kitchen had seemed so familiar. It had sounded just like the stranger he'd encountered early Friday morning. Why would Deana be speaking to him? Who was he? But if he had been in the kitchen talking to Deana, where had he gone?

Deana said the letter would explain everything but it only made things more confusing. Perhaps she could shed some light on this. She seemed to know what was going on. But would she start explaining things to him? He had no choice: he had no one else to talk to but her.

He didn't know how long he'd sat staring at the blank walls. All he knew was his legs were numb with pins and needles.

A shiver extended down his spine. On the other hand, perhaps if he went back to bed and buried his head under his duvet the problems would sort themselves out and go away on their own. Connor went to the window and peered beneath his dusty net curtains.

There was a knock on his bedroom door. Connor didn't turn round. His eyes remained fixed on a sparrow sitting on the fence, staring straight back at him.

'Come in,' he said, watching the bird curiously. Its twig-like legs appeared to be dancing. 'I read the letter, Deana. It's weird. I don't know what to believe any more. It's meant to be from my parents, but they're dead, or at least that's what I thought. If that letter has any grain of truth it means my uncle was right all along. I really was abandoned.'

'You weren't abandoned, Connor. Your parents wanted you safe.'

Connor spun round fast. His breath stopped in his throat. Standing a foot taller than him, a man with straggly brown hair stood in the doorway. For a horrible moment Connor was rooted to the spot in fear.

CHAPTER THREE

The Starstone

'Get out!' Connor screamed. 'Deana! Help!'

Deana immediately rushed into the room, pushing the man aside. She was frowning heavily at the stranger, her expression angry and annoyed. But she didn't appear surprised by his presence.

'Tookar! I should've known you couldn't wait before you made your introduction,' she said sharply.

'We don't have time. Besides, you decided … I didn't,' Tookar replied.

'You know this creep?' quizzed Connor.

'Yes, I'm afraid I do. Connor, I'd like you to meet Tookar, your entrusted guardian from now on,' she said in a calmer voice.

Connor gulped loudly. 'But he can't be my guardian. He attacked me the other day!'

'I did not attack you!' the man declared.

'We've got some explaining to do,' said Deana, giving Connor a reassuring hug and rubbing his back. 'Perhaps we should talk over a drink and some biscuits.'

'Talk?' Connor gasped, finding it difficult to piece together.

'Yes, talk,' Deana repeated sternly. 'We have a few matters to clear up. Come down when you feel ready but don't leave it too late.'

As Deana left the room, the man lingered behind. His dark brown eyes were fatigued. Dirty stains streaked his face and clothing.

'Eh – this is for you,' Tookar said awkwardly. From the inside pocket of his coat, he pulled out a small parcel and handed it to Connor. 'It's good to see you again.'

With that, Tookar quickly left the room. Connor didn't open the small parcel straightaway. Anyway, it wasn't his birthday until tomorrow. Feeling utterly confused, he began pacing his room, chewing his fingernails and telling himself that everything was going to be all right.

By the time Connor gathered courage to go downstairs, Deana and Tookar were sitting in the kitchen with empty cups and a packet of biscuits. Tookar was finishing a sandwich Deana had made for him.

'He needs a bath,' Connor said to Deana. 'He really smells.'

Without giving Deana a chance to speak, Connor spoke again.

'It's true. He can use the bathroom upstairs if he wants to. There's a clean towel hanging over the radiator.'

Tookar burst out laughing. 'Is he always so truthful?'

Deana nodded. 'Yes.'

'I'm sorry for scaring you the other morning. I never meant to.' Tookar picked up his plate and walked over to the sink. 'Well, I'd better go and get cleaned up. I can take a hint.' He ruffled Connor's hair as he went past. 'It's no secret that I've been hiding in the dirtiest of places.'

Connor quickly moved his head away from Tookar's hands. He didn't feel ready to become friends just yet.

'He's a great person really and very respected where he comes from,' said Deana, once Tookar had left. 'You shouldn't be so rude.'

'Rude!' snapped Connor. 'How am I meant to feel? In case you haven't realised, the man who frightened me out of my skin the other morning has just turned up in my bedroom to scare me senseless again.'

'I'm sorry,' Deana said regretfully. 'He shouldn't have done that, but he was desperate to see you and we kept telling him not to. But perhaps he was right. Time is running out for all of us.'

'What are you talking about?'

'I'm not who you think I am,' began Deana, standing up to make another cup of tea. 'I'm a detective as well as a nurse. I work for a secret organisation known as the AAA.'

'I've heard of that place before!' said Connor. 'The old man at the garage mentioned it to me, when I went to buy some ice cream.'

'You met Sparkie,' she smiled warmly, sitting down again. 'He's a bit eccentric but harmless.'

'Sparkie?'

'He works for the AAA, just like me and Tookar. It stands for Alien Agents Alliance. Hundreds of years ago a small group was formed to help stranded aliens. But over the years the role of the AAA has changed considerably. It now provides warships to help defend neighbouring dimensions and other planets from coming under attack from Definastine and other enemies. It also provides rescue parties to save star-spirits in trouble.'

'Star-spirits?' quizzed Connor.

'The term star-spirit refers to all intelligent life forms, including aliens. Instead of calling everyone an alien, we decided star-spirits was a much more suitable name.' she explained.

'So you're telling me you believe in aliens?'

'Yes. I grew up with them. So did you, Connor. Your best friend was a star-spirit.'

Connor stared at her for what seemed like ages.

'Did you know me when I was little?' he asked.

Deana's face drained of colour. Spilling her drink on her lap she quickly stood up and began dabbing at her clothes with a cloth she'd grabbed from the sideboard. 'Oh, look what I've done!'

'Are you okay?' Connor asked. 'You seem a bit jumpy.'

'No, I'm fine,' she replied.

'Was it something I said?'

'No, honestly, I'm fine. Now, what was I saying…'

'I asked if you knew me when I was a baby,' prompted Connor.

'Yes, I did. My parents knew yours. We were brought up together in the AAA, until you were taken away.'

'Oh,' said Connor.

'There's something else you need to know. Your parents are still alive. For the past year they have been on a mission trying to stop Definastine from closing in on a vulnerable planet. He's bent on destroying everything.'

Connor wasn't sure whether to laugh or cry. 'You knew all along and had me believe they were still dead!'

'I'll explain everything if you'll just shut up and listen for a moment. When you were two, Arbtu foretold you would one day become a saviour for our people. He was the star-spirit who created the AAA. He was vague about the details but very insistent it would happen. He said a living consciousness would become one with you and that your two bodies would merge together and work as one until Definastine was destroyed.'

'And my parents wanted me to stay with my uncle because they were worried about me.' Connor took a deep breath.

'How did you know?' whispered Deana.

'I had the strangest dream last night,' Connor confessed and proceeded to tell Deana the entire dream. He spoke of his mum's pain and his dad's wisdom and the little toddler who was taken away.

'Weird. Your dream was very precise,' she said. 'Unfortunately, we must get you out of here. Definastine knows about you. He knows where you live. Ever since he stole the consulting mirror he has done nothing but cause trouble, especially at the AAA.'

'How come?' asked Connor.

'The consulting mirror reveals the past. They have only to ask about the Starstone to know it is here. Tookar received a warning to move you out of here today.'

'When?' whispered Connor.

Deana reached her hand forward and rested it on top of Connor's. 'After you join forces with the Starstone.'

'Will it hurt? Do I have another choice?' He swallowed.

Deana shook her head. 'If Definastine has the power to find you, he'll be watching your every footstep. This is your only chance.'

'This is crazy. I've never believed in aliens before. And now I'm having a conversation about how I'm meant to allow one to merge bodies with me!' He stood up quickly and began pacing the kitchen. 'I don't understand. My parents are alive. Aliens exist. This is too weird.'

'Connor, the sooner you do it the better. It's going to take a while for you to –,' Deana broke off. She stood up abruptly, causing the chair to topple over and crash to the ground. In the distance a dog was howling. Her voice was rushed and urgent. 'Where's the Starstone, Connor?'

'I don't know!'

'Tookar gave you a parcel with the Starstone in it. Where did you put it?' Deana urged, a look of horror on her face.

'It's on my bed upstairs,' he told her, growing increasingly apprehensive. 'What's wrong Deana? You've gone white.'

'Go upstairs and tell Tookar to meet me down here. We've got trouble. Go into your room. Don't open the door for anyone, including me.'

'I don't understand.'

Deana firmly grabbed hold of Connor's shoulders. Her eyes were frightened and confused. 'Listen carefully. You must open the parcel. Let the Starstone become one with you. Hurry, Connor. Before it's too late!'

Connor turned on his heel, dashing up the stairs. He banged hard on the bathroom door. Shouting urgently he called to Tookar. 'Deana needs you downstairs. Something's wrong!'

The door immediately opened. Tookar, with his hair sleeked back, was holding a strange weapon.

'Go into your room!' he said, his expression grave. 'And lock it!'

Tookar then bolted down the stairs. He disappeared from sight leaving Connor alone. Glass was being smashed in the kitchen. Connor heard a scream. Was that Deana? More yelling and shouting. Doors were being slammed. Objects crashed against walls. Connor dived into his bedroom. Somewhere in the distance a dog was howling.

Connor hugged his knees to his chest. He wanted the terrible sounds to stop. He was scared. As the noise increased, Connor scrambled to the edge of his bed to retrieve the parcel. He ripped off the paper and saw a piece of blue cloth wrapped around an object. He cupped it in his hands.

Connor had never been so terrified. Yet Deana's voice echoed louder than his fear inside his head. *'Become one with the*

31

Starstone before it's too late!' Part of him wanted to bury the Starstone in the garden, like a dog with its bone.

Then something extraordinary happened. The blue cloth began to ripple in gentle waves, very much like water. Its colour began to change in appearance to a more purple hue. His hands grew warm. At the same time the object started pulsating as though he carried his very heart in his hands. His eyes widened, his body stiffened.

Connor grew anxious.

'I didn't ask for any of this to happen to me!' he cried out and hurled the object across the room. The cloth immediately fell off and a ball of light continued whizzing through the air. Instead of ricocheting off the wardrobe doors, it passed through them, leaving a small gaping hole in the wood.

Connor screamed. He wanting to flee his bedroom, but the disturbance downstairs kept him where he was. Reluctantly he locked his door and dived beneath his bed to retrieve his baseball bat.

Seconds later, the small ball of light emerged from the wardrobe, hovering and humming softly like a bee. Slowly it began circling the room. Then, increasing in speed, it began to look like a giant hoop of silvery light. A new sound began to sing out.

After a short while it slowed before resting close to Connor's face. Connor squealed and stepped back towards the window. Perhaps he could jump down into the garden. But to his horror he saw the garden was swarming with small grey-bodied creatures. They were naked apart from small loincloths and moved extremely fast and nimbly on their feet. Some were even beginning to climb the brick walls. Their eyes were large and round with huge black pupils

'What the –?'

Connor retreated from the window and leaped on top of his mattress, still holding the bat. What did he think he was doing? Deana wanted him to join with the Starstone, didn't she? So why was he about to whack it with his bat? He threw the bat aside. He couldn't run from this thing. It wasn't what he was meant to do.

The ball of light slowly approached Connor, until it was just inches away. It appeared to be communicating with him but Connor had no idea what he should do. He shuddered nervously.

'Okay, I'll do it,' he whispered timidly. 'Just hurry up and get on with whatever you're going to do.'

The Starstone shimmered in silvery colours, glittering like a gigantic jewel suspended in the air. As soon as it started pulsating, a wave of calm eased Connor's tense body, stripping away his fears. His muscles went floppy as if his bones had vanished. His back slid down the wall as his legs gave way beneath him. His face slackened and his tongue hung loosely from his mouth. Connor stared in awe at the wondrous star.

His mind was now floating on an enormous ocean of cloud. He didn't feel afraid anymore.

A voice began calling him from far away, *Connor.*

Connor glanced at the Starstone, smiling dreamily.

I am the consciousness of the Starstone and I seek to become one with you. Do not fear. Be not afraid for it is our destiny to become one.

Its hypnotic voice soothed Connor's mind. He tried to speak but couldn't. In his effort to say something, dribble poured gently from his mouth and down his chin.

Just relax and close your eyes, the soft voice spoke.

All thoughts of resistance vanished as peace flooded his senses. The last thing Connor saw before closing his eyes was the Starstone descending towards his stomach, where it disappeared inside his body. It had left no visible mark on his body nor caused him any pain.

Deep inside his mind he began to hear a musical voice singing out gently.

Great Ones rejoice with us here,
The time will soon come with nothing to fear.
Although the Dark Master is very near,
The Starstone had chosen Connor as Seer!

'Goodnight,' Connor whispered, falling asleep on the floor and sucking his thumb for the first time in years.

Goodnight, Connor, the Starstone replied.

CHAPTER FOUR

The Healing Miracle

Two days later Connor woke up to a peculiar smell. It wasn't the smell of his home. It smelt different, like something clean. Unfamiliar noises startled him. Stiff white sheets lay across his body, tucked tightly under his mattress. He tried to move but it wasn't easy. Wriggling hard he managed to get an arm out.

'Hello,' spoke a boy in the next bed. 'You've been asleep for ages.'

'Where am I?' Connor asked.

'In h – h – hospital like the rest of us,' stuttered the boy. Then added, 'If y – y – you're looking for your glasses they're on the table t – t – to your left.'

'Thanks,' Connor stretched out his hand and banged it awkwardly on the cabinet. Putting on his glasses he was surprised to find his vision was blurry. He took them off and found to his amazement he could see perfectly well without them. 'That's weird.'

'Wh – wh – what's weird?' the boy asked.

'Nothing.' Connor was puzzled. He'd been wearing glasses all his life and suddenly he didn't need them anymore. Something extraordinary had happened, but what?

He looked about the ward in confusion. Why was he in hospital? He sat up too quickly and became dizzy. Where was Deana? He cheered up when he noticed a couple of birthday cards on the bedside cabinet. One was from Deana and the other was from Tookar. The name seemed familiar but Connor couldn't quite remember who Tookar was.

'What day is it today?' Connor asked the boy.

'Wed – Wed – Wednesday,' he replied. 'You've been a – asleep for ages.'

So Connor had missed his birthday. Somehow that didn't seem important any more either. He smiled shyly at the boy in the next bed. He had a friendly face with dark circles around mischievous brown eyes. At that moment, a stout looking nurse swiftly approached Connor's bed.

'Ahh. I see you've finally woken up, Connor. You kids will do anything to get out of going to school these days,' she tutted, shaking her head. The plump nurse inspected Connor with her green eyes. She had a habit of peering over her glasses rather than through them. She continued to check his pulse before updating the record at the end of his bed. 'Would you like something to eat or drink perhaps?' she asked eventually.

'I'm not hungry. But I could do with a drink,' Connor replied.

A few minutes later she returned with a jug of orange squash and a clean glass.

'Here, this should do the trick,' she said pouring him a glass.

'Thanks,' said Connor, watching the nurse and wondering when she was going to explain what was wrong with him. But she said little else. As she was about to go, Connor called out, 'Why am I here?'

'I'm sure the doctor will explain everything to you in time,' she smiled, eyeing him curiously before walking away.

Connor groaned impatiently. He didn't want to spend any more time in hospital than was necessary. He glanced over towards a young girl lying on her bed, directly opposite him. She seemed to have difficulty in breathing.

'By the way, I'm Ph –Philip. And that's Mary over there. She's g – g – got asthma,' he said, following Connor's gaze. 'She's been stuck in b – bed all her life.'

'That's horrible,' Connor murmured. Suddenly his life didn't seem so bad. 'I can't imagine never getting out of bed. It would drive me crazy.'

'It d – drives me crazy too. I w – w – wish I could stop growing. Then perhaps m – my muscles would grow to fit my bones. I suffer with a disorder known as giantism, but I – I call it a pain in the butt,' the boy smirked. 'I'm al – already over seven feet tall and

I'm still growing. As long as the d – doctors keep drowning me with painkillers, it's b – bearable to live with.'

Connor noticed Philip's feet were poking out at the end of his bed. They were resting on a table. It would be a lie to say that his feet weren't big. They were huge, at least a shoe size twenty.

'Don't lo – look at me like that,' Philip grumbled.

'Like what?'

'Don't pity me,' he grumbled. 'I get it everywhere I go. People always st – stop and stare at me.'

Connor kept quiet. He didn't know what to say. It was Philip who spoke next.

'So, is it your birthday then?'

'No, it was yesterday.' Connor had missed his birthday but that didn't bother him in the slightest. All he wanted was to see Deana and get out of this dreary place. By the end of the afternoon, Connor was exhausted and he hadn't left his bed.

Deana popped in to see him at four o'clock. She looked exhausted.

'I haven't slept a wink!' she confessed, nervously glancing towards the door. 'Are you okay?'

'A bit tired. I can't seem to remember anything,' he replied. 'Deana, is everything all right?'

'Are you joking?' she whispered seriously. 'We've got some serious talking to do.'

'What's so important?'

'Can't you remember anything about Monday morning?' she asked in surprise.

He shook his head and noticed some bruising on her neck and the small cut on the corner of her lip. 'What happened to you?'

'Forget about that. I need to know what you can remember. What about the things I told you about your parents and the Starstone? Can you remember them?'

'I remember hearing you talk to someone in the kitchen but nothing else. My memory's gone blank.'

'Tookar warned me about this,' she muttered. 'He told me that you might forget.'

'Tookar?' asked Connor.

'The man I was speaking to in the kitchen,' she explained. Deana pulled out the newspaper clipping from her pocket. 'By the way, this is a fake. It was made at the AAA as a cover up operation and was given to your uncle. Your parents are alive, Connor.'

Connor gasped in surprise.

'This is so annoying,' said Deana. 'I spent ages talking to you about your parents but you can't remember any of it. Tookar warned me you might have a temporary memory loss.'

Connor remained silent, with a gaping mouth.

'Tookar wanted you to have this.' Deana took a photograph from her bag and handed it over to Connor. 'He wanted to give it to you personally but he was worried you wouldn't remember him.'

Connor took the photograph. He recognised his parents straightaway. They were standing each side of another man with familiar looking scraggly brown hair.

'It was taken just days ago,' Deana informed him gently. 'They're still alive, Connor.'

Connor shook his head and bit his lip. Tears sprung to his eyes but he wiped them away before Deana saw them.

'That's Tookar,' Deana said, pointing to the stranger in the centre of the photograph.

'I still don't recognise him,' Connor sniffed. 'And I missed my birthday. Apparently I slept through the entire day.'

Deana nodded. 'You did. I was here for two hours and not once did you move. I had to pinch you just to make sure you were still alive. I even sang Happy Birthday to you.'

Connor gave a laugh.

'K should be here tomorrow morning to collect you,' said Deana.

'K? Who's K? Why can't you come and get me?'

'K's a very good friend of mine. I'll come and visit you in the morning but I won't be able to leave with you,' Deana explained. 'It's too dangerous.'

'Dangerous?' Connor almost choked. 'This is a hospital, not a raging river.'

'Anyway, it's all settled.'

'What does K look like?'

'It's hard to say,' Deana said. 'He could be in disguise.'

'That's a big help,' Connor mumbled.

'Don't worry about anything, Connor. Tookar believes your memory will return by tomorrow and you'll be able to understand everything then.'

After Deana had left the ward, Connor felt an overwhelming loss. Although he was lonely, he didn't feel very talkative. His recent conversation with Deana rolled over and over in his mind as he tried to make sense of it all. His parents were alive. This was unbelievable. Where had they been all his life? Connor began to suspect they really did desert him. This played on his mind for the best part of the day.

Philip's parents stayed for an hour and Connor, not wanting to be rude, made polite conversation with them. They seemed nice enough people. They even went downstairs to the hospital shop and bought magazines for the two boys on their return. They were an odd looking couple. Mrs Trout, who insisted on being called Rachel, was incredibly tall. His dad, on the other hand, was the shortest man he'd ever met and made up for lack of height by spreading outwards instead.

'You've got nice parents,' Connor remarked when they had left.

'I sure have,' Philip beamed, his cheeks puffed out after shoving a whole handful of grapes into his mouth at once. He offered some to Connor. 'Where are your parents?'

'I don't know,' said Connor, not wanting to discuss them. 'I really don't know.'

Philip gave him an odd sideways glance, shrugged and continued devouring more tasty grapes. With the empty bowl on his lap, he soon fell deep asleep. The night had slowly arrived. Curtains were closed and the lights on the ward had been dimmed. Connor turned his head. In the main corridor outside the ward, he watched the nurses sipping hot drinks while writing their reports at their desk. Their soft chatter and laughter were comforting. It made Connor believe everything was normal and things were going to be all right.

He glanced across at Mary. She didn't look so good. She'd been unable to talk as she fought her battle to breathe. A mask had been placed on her face and covered both her nose and mouth. Her chest was rising rapidly as she breathed with the aid of extra oxygen. If only something could be done to help her, Connor thought.

Connor gently rubbed the crease of his elbow where the doctors and nurses had performed one blood test after another. He had been pricked like a pincushion all day. Connor was thinking about charging them a fee if they didn't stop: he'd make a fortune.

Two specialists had examined Connor's stomach. There had been several gasps between them. Connor grew concerned. He wanted to retreat into a little ball and scream for them to leave him alone. He wasn't some guinea pig to be experimented on. He wished he could turn back the clock to Sunday, when everything was normal and felt safe. But that was impossible and for now he'd just have to grin and bear it.

Being tucked up in bed wasn't a pleasant experience either. The freshly cleaned blankets were tucked under the mattress so securely that it made Connor feel he were an insect in a cocoon. It did cross his mind that they were trying to keep him a prisoner. He soon became frustrated. His life didn't seem his own. He was losing control of it. There was no room for him to make decisions. Deana wanted him to do one thing and the doctors and nurses wanted him to do something else.

By the time Connor put his worries to one side and closed his eyes, he was one of the last children to fall asleep. It didn't take long for him to start dreaming. He dreamt he was falling into a bottomless pit, before coming to a slow grinding halt. Then his body catapulted in the opposite direction, flying him up like a bullet. With a loud pop he found himself floating above his body, staring down at the familiar face he'd come to know so well. A purple thread of light was safely linking both his bodies. His head was tipped on the side so that his cheek was squashed against the pillow. His mouth was opening and closing in a gentle snore. He reached out to touch his face but his hand went right through his skin.

Connor felt invigorated. He felt free. Yet somehow he knew it wasn't a dream as whirls of different colours began surrounding all the other children. Without any warning Connor was sucked back into his body, where his dreams were restful. He continued sleeping well throughout the night.

But unknown to Connor, his desire to help Mary was causing something to happen inside him. The Starstone, which was nested inside his stomach, was leaking light and an invisible force was flowing unconditionally out from his body. It was sending a healing thought wave to every patient in the children's ward. Connor's compassion alone had energised this strange alien life form, which continued to feed the patients until every last person became cured of their complaint.

The next day at sunrise, the children's section of the hospital was brimming with excitement. Joyous faces were at every turn.

'It's a miracle!' exclaimed the day nurses, who had arrived at work to find the ward in absolute chaos with previously bedridden children jumping on their beds and running around excitedly.

'My cancer has disappeared. Father Christmas gave me my present a month early,' a young boy was telling everyone who would listen.

'Look what I can do,' another child shouted across the room, bouncing on the bed. His broken legs had rapidly mended.

'And me,' another cried out.

Mary was also cured. For the very first time in her life she got out of bed and with the assistance of the nurses she was attempting to walk. 'Look at me!' she grinned. 'I'm walking. Soon I'll be running!'

Connor was flabbergasted. 'Unbelievable!'

Philip spent most of the day in shock. Already he had reduced by four inches in height. His pain had completely vanished and for the first time in months he was able to swing his long legs to the side of his bed as he sat up. 'I'm shrinking!'

'That's incredible!' Connor managed to say.

Broken bones had mended overnight. Cancers and tumours had simply vanished. Burns had been replaced with new skin leaving no scars behind. Children waiting for organ transplants no longer needed them. Those children simply needing time to recover had recovered. The list of complaints healed was endless. But the healing didn't just extend to the children. Any nurses working last night were also cured of any complaint.

'My warts have vanished,' Connor heard one nurse say. 'I've had them for years and they've simply vanished.'

Connor dressed quickly and patiently waited for Deana to arrive. He had something to tell her. Last night his dreams were occupied with people being healed. Surely his dreams and what had happened in the hospital weren't pure coincidence.

'What happened to us all?' Philip was lost for words and no longer seemed to stutter.

'I haven't got a clue,' Connor murmured, still wondering if he was the cause of it all.

CHAPTER FIVE

Hunted

Throughout the morning, vast crowds of people had flooded the children's ward. Doctors, surgeons, nurses, news reporters, family and friends. Every child had been miraculously cured of illness.

One by one the children were discharged. Philip saw the doctor at ten o'clock. Fifteen minutes later and beaming, Philip emerged from behind the curtains.

'It's official!' Philip told Connor. 'I'm shrinking. I'm four inches shorter than yesterday!'

'That's great!' said Connor, trying to keep his eye on the door in case Deana arrived. It was hard to hide his disappointment when every time the doors swung open, Deana wasn't the one walking through them. Instead it was someone else's parents.

Philip's mum and dad arrived at eleven o'clock to collect their son.

'I can't believe it!' Rachel was beside herself with emotion, while showering Philip with affection. 'You're shrinking! Whoever heard of such a thing? And they say miracles never happen. Blah!'

'Get off, mum!' Philip mumbled, trying to duck his head from his mum's overly affectionate hands.

Philip's dad was reacting quite differently. He was standing in shock with a funny lopsided grin that could almost be mistaken for a snarl, except his eyes were deeply puzzled and not angry. He had one hand placed on his dumpy waist and the other scratching his head.

'I can't believe you've lost height!' said Rachel in disbelief. 'Four whole inches.'

Connor grinned at her comment, since most people comment on losing weight and not height.

'Don't worry love, I'm sure your sister will turn up soon,' she said, smiling kindly towards Connor.

'She's not my sister,' corrected Connor. 'She's just a friend.'

'Well, you've got a good friend there,' she replied. 'Come on Philip. Get your things together. We'll be waiting for you outside in the corridor while you say your goodbyes to your new friend. Don't be too long though. By the way Connor, please come and stay with us sometime.'

'Thanks. I'd like that.' Connor gave them a wave as they walked out of the ward.

Philip wrenched a pad of notepaper from his bulky carrier bag. His clothes were spilling out of the top.

'Here. I'll give you my phone number and address. It would be good to hear from you. I've never had a pen pal before,' said Philip, scribbling frantically.

'I've never had any kind of pal,' Connor replied.

They exchanged addresses and Connor cheered up considerably. Visiting a friend was something to really look forward to.

'You never know, but next time I see you I might be a little shorter,' Philip grinned. 'Well, see you soon, hopefully.'

As Philip left the ward, Connor found himself alone. It was now twelve o'clock and he felt truly abandoned. Where was Deana? He desperately wanted to go home but the doctor insisted that he should stay.

'But I feel so well,' Connor groaned.

'Your scan is set for this afternoon. I'll come back for you then.'

It was one o'clock in the afternoon when Connor saw Deana walk through the door.

'At last,' he said cheerfully. 'I thought you'd never show.' He offered her fresh grapes from Philip's abandoned fruit bowl.

'What's been going on here then?' she breathed excitedly. 'It's on the news and everything. I had to fight through the crowd to get in here. Don't worry. I went on all fours and crawled between their legs, hence my dirty knees.' She dusted the knees of her trousers.

'It doesn't make sense. Why can't I go home? Everyone else has. I'm the last person left in this miserable place!'

'Don't worry, but I think the Starstone may have changed you in some way.'

'What?' Connor made a face. He hadn't a clue what she was talking about.

'Oh, haven't you remembered yet?' Deana said, looking disappointed. 'I shouldn't have brought you here. If the AAA were more secure, I'd have taken you there. That's where you should've gone. They've got the best hospital, but it's madness in that place at the moment. Someone let those damn devlins loose again. I told them they should never have had them there in the first place. But Madam Gripe insists that lessons in identifying monsters are most important if we are to know what we're fighting against. I suppose it's true but they cause nothing but trouble. They happily munch away at wires and destroy the computer systems. They do it every time. The worse thing is they reproduce so rapidly. Every minute another ten devlins are born. It's ridiculous.'

Connor was frowning. Deana paused for breath.

'Oh, sorry. I forgot you don't know what devlins are. You'll see them later and then you'll know what I'm talking about.'

'I doubt that,' Connor muttered.

'K's coming later to get you out of here.' She paused. 'This might come as a bit of a surprise to you, but both Tookar and K are shape-shifters. They can transform into any living form they want.'

'You should be in here, not me. Better still, you ought to go to the funny farm and get your head examined,' Connor replied, shaking his head. 'You're losing the plot, woman.'

'I knew you wouldn't believe me. But think about it. And what about the letter you received? The one that you couldn't destroy – it was a shrouded letter. Don't you remember? Only the person who it is sent to can read it.'

Connor closed his eyes. Didn't Deana realise how absurd she sounded? 'I'm sorry Deana. I can't remember anything apart from some strange dreams I've been having.'

'I wish you could remember. It would make my job of explaining things to you a lot simpler. What about the Starstone that entered you. It's an intelligent life form with incredible powers. Whether or not you want to believe it, I think you had something to do with this healing business,' Deana continued, as Connor remained quiet. 'Apparently the Starstone can do anything. More than we can ever imagine and it's your mind that helps control it.'

'This is going to sound just crazy, but I do think I had some connection with what happened here last night. I had a dream I was healing loads of people. I only had to touch someone and they got better.'

'I knew it!' Deana grinned. 'By the way, what happened to your glasses? Why aren't you wearing them?'

'I'm not sure,' Connor admitted. 'I can see better without them.'

'That's amazing,' breathed Deana. 'I bet it's the Starstone's doing.'

The doors banged loudly and a doctor with wild frizzy hair came into the room. He coughed loudly to gain their attention.

'I'm sorry, Miss, but visiting times are over,' he said. 'You'll have to leave now.'

Connor's stomach lurched. He didn't want Deana to go. He didn't want to be alone. The hospital was really spooky since he was the only patient left in the ward.

'Remember what I said – trust K,' Deana whispered, giving Connor a quick kiss on his forehead.

He watched her walk away. She turned and waved as she disappeared through the doors. Heavy hearted, Connor waved back. He felt empty and lost now she'd gone. The doctor quickly whisked him away for a scan. It turned out to be a painless ordeal that left Connor none the wiser.

He was later moved to a single room. This was much better and far less scary than being in the large ward alone. He was also pleased to see a television hoisted high on the wall. At least he had something to occupy his mind now that he didn't have Philip to talk to.

A few hours later another female nurse, whom Connor had never seen before, showed two men into his room. She left, snapping the door shut behind her. He was now alone in the room with them.

The hairs on the back of Connor's neck prickled uneasily. He switched his gaze from one man to the other. They both appeared to be in their forties, wearing suits and carrying briefcases.

The larger man had broad shoulders as square as his jaw and as wide as the doorway. He introduced himself as Marty. His proud baldhead shone like a gem, in direct contrast to the amount of hair he had growing on his face. Taking off his sunglasses, he revealed small dark eyes, which were out of proportion to the rest of his face. A golden suntan warmed his skin and Connor wondered if he'd been on holiday or visited a sun bed. He chewed noisily on some gum and eyed Connor dubiously.

The other man's name was Joe. He was an extremely gaunt looking man with thin serious lips. Connor wondered if he'd ever laughed in his whole life. Perched like a bird on the end of his bed and with a beak like nose, Joe eyed him with piercing blue eyes.

'We work for the government, son, and we want you to tell us everything you know about the miracle healing business which took place here last night,' Marty said, taking a seat and resting his hands on his knees in a relaxed manner.

'I don't know anything.' Connor whispered in a small voice, turning his attention to Marty.

'We were hoping you might have something to tell us,' Marty continued, leaning forward in his chair. 'We've spoken to quite a few people from last night. They were all more than happy to tell us their stories. We were hoping you would be just as co-operative. Perhaps you can tell us how you were affected last night?'

Connor squirmed under his gaze and gave a shrug.

'Don't look so frightened. Everything you tell us will remain confidential. We have your best interests at heart. In your own words, please tell us your experience.'

Marty smiled too coldly for Connor to ignore. He recognised a snake when he saw one. His stomach flipped backwards. He shrugged, not knowing what to say.

'All I know is, I feel much better,' he said.

'Come on!' Joe snapped. He turned from the window and slammed his hand down hard on his briefcase. Connor's heart skipped a beat. 'Tell us what *really* happened.'

Marty scowled at Joe.

'I apologise for my colleague. We've both had very hectic days. So what *do* you think happened?' Marty continued smoothly. 'I mean, it's not every day things like this happen.'

'I don't know,' Connor replied carefully.

He was beginning to feel fidgety. He wondered where K was. It was getting late. Surely he should be here by now. But perhaps he wouldn't be able to find this room. He began to panic.

'Let's talk about aliens. Do you believe in aliens?' Joe asked smugly. 'Judging by your latest scan that we had access to, I think you know exactly what took place here last night. We know your body isn't normal. We know you're not normal. We know you're one of *them*.'

Joe made that last word drag on for longer than necessary but Connor understood the meaning. Whatever the scan showed, these men really thought he was an alien. Marty passed Joe a scornful glance as if he'd said something he shouldn't have. These men were relentless. They wanted to implicate him with the recent events happening in the hospital. It seemed they wanted his blood and at this moment Connor felt he was a mouse being eyed by two great hawks.

The next forty-five minutes were the longest of Connor's life as the two interrogators probed and accused in an attempt to make him confess that he really was a creature from outer space.

'You're an alien! So why don't you just tell us the truth!' Joe screamed angrily.

'I'm not an alien!' Connor blurted out. 'I'm a boy!'

Their faces darkened like thunderous clouds.

'A boy,' Joe mocked, leaning forwards so Connor could feel his breath on his face. 'I haven't seen a boy like you before.'

Marty raised his hand gently and looked directly at Joe, who quickly quietened down.

'What my colleague is trying to say is – we know the truth. We know you are an alien trying to survive on this planet while you're waiting for your family to come down in their little spaceship and rescue you. What we want to know is where and when will you be meeting them.'

'You're both mad!' Connor cried out. 'I am *not* an alien!'

'Well, we do have the evidence to prove contrary,' said Marty, rubbing his hands impatiently.

'I don't even believe in aliens,' Connor replied, not liking the tone in Marty's voice. It sounded even more deceitful, if that was possible.

'We're not going to let you go, you know,' snarled Joe, suddenly pinning Connor's arms to the chair.

'Get off me, you creep!' Connor screamed, kicking out with his legs. With all the strength he could muster he tried to fight back.

'Perhaps you should tell my friend the truth,' Marty smiled, watching Connor struggle. 'Then he might let you go.'

'I won't lie for anyone!' spat Connor.

'This is ridiculous!' Joe shouted, holding Connor's wrists so tightly they began to bruise. 'We're wasting time!'

Connor was trapped. But he wasn't giving up easily. He'd make them suffer as much as he was. He curled his spine forwards and bit Joe's hand.

'Ahh,' Joe yelled, releasing Connor's wrists. He brought his hand high in the air and struck Connor hard across his face.

The burning blow left Connor shaking, but he refused to let them see his tears. In his mouth he tasted blood.

A loud dialling tone broke the silence. Marty pulled out his mobile phone and looked directly at Connor. 'Yes… all right… we'll do that… okay… see you in a moment.'

He hung up and turned to Joe.

'Everything is ready. Zelda is waiting for us in the car park. Apparently they've tracked the girl down as well.'

'What girl?' Connor blurted out and a horrible realisation dawned on him. 'No! Not Deana!'

'Shut up, brat,' Joe laughed, plucking a handkerchief from his pocket and a small bottle labelled with a skull and crossbones.

'You leave her alone – she hasn't done anything!' Connor responded.

'It's not as easy as that,' Joe sneered. 'But if you come with us, we'll see about having her released.'

'That's blackmail!' Connor spat.

Joe quickly unscrewed the lid and dabbed some clear liquid on the handkerchief. Connor wasn't thinking properly. Everything was happening so fast. He was concerned for Deana. What were they going to do with her?

'W… what are you doing?' Connor stammered, jumping out from the chair and knocking it over. 'Get away from me!'

'Pin him down, Marty,' Joe sneered. 'You're coming with us. This won't hurt.'

Marty stepped forward and grasped Connor's arm.

'Get off me!' Connor cried, struggling to release his arm. 'Help!'

Marty placed his hand over Connor's mouth. Connor kicked him hard. 'Quick. Bring it here. This will knock him out!'

But before Joe reached him, the door opened, slamming heavily against the wall. Connor was speechless. He fell to his knees as a large silverback gorilla stood on its hind legs, blocking the doorway. It pounded its mighty chest and waved its muscular arms. At almost seven feet tall, it looked terrifyingly huge. It gave a sudden cry and charged into the room with all the power of a steam train.

'What the –?' Marty spun around.

Joe pulled out a gun. But it was too late. The gorilla picked him up and threw him like a puppet against the wall. Something snapped when he crashed to the floor unconscious.

Marty released Connor and pushed him towards the gorilla, as he tried to make a run for it. Much to Connor's surprise, the gorilla moved him gently out of the way. It lurched towards Marty and grabbed him before he fled the room. Connor placed his hands over his ears and hid under the bed.

The next thing he knew the same silverback gorilla was gently pulling him from under the bed and helping him to his feet.

Connor was shaking. He thought he was going to be sick. He caught sight of Marty's body lying on the floor, lifeless next to Joe's. A wide, gentle grin appeared on the gorilla's face and his belly started vibrating like a cat. His broad chest heaved with exertion and his large nostrils were flaring.

'Are you okay?' asked a deep rumbling voice.

Connor stared in fright and nodded dumbly. The gorilla could speak. How was that possible? Slowly, in front of his eyes, the gorilla began changing shape. Its hair was sucked into the skin, which turned a paler colour. Its jaw and facial shape transformed to one more human looking. Clothes instantly appeared on the human form and longer brown hair sprouted out from the top of his head.

Connor stood with his mouth wide open, quivering on the spot.

'I'm sorry about that,' the man apologised. 'But those two idiots were going to kill you. They work for an organisation called ACE, Alien Control Exterminators. Don't worry. I'm here to rescue you. People like that have to be detained, otherwise they'll continue to do harm. By the way my name is K. I'm a…' he hesitated. 'I'm a…'

'Alien?' Connor whispered.

'Half alien, to be perfectly honest. But I'm the best shape-shifter in town.'

'The only one, I expect,' Connor replied, watching him uneasily. 'So you can change your shape into anything?'

'Well, almost. Anything living. Choose an animal for me to turn into and I'll prove it to you. Better still, I'll become you. Don't be afraid.'

K's body began jolting and very slowly Connor saw him changing shape. He watched aghast, as K's face became more oval. Loud cracking noises, which sounded like bones breaking, filled the room. His hair changed in colour from a rich dark brown to a mousy blond. At the same time his height instantly decreased by several inches. Within a couple of seconds, K had finished his transformation. Connor was now staring at a duplicate image of himself with the same familiar blue eyes shining back at him.

'This is weird!' said Connor, shaking his head. 'You look like me. How is that possible?'

'No time to explain. Now, listen to me carefully,' he ordered, grabbing Connor's shoulders firmly. 'I've got to get you out of here. Another friend of mine will be waiting for us in a van. He'll take us to a place of safety.'

'What sort of trouble am I in?' Connor asked.

'You've had a scan at the hospital. Someone has leaked information to the ACE,' he said bluntly. 'I don't know who it was but they obviously have an informant here working for them. The Starstone has distorted your body slightly, for you to be the perfect host. The scan revealed that your heart has doubled in size and your other organs appear to have vanished. But don't worry. It's only temporary.'

'I'm a host and my organs have disappeared?'

'There's so much to tell you but so little time to explain,' said K.

Connor had never felt as vulnerable in his life as he did now. His entire being felt stripped to the core. Nothing would ever be the same again. His safe little world had been turned upside down and placed inside a cement mixer.

How could these things happen to him? He hadn't a clue his body was any different. His organs had vanished. His heart had doubled in size. He eyed K nervously. Could he be trusted? Connor had to rely on his gut instincts. Right now they were telling him to go with K. He had no other choice.

'Our time is short,' K explained. 'Men from the ACE are crawling all over this joint like ants. Quick put your coat on. It's cold outside.'

Connor gulped rather loudly and did as he was told. 'What if I get caught?'

'That's why I'm here. Don't worry. Now that I'm disguised as you, they won't know who to chase,' said K softly, looking directly into Connor's eyes. 'Now follow me. And Connor –'

'Yes.'

'Be careful. I don't think it's just the ACE that are after you.'

'What do you mean?'

'I'll explain later, just be wary of everyone for the time being!' he warned.

'But –'

'What is it?'

'I think Deana's been kidnapped,' Connor told him.

'Nah!' K grinned reassuringly. 'She's okay, I've just seen her.' K opened the door. 'Come on. It's all clear!'

Connor felt a burden lifting. He truly hoped K was right about Deana.

K hastily left the room with Connor following close behind. In the corridor and standing a few feet away from the door, K quickly ran back. Pulling out a gun from his pocket, K shot it twice in the room. Connor froze, his heart thumping heavily. He couldn't believe what he'd seen. K had shot those two men in cold blood and apart from looking anxious but there was nothing else in his expression to reveal the deadly act he'd just performed.

'Come on!' urged K, running ahead. He grabbed hold of Connor's top and dragged the boy reluctantly.

They ran blindly towards the door.

Being a host for a Starstone – having no organs – on the verge of being drugged and kidnapped – meeting a half-alien – being hunted down – seeing K shoot two men – all these were enough ingredients to cause a tornado of chaos inside Connor's head.

K pushed open the heavy, squeaky doors that led down the stairs. They were on the twentieth floor of the hospital. Connor peered over the banister and started panicking.

'Breathe deeply,' whispered K. 'You'll be fine.'

Connor nodded shakily. He took a deep breath. Slowly, he felt his anxiety coming under control.

'Can't we go down in the lift?' he asked

K shook his head and gave a laugh. 'The exercise will do you good, you lazy toad.'

CHAPTER SIX

The Ghoul

They successfully descended to level ten before encountering any serious dilemma. Connor jumped as the back door of the hospital burst open, allowing a tidal wave of commotion to sweep up the stairs towards them. K wasted no time. He grabbed Connor and shoved him through the doors on level ten.

'Keep down!' K hissed.

As the thunderous footsteps passed them, K and Connor peered discreetly out of the glass doors. A troop of soldiers, armed with guns, was disappearing up the stairs. Connor managed to count seven men dressed in distasteful green uniforms but had no idea how many more were in front.

'So, they think they can stop us by bringing in the troops, do they?' K whispered, too preoccupied to notice a rather large lady standing over them.

'What are you two boys doing down here in this maternity ward? I don't remember seeing you two before.'

They turned to face a large woman wearing a blue uniform. Her grey hair was swept into a bun with wispy strands poking out. Her murky coloured eyes narrowed suspiciously. Connor wasn't sure what was scariest, a handful of soldiers or the nasty looking woman looming over them.

'Identical twins,' she tutted impatiently. 'Double trouble.'

'We're looking for level nine,' said K, pushing open the doors and running down to the next level before she could say anything else.

'Kids!' the nurse muttered as she returned to her patients. 'Who in their right mind would have them!'

They leaped down the stairs, two at a time, and descended a further four levels.

On a higher level a loud shout rang out.

'There they are, men!' cried a commanding voice.

Connor saw several white faces, staring down at them. One of them was distinctly pointing at him.

'Run!' shouted K.

Connor raced down the stairs, jumping five at a go. The soldiers followed hot on their tail and appeared to be gaining on them. When they arrived on level four the door once again crashed open and more soldiers swarmed into the building like flies.

Connor didn't know what to do. They were trapped and his legs had frozen in fear, making him a prisoner inside his own body. His eyes were dancing fleetingly in alarm. There was no escape. The enemy was storming towards them from both sides. Everything was happening too fast as if he were a video being fast-forwarded. Yet, at the crucial time when the enemy was almost upon them, time suddenly slowed down and almost stopped.

'Huh?' K frowned in puzzlement as Connor searched his face in an urgent appeal for help. 'Jump!' he shouted, yanking Connor towards the banister. 'Trust me! You'll be all right!'

Connor hadn't time to think. This was a situation of flight or fight and it seemed they were going to take flight over the railings. This was no time to reason or ask questions. It was the only escape route. Connor clambered on to the railing and as he looked down towards the ground on level four he closed his eyes.

'Now!' urged K, with a firm grip on Connor's hand. Together they made the jump.

Gunfire exploded around them. Down Connor fell towards the ground with K at his side. He gritted his teeth as his stomach rolled over. They seemed to be falling forever. The air whizzed past his ears as he fell helplessly towards the concrete floor below. Then a loud sound entered his ears – he was screaming. At that crucial moment, K released his hand.

Through his screaming, Connor began to hear a thunderous applause above him. Just before he crashed to the floor he glanced up to see a magnificent creature with massive wings flying above him. Huge talons closed on his shoulders and before he knew what was going on, he was lowered to the ground, in one piece. Connor gulped. The bird was bigger than an ostrich and could fly. It looked more like a griffin with emerald green wings and a shiny orange beak.

And if that wasn't amazing enough, the creature spoke to him in a squawky voice.

'Get out of here! I'll keep these men at bay!'

And suddenly it dawned on Connor that it was K, coming to his rescue: the best shape-shifter in town. Connor's mouth fell open wide as he turned on his heels and ran out of the door into the night. Gunfire erupted behind him and Connor ran for his life. He sprinted along the path, skidding as he turned a corner. Before he could stop himself, he suddenly collided with someone.

'Ow!' a familiar cry echoed.

A woman stood rubbing her head.

'Deana – you're safe! What are you doing here? Boy, am I glad to see you! We've got to get out of here!'

'I know,' she smiled, taking his hand and pulling him after her. 'I've got some bad news. Your aunt and uncle have been kidnapped.'

'What?' he panted, struggling to keep pace.

'A portal was used to enter your home. Definastine's servants didn't just take them, they took the sofa as well.'

Strangely, Connor wasn't too bothered by this news. 'Why couldn't he have taken them a few years ago.'

'Connor!' Deana scolded. 'That's a horrible thing to say.'

'I know,' said Connor, not regretting a single word of it.

'Come on. Sparkie's waiting for us in his van.' Deana stretched her head forward. Squinting into the darkness, she cautiously checked the area.

'He's not here,' Deana noted in a whisper. 'Perhaps he parked round the corner. Keep close to the wall. We'll be able to hide behind those bushes for cover if we need to.'

The air was cool and refreshing after the stuffy atmosphere of the hospital. Connor felt free for the first time since he'd arrived at the hospital. He was glad to be outside but felt a pang of horror having left K behind. K had done something awful in the hospital; he'd killed two men. Yet, Connor still felt a sense of gratitude towards him. Without K, he wouldn't have stood a chance of escaping. Those men were going to do something awful to him, maybe even kill him. Goodness knows what would have happened if K hadn't turned up when he did. It didn't bear thinking about.

'I met your friend, K,' whispered Connor, not wanting to expose K's heartless deed, of killing in cold blood.

'Was he all right?' asked Deana, looking genuinely worried.

Connor nodded and said nothing else. Deana became concerned.

'What's wrong?'

'Nothing,' Connor lied. How could he tell Deana that her friend was a murderer?

'You would tell me if something was wrong, wouldn't you?' she said with a pleading look in her eyes. 'K's a really good friend of mine. If he's hurt or something I need to know.'

'No, he's fine,' Connor replied coolly.

'Good.' Deana relaxed and continued along the path.

Every now and then, Deana froze her position whenever she spotted anyone walking across the car park. When it was safe to move on, she silently resumed along the path. Connor followed quietly, his eyes wide and frightened like a scared kitten. Nearby lampposts stood tall and erect as if watching them with empty eyes.

'Sparkie fixed it so the lights wouldn't give us away,' Deana explained. 'He's good with things like that.'

Suddenly Deana grabbed Connor and pushed him down to the ground. He fell face first in some mud.

'What did you do that for?' he complained, wiping his eyes clean.

Deana hushed him at once, her eyes focussed ahead. Connor followed her gaze to a black car parked a few feet away, with blackened windows. He peered through a small gap in the shrub. Clouds of smoke drifted out from a small opening in the back window. A tall man dressed in a black suit was walking across the car park towards the car and opened the back door. The interior light of the car revealed a tall, skinny woman stepping out of the vehicle. She had sleeked bleached hair and was wearing a bright red mini skirt and high heel shoes. She had a cigar between her lips and was blowing circles of smoke into the night air.

'Who's that?' Connor murmured.

'Keep down!' hissed Deana, forcing Connor's head lower.

'Any sign of that little creep?' they heard the woman speak.

'Not yet,' the man replied. 'But your men *will* find him.'

'It's been a long time since we caught an alien for ourselves. I'm not going to let this one get away,' the woman replied coldly and wrapped her jacket around her shoulders.

'The girl escaped though. She put five of our officers out of action. We think she may be one of them, but we're not sure. There was no one else at the house.'

'How dare she!' the woman raged, throwing her arms up in the air and stamping her feet. Her black leather jacket fell to the ground. 'I'll kill her myself!'

The man retrieved the jacket for her, placing it over her skinny shoulders once more. 'You could do it very easily,' he praised.

'Thank you, Doug,' the woman drooled, stroking her finger along his jaw. 'I think you're a great asset to the ACE. I'm thinking of getting rid of Pierre so I can have you as my personal bodyguard. What do you say?'

'It would be an honour to serve you so closely,' he replied smugly.

'Huh! I've seen enough of this,' said Deana, pulling Connor with her. 'Let's get out of here.'

Deana, keeping low, headed back towards the corner of the car park. From there they hoped to spot Sparkie's van. Crouching within the shadows of a bush, Connor soon began to ache.

'Did you really put five of her men out of action?' he asked quietly.

Deana nodded.

'What happened? How did you do it?'

'What? You want the gory details?' There was amusement in her voice.

'No, I just wondered what happened, that's all.'

'I'll tell you later,' she replied.

Connor frowned and looked away. They had only been there for a couple of minutes when an unexpected flash of light startled them from behind.

Deana turned, losing her balance. 'Sparkie?'

But it wasn't Sparkie. Connor smelt it before he saw it. A raw, decaying stench burned the inside of his nostrils. Connor wanted to be sick. To his horror, a tall hooded figure wearing a robe stepped out from the solid brick wall, or rather through it.

'Give me the Starstone!' its cruel voice spoke with authority.

A shrivelled hand reached out with lightning speed and gripped Connor's throat. The faceless creature towered before him.

Deana gasped. The creature turned its gaze to her. She reached for something inside her pocket but whatever she wanted to do, it was too late. Two shafts of red light pierced out from the creature's eyes as it stared hard at her. Deana immediately slumped lifeless to the ground. Connor screamed. Was Deana dead?

'Deana!' he croaked. 'Deana!'

She remained unresponsive.

'What did you do to her? Get off me!' Connor squirmed desperately but to no avail. The more he struggled, the more sinister the grip. The creature then altered the positions of its hands. It grasped hold of Connor's coat and suddenly hoisted him high in the air. Connor's feet dangled from the ground. 'Let me go. You're hurting me!'

'Give me the Starstone,' it repeated coldly, 'and I'll let you live!'

'I haven't got it! You've got the wrong person. Let me go!'

'Ahhh,' the creature screamed. 'Don't play me for a fool. Surrender it now or I will take it myself.'

Connor started to choke. He could hardly breathe anymore. 'You're hurting me!' he rasped.

'That's the whole idea!'

Connor was beyond fear. He thought he was going to die.

CHAPTER SEVEN

A Leap into the Unknown

Death. It wasn't something Connor had even thought much about in the past but now he seemed to be coming closer to it every minute. He was dangling in mid-air and began viewing his life in a disconnected kind of way. He was able to note the pains in his body without actually feeling them. Was this what dying was like? He didn't feel frightened anymore. He felt free and strangely peaceful. He hung above the ground helplessly and waited for the moment when he would take his final breath.

But something began talking him out of surrendering. A soft angelic voice began speaking to him.

Don't give up. Fight with all your might!

Connor's body shuddered with a jolt, as if a switch had been turned on inside his body. With a sudden powerful force he realised he wasn't prepared to give up. With all his strength, he kicked the foul creature. He repeatedly swung his dangling feet and struck at the body beneath the robes. Although Connor was held at arm's length by the scruff of his neck, he did at one point make contact with the creature's body and felt it stiffen.

The monster snarled and raised a hand into the air, bringing it down hard across Connor's face, tearing his cheek. Blood flowed from the open wound.

Connor felt no pain. Numb with fright, resentment soon built up in the pit of his stomach until he was burning with an anger that engulfed all terror.

The creature snarled. Shaking Connor like a rag doll, it stared with its piercing eyes. The beams of blood red light burned deep inside Connor, but had no effect.

'Get off me!' Connor screamed angrily.

The creature held Connor warily. Why hadn't the boy reacted to his chilling glare? Was the Starstone helping him?

'Give the Starstone to me and I'll release you!' the creature bartered.

'No, you won't!' Connor gasped for breath. 'I'm not stupid! You'll kill me anyway.'

'I'm losing my patience,' a warning note appeared in the chilling voice.

The creature paused for a moment. Then, without any warning it released one hand and reached it forward. It was going to try to take the Starstone from inside Connor's stomach – even if it meant slicing him open.

Deep purple veins poked out from the deadly grey skin on the hand where large knotted lumps covered it like a miniature range of mountains. With fingernails like dirty yellow claws, long and curled, it attempted to rip the boy's stomach open.

Unknown to Connor, his muscles were rapidly knitting together, forming a surface so tough that the ghoul broke all its fingernails.

'Ahhh!' it cried.

Connor's muscles were as strong as concrete and although his clothing had been ripped the ghoul made no scratch on his body whatsoever. Startled, it cursed the boy and held him up with both hands again.

'What strange magic is this?' it whispered. 'No one encounters Definastine and lives to tell the tale!'

'Definastine?' croaked Connor.

But something extraordinary was happening inside Connor, something he had little control of. His cloudy blue eyes became speckled with dashes of golden light, like sunlight reflecting on water. His pale skin hardened. His muscles grew in size and strength.

Deana slowly gained consciousness and scrambled to her feet. When she noticed the physical changes in Connor, her eyes widened in fear. She panicked, believing the creature was killing him.

She whispered Connor's name, her voice distressed.

Connor didn't respond. Responding would be catastrophic. He couldn't afford to lose concentration. His survival mechanism was operating at full power. With the Starstone giving him incredible strength, Connor knew this was his only chance of escape. He had to focus.

Deana was free to run away at any time. But she didn't. She wanted to stop Definastine before he killed her friend. She wanted to use her weapon, the latest Zap-Fire laser model, but she was afraid of harming Connor. She frantically searched the ground and stumbled across a rusty metal pole. She raised it above her head and made a swing for Definastine's head. It surged through the air knocking Definastine backwards. She struck him again.

Definastine groaned loudly. Losing his footing he dropped Connor to the ground. Deana pulled out her Zap-Fire and fired several shots at Definastine's leg. The first one struck him and he fell to his knees. Immediately a red tinted shield encompassed his body, sheltering him from further harm.

'Run!' Deana screamed at Connor.

He did. Together they ran for their lives. Definastine watched them flee into the distance. Snarling viciously he gave orders to another figure hiding in the shadows.

'Razor, you saw what that child did. Destroy him and the girl!' he demanded. 'Do it quickly and bring me the Starstone!'

Stepping out from the darkness was another powerfully built tall, hooded figure.

'Yes, master,' it bowed respectfully, before turning on its heels to pursue the boy and the young woman.

With longer strides it gained with every step. Connor and Deana were petrified. Deana turned and fired several more shots but they all missed as the creature dodged them with lightning speed.

They sprinted across the car park, weaving between the cars. Connor lost sight of Deana as she stooped down behind a parked vehicle. He darted in between the parked cars but he couldn't see her. Connor knew he couldn't outrun the creature, so he lay flat on the ground and rolled under a parked Range Rover.

Footsteps swiftly approached just yards away. The creature

paused and sniffed the air. It then came closer to where Connor was hiding. Suddenly the creature knelt down and lowered its face flat to the ground.

The hideous face came into view. It was bony and covered in grey skin stretched over a pointed jaw. There was no fleshy nose, just a hole in the skull. The eyes were glowing orange and staring straight at Connor. A cruel grin appeared on its face, revealing razor sharp teeth.

Connor kicked out at the monstrous face. The creature screamed and retreated quickly.

Then another sudden scream erupted a few yards behind him. Connor stiffened. It was Deana. The creature stood up but was flung back to the ground. It stood up a second time and gave a chilling scream. It began waving its claw-like hands wildly in mid air. It seemed to be fighting something. Connor remained where he was. After a moment's struggle the creature fled back in the direction from which it had come.

Connor heard a car tearing across the car park, followed by screeching brakes and loud shouting.

'Get him, men!' screeched a woman's voice.

The car, followed by several others, raced away in pursuit. Connor had no idea what was happening but guessed it had something to do with the creature that had almost caught him. Once he felt the danger had passed, he wriggled out from under the sanctuary of the Range Rover.

'Ahoy there, Connor!' a high pitched voice rang out. 'Giddy up. We have to get you out of here!'

It wasn't obvious at first, but floating in the air just above the cars was a van partially invisible in the surrounding darkness. An old man poked his head out of the window, grinning wildly.

Connor gulped, immediately recognising the man from the garage where he'd bought his ice cream. The back door swung open. Deana was leaning out with her arms outstretched.

'Come on, Connor!' Deana yelled urgently. 'Before it comes back!'

Connor scrambled onto a car roof. Grasping hold of Deana's hand, he clambered into the hovering vehicle.

Deana hugged him tightly and, noticing his wound, pulled out a handkerchief from her pocket. She tried to stop the flow of blood by applying firm pressure.

'Does it hurt?' she asked.

'Not really,' Connor replied shakily. 'I can't feel much at the moment.'

'Thank goodness you had the sense to hide,' she said. 'Well done. I don't know how long I was knocked out back there but you must be a right little warrior to survive.'

'Just like your mum and dad. You certainly led them a merry chase, didn't you?' the old man chuckled. 'So, aliens don't exist, eh? Have you changed your mind yet?'

Connor nodded dumbly. He noticed for the first time what bright blue eyes and white teeth Sparkie had.

'You had brown teeth when I first met you,' Connor observed.

'I was in disguise,' Sparkie giggled excitedly.

Deana started laughing and threw her head back. 'This has been a night I won't forget in a hurry!'

'Same here,' Connor mumbled. 'I thought that creep had killed you!'

'Knocked me out pretty bad – but didn't kill me.'

The old man was still chuckling happily. When he finally calmed down he said, 'Well, I expect Deana told you lots about me.'

'No,' said Connor honestly. 'There's a lot Deana hasn't told me.'

'It's not my fault you forgot everything I explained to you on Monday morning,' she replied sulkily.

'As I understand it, it's not his either,' Sparkie reminded her. 'Anyway, I'm Sparkie. It's good to meet you properly at last. I'm sorry I wasn't parked where I said I would be, but other unforeseen problems presented themselves to me – such as the black car. Trust Zelda to park in the spot I'd planned to be. Typical women, always spoiling things for others.'

Deana gave a disapproving grunt.

'Oh, apart from you, my dear. You're no problem. You're like one of the men! But that woman finally came through for us in the end, I must admit.'

'But not deliberately,' Deana muttered. 'She wasn't helping us.'

'But that's the beauty of it. She helped us without even knowing it. Did you see Zelda chasing Razor away in her car? At least that took both their minds off you two for a while.'

'Who's Zelda?' asked Connor, taking things slowly. 'Two men who came to interrogate me at the hospital mentioned that name. They said she was waiting for me.'

'She's the woman you saw coming out of that black car. She's in charge of the ACE,' Deana explained. 'She's a complete nut case.'

'The ACE soldiers are swarming all over that place but if I know K, he's sorting out the problem.' Sparkie showed them a pocket-sized television screen.

K had changed back into his human form and quite mystifyingly was dodging numerous bullets with a speed that must have been faster than light. He was holding his gun and was firing it directly at the attacking party. They were vanishing one by one.

'Huh?' grunted Connor. 'What's happening to them? Where are they going?'

'Straight to the interrogating unit at the AAA,' said Deana.

'You mean – he isn't killing them?' Connor gasped, slowly coming to realise that K hadn't killed Marty and Joe in the hospital; he had merely transported them to another place. Connor hadn't been close enough to see their bodies disappear. He'd assumed K had killed them. He had jumped to a conclusion without knowing the facts.

'K wouldn't kill anyone. That young man believes in giving people a second chance. If it weren't for him many lives would have been unnecessarily ruined. K has helped many people in his short life. He's a Star-Lord in the making, he is,' said Sparkie proudly.

'Star-Lord?' quizzed Connor.

'It's the highest rank a person can ever achieve in the AAA. It's what most star-spirits strive for,' Deana explained.

'He'll make someone a proud husband one day,' Sparkie smiled and winked at Deana.

Her face flushed crimson.

'The ACE must've tracked you down anyway after hearing about the bizarre events in the hospital last night. Never mind, from now on we'll just have to be extra careful.'

'Who was the strange creature that tried to kill me?' Connor asked, touching his cheek.

'There were two after you tonight,' Deana told him. 'The one wanting the Starstone was Definastine, otherwise known as the Dark Master. It's amazing that he didn't kill you. Not many people have ever seen him before and lived to tell the tale.'

Connor looked out of the window. He could believe that. If it weren't for the Starstone, he'd have been killed easily. On the other hand, if the Starstone hadn't placed him in this predicament in the first place, he wouldn't have to worry about such things.

'When we started running he sent one of his servants after us,' Deana explained.

'It was Razor,' said Sparkie sadly. 'Poor soul.'

'Poor soul!' gasped Connor. 'He wanted me dead!'

'Yes, that is true but he wasn't always like that. Let me explain. Razor used to be a top secret agent, working for the AAA. He was a fantastic man. He wouldn't think twice about placing his life in danger to save others. He was one of four men who disappeared several years ago. After an operation went wrong, Definastine managed to capture them. He changed everything about them. He trapped their souls and distorted their bodies. Now, they can't even remember their pasts,' explained Sparkie. 'They are lost souls.'

Connor said nothing. He felt emotionally numb. At this moment he didn't care about anything. He leaned back, relaxed his head against the cushioned headrest and breathed normally at last. He began to wonder if it was all a very strange dream; every now and then, he expected to wake up to the bellowing of his uncle's demands.

Connor observed Sparkie placing a strange hat on his head, which strongly resembled an upside-down kitchen sieve. Thin blue wires poked out from the top and streams of blue electric currents randomly pulsated between them. Several times, he blinked, just in case his eyes were playing tricks on him. It was like watching a lightning storm on a miniature scale.

'What's that you're wearing?' Connor asked.

'What? This old thing?' Sparkie pointed to his hat. 'It's a communication link with other star-spirits. I invented it.'

'Very trendy,' mocked Deana.

'What does it do?' asked Connor.

'Apart from making me look trendy,' he looked across at Deana, 'it also helps me pick up various messages. I'm waiting to hear from Tookar at the moment.'

'Oh,' Connor replied.

Sparkie then attached small suction caps to his temples. Connor began to think what a very odd little man he was and continued watching him with interest.

Everything about Sparkie was odd. He had a peculiar shaped face, with a wider than average forehead. His long pointed chin stuck out sharply and hanging proudly from it was a long, silvery goatee, which was curled perfectly near the end to form a complete loop. It was difficult to see where his chin ended and where the goatee began.

He also wore red framed glasses that were far too big for his face, resting on a very large nose. Fluffy white tufts of hair stuck out from under his hat. He was of slender build with unusually small feet and his little knobbly knees looked more like skin coloured tennis balls stuck firmly on to his legs.

He wore a T-shirt and shorts in the middle of winter but since the van was warm, it wasn't too surprising. It was difficult to tell his age. Connor placed him in his seventies since he had many wrinkles.

Sparkie continued fiddling in the front seat. A warm golden light suddenly filled the van, revealing strange fish swimming above their heads. The van had magically become a fish tank on wheels. Instead of metal bodywork, it was made from transparent material filled with clear liquid that softly changed colour. Even the fish seemed to change colour. The warm glow in the van was reflected within the tank, emphasising the shimmering scales of the fish.

Connor was slowly hypnotised watching the fish swimming all around him. It had an instant calming effect and seemed very surreal after his recent encounters.

'How is it possible?' Connor whispered under his breath. He was soon gaping like a goldfish himself. 'They're beautiful! Where did you get them from?'

'From another planet. Some friends gave them to me.'

'From another planet?' Connor whispered in awe.

'That one is my favourite.' Deana drew Connor's attention to a large red and pink striped fish, that looked as if it were wearing a magnificent ball grown.

Connor rather liked the blue and orange striped one. It was as round as a ball with teeth that stuck out.

'I don't think we should hover above these cars so low down. We should go higher. Put your seat belts on,' Sparkie said, immediately pulling a lever.

The van zoomed up into the sky.

Connor's stomach churned. The acceleration made him stick fast to his seat. At last when the van stopped, Connor banged his head on the roof.

'Ow!'

'Sparkie!' said Deana crossly. 'You could have given him time to put the seat belt on first! You should make sure all your passengers survive your trips instead of coming close to death.'

'Sorry about that!' Sparkie replied sheepishly.

'Are you all right?' she asked.

'I'll live,' replied Connor, who was feeling rather light-headed.

Deana helped adjust his belt so it fitted more securely.

Meanwhile Connor had started exploring the door to his right. The surface felt horrible and rubbery. He turned around and noticed that the van was twice as big on the inside as it was on the outside. It was amazing. Neither did it possess a steering wheel or handbrake.

Connor stretched out his legs, feeling surprisingly happy.

'This is great!' he smiled. 'I bet this is better than flying in an aeroplane.'

'How's your head feeling?' Deana asked loudly, glancing hard at Sparkie.

'Fine,' said Connor. 'No damage done.'

'No, but there could have been,' Deana said sternly. 'It says in the code of conduct, to always consider your passengers first and make sure they understand what's going to happen next.'

Ignoring Deana's remarks, Sparkie occupied himself with some buttons on the dashboard. He amazed Connor. If someone were nagging at him like that, he wouldn't be able to concentrate on anything else.

A flat television screen sprung up from the middle of the dashboard. Sparkie turned a dial and the screen became a virtual reality map, revealing the entire area of the hospital car park. It showed everything from the viewpoint of a helicopter suspended fifty feet up in the air.

Suddenly the floor disappeared.

Connor screamed.

'Sparkie!' Deana yelled. 'You must explain to Connor what you're going to do next. You just frightened the life out of him! Don't worry, Connor, the floor has turned transparent but it's still there.'

'Connor, please forgive me. I rarely have passengers. I'm not used to speaking about what I'm going to do next. I'll try to be more considerate and inform you as I go along.'

Connor grinned. As long as he was safe, he could put up with anything, including a nutty old man. He tentatively touched the floor with his foot and was surprised to feel something solid beneath it. He rounded his body forward and peered between his knees to observe the hospital ground below.

'Wow!' Connor said, feeling giddy with vertigo. 'Can anyone see us up here?'

Sparkie laughed. 'No, we're partly transparent at the moment.'

'What else does it do?' Connor said, sitting excited on the edge of his seat.

'Many things. This van is based on a typical spaceship, which I invented. It can fly, hover, float, travel underwater, cross galaxies, turn us invisible. It can even change its shape. Its design is based entirely on energy and vibrations. The Mookie Zensa people passed on all their advanced knowledge to me.'

'The Mookie Zensa people?' Connor queried, frowning quizzically.

'Star-spirits I met a long time ago. That's good. K's coming now,' announced Sparkie, who was focussing on the screen. 'We'd better open the window. We don't want him slamming into it now, do we?'

'I don't see anyone,' said Connor, wrinkling his eyes.

Apart from a small bird flying through the sky, he saw nothing else. It flew with speed straight towards the van. Sparkie opened the window and the bird fluttered in, flapping its wings. It hopped on the back of the seats until it came to rest in the rear of the van.

'Excellent work, K,' Sparkie congratulated him. 'Well done!'

The bird slowly began changing shape. Several loud cracking noises were heard before a handsome young man with short brown hair and dark brown eyes was sitting in its place. Connor shivered at the now familiar noise. It was like hearing a long fingernail scratching across a blackboard.

CHAPTER EIGHT

K the Shape-Shifter

'Wow!' Connor breathed. 'Thanks for rescuing me.'

'I'm glad you made it!' K smiled at Connor, grasping his hand and holding it tightly for several seconds. He turned to Deana and planted a kiss on her cheek. 'How's my favourite lady?'

'As good as can be expected,' she blushed. 'How did it go down there?'

'Altogether about forty ACE men out of action,' he told her.

'I sorted out another five,' Deana informed him.

'They can't cause trouble where they've been sent to,' smiled K.

'What will happen to those men?' asked Connor.

'They'll get a fair hearing,' explained Deana, 'to decide on what level of mind sweeping is required for them to become better citizens.'

'You mean wipe their minds!' replied Connor, startled. 'You can't go round messing with people's minds! It's not right.'

'People have been doing it for centuries. You've heard of people being hypnotised, haven't you?' Connor nodded.

'Well, it's a similar thing. It's a completely harmless process and a very effective way of dealing with traumatic memories. Not only do we help people come to terms with grief and pain but we also help them remember things they have long forgotten,' Deana explained.

'What right do you have to tell someone what they can and can't remember?' Connor argued.

'Don't you want to remember your past?' Deana asked softly. 'To remember the first two years of your life. We could make that happen for you.'

Connor opened his mouth to say something but closed it again and remained quiet. How could he argue against that? He'd be a hypocrite. Of course he wanted to remember.

'You see, Connor, there's a lot to learn,' Deana smiled gently. 'Look at me. I'm a warrior and a nurse. Sometimes I find myself battling for survival. Sometimes the very people I fight against get hurt. But I'm there for them in case of emergency treatment. These people have been brainwashed in a sense too. They believe fighting against other star-spirits is a good thing. "Rid the world of anything that *might* be a threat!" they say.'

'But the mind sweeping business,' said Connor, 'it doesn't sound right.'

'Can you imagine what it would be like to have witnessed a terrible crime and remember it day after day? You'd never rest. Never have peace of mind. Sometimes intervening and helping people forget is a healing process in itself. Sometimes a person who has done terrible crimes in the past wants a chance to change. Mind sweeping gives a person the opportunity to start again. It can be very difficult for someone to change without help. But everyone gets a second chance at the AAA.'

'I'm sorry I snapped,' grumbled Connor. 'I'm feeling a little tired.'

'Try and get some sleep,' Deana soothed. She began giving orders. 'Sparkie, recline Connor's seat so he can relax, – K, grab a pillow from the back for Connor.' She whispered something to Sparkie. From the glove compartment he pulled out a small flask and passed it to her.

'Here, drink this,' she smiled. 'You'll feel better when you wake up.'

Connor held the flask to his lips and sipped gently. He hadn't realised how thirsty he'd become. The sweet tasting liquid was thick and juicy. Before he knew it, he'd consumed the entire contents. It was certainly delicious and somehow made Connor feel more tired than before.

His seat slowly reclined backwards. K passed Deana the pillow to place under Connor's head.

'Are you really half-alien?' Connor whispered to K.

'Yes. My father is an alien but my mother is human like you,' K explained. 'And because I'm both, I'm mixed.'

'Mixed-up in the head,' Sparkie added.

'But how is that possible?' asked Connor, his eyelids drooping heavily.

'I'm sure I don't have to explain to you the ins and outs of the biological process of having a baby,' K smirked.

Connor's face burned with embarrassment. 'No, of course not.'

'Sleep well, Connor,' Deana whispered, stroking his head.

That was the last thing he heard before closing his eyes and drifting off into a world of dreams that twisted and entwined with each other.

His parents entered his dreams again. But this time it was different. He was able to see faces behind his parents. As he hugged his mum he saw a teenage girl grabbing his hand crying. Between her sobs, she whimpered, 'Don't forget me. I'll always be your big sister.'

There were more solemn faces coming to stroke his hair or hold his hand. People were saying goodbye. He was feeling confused. He couldn't understand what was going on. Why were they looking so distressed? But then, as strong arms held him securely and took him away from his parents, he felt something was very wrong and he grew frightened.

Next a young puppy was scampering after him, bouncing up to where he was being held. He seemed to be a long way off the ground and the puppy was finding it difficult to reach him. Suddenly the puppy changed shape to become a teenage boy.

He heard himself calling the boy's name. 'K!'

The boy waved sadly, watching him being taken away.

He was calling for his mum. She'd collapsed to the ground, heartbroken.

Everyone was watching, but no one came to help him. He glanced into the face of the person carrying him. It was a hairy faced man with warm, deep-set eyes. Connor hugged the man tightly.

The dream faded and Connor found himself in a second dream with a man and a dog. Connor was running home, desperate to escape from them. He was about to open the door, but they'd followed him home. Connor was petrified. A large hand was smothering his mouth. He couldn't scream. The man wanted to give him a letter, but a struggle broke out and the man had somehow vanished in mid-air. Then the dog took off down the road.

He dreamt of Deana talking to someone in the kitchen but when he entered the room she was alone. She looked surprised when she saw him clasping a letter. She told him to go and read it.

But it wasn't an ordinary letter and he had to hold it for several seconds until he could understand the words. It was from his parents. They were warning him of danger. Then a strange man turned up at his house with a gift that turned out to be the Starstone.

Now Connor was alone in his bedroom. Deana was screaming downstairs. Looking through his window, he could see little grey men with large, black eyes climbing up the walls to his bedroom.

A ball of light was floating in front of him. He was feeling peaceful. The Starstone was entering his body and he was falling unconscious. Then he was waking to find his window smashed and little grey men with cruel expressions clambering through it. They were odd looking creatures with long rubbery noses like elephant seals. He picked up a bat and began whacking the creatures with it as they tried to take him away. He jumped on his bed and kept hitting them. Suddenly the door burst open and Tookar was standing in the doorway, his face glowering.

'Get away from him!' he yelled, shooting at them with a strange weapon. They vanished in seconds.

But Connor was wounded, although he hadn't felt any pain. The little creatures were cutting him with their daggers. He was soaked in blood. He felt weak. Deana was crying.

'We'll have to take him to the hospital!' she screamed.

Connor woke with a jolt. Deana was sitting next to him, resting her eyes and holding his hand. The flowery scent of her perfume, which he hadn't really noticed before, was strangely comforting. With the dreams still fresh in his mind, it took him a minute to recall where he was.

K was talking to Sparkie. They were discussing Tookar and voicing their concerns about where he was.

'Any luck?' K asked.

'No, nothing. Something must've happened,' Sparkie said. 'Perhaps we should go and look for him. It's not like him to leave it this long.'

'But what about Connor? It might not be safe for him,' K urged.

'Is anywhere safe for that poor child at the moment? At least he has us to protect him.'

Connor frowned, feeling suddenly insecure. 'What are you talking about?'

K spun round. 'Hey – how are you feeling?'

'Okay, thanks. How long was I asleep for?' Connor thought it must have been for hours.

'Half an hour,' replied Deana, opening her eyes and stretching. She rested her hand on Connor's forehead and smiled with relief. 'That's good. Your temperature is down.'

'I know what happened at the house,' Connor said seriously. 'I know about those grey men. Who were they?'

Deana closed her eyes and nodded reassuringly. 'That drink we gave you was meant to relax you to the point where you'd start remembering things. Those grey men you saw were rock dwellers. Someone must've opened a portal directly from Dramian to your home. They were after the Starstone.'

'I thought so,' said Connor shakily. 'But there's something I don't quite understand. Those rock dwellers cut me with their daggers, didn't they?'

Deana nodded.

'But I don't have any knife wounds on my body.' Connor frowned. 'I don't have any wounds at all.'

'Tookar used all his healing ointment to close your wounds before you lost any more blood. We washed your body and changed your clothes before taking you to the hospital so they didn't get too suspicious.'

'You washed me!' frowned Connor, feeling highly embarrassed.

'Don't worry about it,' smiled Deana.

Easier said than done, thought Connor, turning to K. 'I dreamt of you, too.'

'Me?' K said, raising his eyebrows. 'How did I end up in your dreams?'

'It must've been a nightmare,' Sparkie added.

'I remember saying goodbye to you when I was taken from my parents. You had shape-shifted into a puppy.'

K's face went pale. 'I can't believe you remembered that. It was so long ago. We used to play together all the time.' His eyes softened. 'When you were a little kid you always insisted I change my shape before we played. When you were living with your parents you always came to visit me, with your sis...' K quickly broke off looking nervously at Deana. She was shaking her head.

'My sister,' finished Connor. 'I dreamt about her too. I can't believe I've got a sister. Why hasn't anyone mentioned her to me as yet? Is she dead or something?'

The van went uncomfortably quiet.

'Well – is she?' Connor persisted, glancing from one face to another. 'Tell me about her, *please*?'

It was Deana who spoke. 'She's alive and well but we've had strict instructions to keep her identity secret in case Definastine became aware of her. If he knew you had a sister he might want to blackmail you. If he ever kidnapped her he'd place you in a position to rescue her. We can't afford to let that happen. You're too important.'

'What is she like? Do I have any other brothers or sisters?'

'No, but you can be sure that your sister is a very nice person,' smiled Deana.

'She's brave like you and misses you like mad,' K told him.

Connor smiled. He couldn't believe it. He had a sister as well. He felt like the luckiest boy alive. He wasn't an only child and he hadn't been abandoned. Giving him up had broken his mum and dad's heart. With these warm thoughts, a glimmer of hope began to grow; perhaps one day soon he'd have the chance to see his parents and sister again.

'I've been helping Tookar look after your welfare for some time now,' K said.

'You have?' Connor replied.

'Tookar used to turn himself invisible and watch over you from time to time. I'd sometimes go with him. I particularly remember him being good at dealing with nasty little boys who picked on you. He'd accidentally trip them over so they fell into a nice dirty puddle.'

'Tookar did that?' Connor gulped. Something unfavourable would often happen to anyone trying to bully him. He had developed a reputation of sorts. For this reason he was picked on less frequently.

'Tookar was also there when a speeding car almost ran you over. He pushed you out of the way, saving your life.'

Connor gasped. His face turned deadly pale. Connor recalled the incident with clarity. He'd spent many sleepless nights thinking about it. And no matter how hard he tried to make sense of it, he couldn't forget the two hands on his upper back, pushing him to safety. It had spooked him for weeks. The car had missed him by inches.

'So how long have you been watching me?' Connor asked quietly.

'We weren't always watching you. Just every now and then.'

'How long?'

'A few years,' K told him.

'How many years?'

'Oh, for goodness sake, just tell him the truth,' snapped Deana.

'All your life,' K whispered.

Connor recalled the time he had almost fallen down the stairs at school. He could have sworn someone had grabbed his arm. But there was no one there.

'I thought I was imagining it all,' Connor confessed. 'Why you and Tookar?'

'You were one of my best friends. I didn't want to lose contact with you,' K glanced over at Deana. She smiled bashfully in return. 'Tookar was keeping his promise to a friend. To watch over you like a guardian angel.'

'He did that all right,' said Connor quietly, remembering how he'd previously treated Tookar and feeling ashamed by it.

'By the way, Connor had the pleasure of meeting Definastine tonight,' Sparkie told him.

'Huh? What happened? Were you hurt? Did he say anything to you? How did you get away? Why didn't anyone tell me?'

'Because we have been concerned about Tookar!' Sparkie answered.

Connor was laughing.

'He could've killed you!' gasped K.

'But he didn't,' Deana reminded him.

'So. What happened?'

'This creature came out from the wall and took one look at Deana and she collapsed on the ground.'

K's expression turned more serious. He turned to Deana. 'Are you all right? Were you hurt?'

'I'm fine,' she smiled calmly. 'Connor was the hero.'

Connor began talking excitedly. Within the company of his friends, his fear was long forgotten. 'He tried to take out the Starstone from my stomach but he couldn't – my body toughened up like concrete. He dropped me after Deana knocked him on the head with something. Then we ran for our lives.'

'Everyone wants the Starstone. It's amazing Tookar was able to keep it secret for as long as he did,' Sparkie muttered.

'What is it exactly?' asked Connor.

'The Starstone is an intelligent alien life form. In the two thousand years that Tookar has been stranded on this planet it had never chosen anyone until you came along.'

'Stranded for two thousand years!' gasped Connor. 'But why didn't you take him back in this van?'

'I couldn't. As long as Tookar is Guardian of the Starstone, the Tinxshians are in grave danger. Tookar bravely made his choice and left his planet to hide with the Starstone. In doing so, he's protecting his people. When his spacecraft crashed to earth, Tookar remained here.'

Connor struggled with his thoughts, which were swarming like bees inside his head.

'Why did it choose me? And why do you think Definastine kidnapped my aunt and uncle?' Connor asked.

'Blackmail,' Sparkie replied. 'He's using your relatives like bait to snare you. But I think I can rescue them. I've tracked them down to a secret underground hideout used by Definastine's servants. And to answer your first question I can honestly say, I don't know. Things happen in life and sometimes it's best if we go with the flow. Is everyone strapped in?'

'No!' yelled Deana.

Sparkie pulled out a silver pen from his trouser pocket and skilfully traced a route. He moved so quickly, Connor wasn't able to see where they were going. He glanced out of the windows. The view was blurry. The only things that could clearly be seen were the beautiful exotic fish with bulging eyes.

'Right. Is everyone ready? We're going to use the transporter.'

'Yes,' rang a chorus of voices.

The button was pressed and the van gave a slight shudder. Sparkie undid his seat belt and was about to unlock his door, when Connor spoke. 'Has it broken down?'

Sparkie almost choked. 'Things aren't always what they seem. We've been transported to the woods behind Tookar's cottage.'

'What!' Connor gasped in disbelief.

'Learn to believe in the impossible and you'll begin to live. This van has an auto driver mechanism. Once you give it the information it requires, such as the place we want to go and how we wish to travel, it will then do everything else itself. The screen is the brain behind this van. I can see more looking at this small screen than through an ordinary car windscreen. As you are already aware this van can partly disappear,' Sparkie explained. 'It can travel on roads, in the air, beneath water, or even underground. It depends how urgent my destination is. Anyway, enough time has been wasted. Let's go and find Tookar.'

Stepping out of the vehicle, Sparkie gasped loudly. The others, hurrying to join him, all stood gaping too. Their breaths stopped in their throats, for in front of them a building was overwhelmed with fire, burning ablaze. Smoke poured upwards through the air.

The flames tearing into the night. Shadows in the woods flickered and danced in the furious blaze.

'Oh my. Oh my,' Sparkie repeated. 'This can't be true.'

'They found his home!' Deana panicked.

'But did they find him?' muttered Sparkie, his eyes heavy with concern.

They all stood silent as the flames rose higher. Amidst the snapping and crackling of burning material, a siren could be heard in the distance.

'This is terrible,' gasped Deana, her eyes desperately searching for any sign of Tookar. 'I wonder where he is now.'

'Who do you think did this?' Connor asked timidly. Everyone seemed to know who was responsible, except him.

'Definastine's servants.' Sparkie spat the words out as if they were something that tasted foul and stroked his fingers through his tufts of hair, pondering on what to do next.

A few trees bordering the edge of the garden had begun to burn. The bark had turned black and was smouldering with thick smoke. At that moment, approaching sirens filled the smoke thickened night.

'Where should we go now?' Connor asked, his eyes becoming sore.

'Why, to find Tookar of course,' replied Sparkie, after a quick cough to clear his throat.

CHAPTER NINE

The Secret Hideout

Connor, Deana and K followed Sparkie back into the van, strapped themselves in and waited anxiously. Connor had no idea what would happen next but he sat comfortably in the back seat next to Deana, watching Sparkie and K in the front.

No one made a noise as Sparkie pressed an orange button. Headrests immediately sprung up at the back of their seats. Deana jumped in surprise.

'Oh, no!' she screamed, trying to undo her seat belt. 'Not this!'

'Keep it on!' urged K, his voice serious.

'What's going on?' whispered Connor, staring into Deana's petrified eyes.

'He's going to turn us invisible!' she screeched.

'Invisible!' Connor gasped. 'Is that really so bad?'

Very slowly to Connor's surprise, the van began spinning pleasantly in a complete circle.

'This is okay,' Connor grinned.

'You haven't seen anything yet!' Deana squealed, grabbing his hand quickly.

'Ow!' Connor cried, trying to wriggle his hand free from Deana's grasp. She squeezed it even tighter, like a clamp. No matter how hard Connor begged her to let go she continued holding it fast, staring blankly ahead and whispering a prayer. The van started jolting and rumbling, steadily increasing in speed. Connor began to panic.

'We are changing to a new vibration. We will be operating on a new frequency. Don't fight it. Go with it. It's going to spin much faster in a minute or two!' Sparkie squeaked, sounding like a choirboy.

And sure enough, just as Sparkie warned, the van began to spin rapidly. Connor cringed. He tightened his stomach. He grunted and gritted his teeth. His cheeks were flapping and his head stuck fast to the headrest. A nauseous feeling overwhelmed him. It seemed the van would never stop. At this moment there was little difference between the van and a washing machine on full spin.

Sparkie looked positively scary. You could hardly see his face, since his beard had wrapped about it like a winter scarf. His hat was levitating above his head but was still attached by the suction caps on his temples. These suction caps were so powerful that they stretched his skin to maximum capacity.

Deana was producing noises like a deranged animal and her fingers were still fixed on Connor's hand. At this point he barely noticed her fingernails sinking into his flesh. After a horrendous two minutes the van slowed down before finally coming to a standstill.

'Now, that wasn't so bad, was it?' Sparkie smiled, excitedly. He began smoothing his beard down.

Connor shook his head. How could Sparkie be so excited by what just happened? He took a deep breath and belched loudly instead. 'I don't understand. I can still see you all. Why aren't we invisible?'

'We are,' smiled Sparkie. 'We are all operating on the same frequency as one another. That's why we can still see each other.'

K was busy trying to get his eyes looking straight ahead. He'd gone cross-eyed and was blinking furiously in an effort to focus properly.

'Is everyone okay to continue?' Sparkie asked lightly, noticing Deana still had her eyes tightly shut. 'What about you Deana? Are you all right?'

She slowly opened her bloodshot eyes.

'Don't you ever do that to me again!' she screeched.

'Ah, it's good to see you're with us,' Sparkie smirked and pressed the orange button, which controlled the headrests. They swiftly disappeared and Deana's head flopped backwards.

'Ow!' she complained.

But Sparkie shook his head and stepped out of the van before she could answer.

Deana peered at Connor. Seeing his horrified expression she quickly lowered her head.

'Do I look that bad?' she whispered, taking some tissue out from her pocket.

'Worse,' Connor replied, and whispered discreetly. 'Use it around your eyes.'

She looked awful. Her eye make up had trickled on to her cheeks, staining them like black tears.

Deana corrected her appearance but wasn't aware K was watching her.

'You don't need to wear make-up. You're beautiful without it,' he told her.

'Oh, stop it,' said Deana, blushing.

Further into the wood, they were in a place far distant from the threatening fire. An unseen carpet of damp vegetation extensively covered the woodland floor. The leaves that had once covered the trees in a golden array of different tones during autumn had now fallen to smother the ground.

Stepping out from the van, Connor soon found himself slipping on the slimy leaves before sinking deeply into the mud below.

'Urgh!' he grunted.

From inside the van, he heard Deana chuckling. She leapt from the step of the van and missed the soggy patch of mud that Connor was standing in. But where she landed her foot quickly sunk too. Then it was Connor's turn to start laughing. Deana, feeling mischievous, scooped up some mud and threw it at Connor. A large lump landed with a splat, right on his cheek.

'Deana!' he squealed, wiping his cheek.

But Deana wasn't hanging around. If she knew Connor, he'd be throwing mud at her too. So she quickly dragged her feet from the mud and dived behind a tree for shelter. A moment later her face peered from behind the trunk.

'Bit old to be playing hide and seek, aren't you?' he shouted.

With force, Connor heaved his feet out too, making squelching sounds on removal. Thick mud stuck to his feet, making them heavy and uncomfortable.

His sole intention was to pay Deana back for her dirty trick, but then, to his surprise, his hand accidentally flew towards the van door and instead of making contact with the van, travelled through the transparent material. For a couple of seconds his hand was occupying the same water as the fish. He was quite amazed by this, until Sparkie shouted a warning.

'Quick! Take your hand out, Connor!'

Connor glanced at Sparkie and saw a look of horror on his face. Connor followed his gaze. He gulped in dismay as a very large, grumpy fish was swimming straight towards his hand. Fighting against a strong sucking force, he managed to pull his hand out just in time before the fish snapped its jaws around his fingers.

'Lucky he didn't bite you,' said Sparkie, resting his hand on Connor's shoulder. 'Nasty little blighter, that one – almost had my finger off once. When he'd finished with it, it was hanging by a thread.' Sparkie lifted up his index finger to show Connor a thick white scar. 'But I got to hospital in the nick of time and they sewed it back on.'

Connor swallowed hard. Without Sparkie's warning, he'd probably have one finger less by now.

Sparkie, chuckling with relief, pressed a small remote control device that was dangling from a chain around his neck. Connor watched in disbelief as the van miniaturised to the size of a matchbox vehicle.

'How on earth –?' gasped Connor, wrinkling his nose in puzzlement.

'Don't bother to ask,' replied Deana, quietly coming up behind him.

'That's another good thing about having this van; it fits nicely in my pocket.'

Sparkie walked off, leaving Connor staring behind him. Numbly shaking his head, Connor followed unsteadily. K quickly caught up with Deana and wrapped his arm about her shoulders, giving her a squeeze. Connor raised his eyebrows. Grinning widely, he staggered behind them. Love was in the air, he thought.

'He'd better be here,' muttered Sparkie.

Connor looked ahead, expecting to see a little hut or shed amidst the trees, yet he could see nothing but more woodland. Sparkie was now moving faster.

'Keep quiet now. Follow me and don't make a sound,' ordered Sparkie, his face serious.

By now, everyone was slipping on the damp, decaying leaves like amateur ice skaters. Treading carefully they managed to avoid the muddiest areas. Hiking a little farther through the woods they eventually came to a large oak tree; a slanted gravestone rested against it.

'Here we are,' announced Sparkie, looking slightly happier.

'It's a gravestone,' said Connor bluntly, clearly unimpressed.

The gravestone was tilted forwards at a slight angle. It felt cold to the touch and was covered in a soft green moss. There was nothing special about it. Connor continued looking about, still expecting to see some kind of building. To his surprise, Sparkie was touching the gravestone. Placing one hand on each side he gave a little push. Suddenly the gravestone shifted a fraction.

'This is Tookar's secret hideout. If there's a chance that he's alive, he'll be found in this place,' Sparkie declared, sounding more confident. 'Tookar spends more time here than anywhere. Especially if he senses trouble.'

'I didn't know about his secret hideout,' gasped Deana. 'Why didn't anyone tell me?'

'Because it's a secret!' groaned K.

'So, is he dead or something?' asked Connor nervously. 'I mean he doesn't live in a coffin for specific parts of the day, does he? That would explain why he came after me in the dark.'

'No, he's not a vampire,' Sparkie smiled. 'Although I can see why you might think so.'

'How can anyone live here?' Connor carried on. He wrinkled his face in puzzlement and continued looking for signs of a hideout. 'I mean – it's not what I'd call a homely place, is it?'

'Everything will soon become clear, young Connor,' Sparkie told him. 'K, I need your help. Time to put your muscles to good use.'

Sparkie positioned both his hands on one side of the heavy slab of stone, leaving extra room for K. 'We have to push it until it's upright. Stand over there you two.' Sparkie pointed to an area behind him. Deana and Connor wasted no time changing their location as they watched the two men push the gravestone.

The scent of burning fumes wafted through the woods, drying Connor's throat. Where they stood, tentacles of smoke twisted feebly through the cluster of trees, pointing like crooked fingers. Connor shivered. It was eerie how the smoke resembled mist as it circled the old gravestone.

There was another strong scent in the proximity too, drifting from a semicircle of pine trees surrounding the old oak tree. In some ways, they were like protective parents, tall and dominating.

Grunting like a pig, K pushed with all his strength. Connor turned his attention to Sparkie. He didn't appear to be making much effort. He seemed oddly relaxed and although he was in the position for pushing, Connor suspected the crafty old man was just leaning on the stone.

K was performing most of the work. His strength alone was causing the slab of stone to move. Eventually the gravestone shifted a small distance while groaning in resistance. Deana gave a scream. A deep rumble began vibrating from the ground. In front of their eyes the earth began to open. Gradually, the gap widened to such a width the group could see the entrance to a secret tunnel. Cobbled stone steps led deep below the ground vanishing in darkness.

'Yes!' Sparkie cried excitedly. 'It's opened!'

'It would have opened quicker, if you'd assisted me,' K growled, rubbing his sore hands.

'I'm getting old – my muscles aren't like yours,' he said, slapping K on his back with such force, it sent him flying down into the dark chasm below.

'K!' Deana squealed in fright.

'You seem strong enough to me,' K's voice echoed from the abyss below.

'Oh, sorry about that, young chap,' Sparkie called down. 'It was a bit harder than I intended.'

K was still grumbling when the others came down the stairs to join him. He was nursing a bruise on his arm.

'You poor thing,' cooed Deana.

'Let's hurry inside. Never know who might be watching us. Definastine has his spies everywhere.'

'But we're invisible,' Connor reminded him.

'We might be invisible – but the ground isn't,' Sparkie reminded him. 'Not to mention our voices. Come on. Let's get moving before we're tracked down – not that the enemy would get very far in this place. These tunnels are riddled with traps, designed like a labyrinth. Don't worry, I'll be your guide. I know this place extremely well.'

Connor froze. He wasn't very keen to rely on someone else for directions. What if he got lost? What if he came across one of those traps Sparkie had spoken about?

There was a metal lever in the wall and Sparkie pulled down hard on it. The ground slowly began closing with a deep rumble. Connor imagined the earth caving in above their heads. He jumped when it finally sealed shut with a loud clank. His hands went clammy. His pulse raced. They were now in complete darkness.

A soft hand suddenly clasped his. It was Deana's hand. He was so frightened that he held tight, wondering how far they would be travelling in these confined tunnels.

Sparkie stroked his hand along the wall. Small circular lights appeared from inside the walls, radiating enough light to allow them to see where they were going.

Deana smiled bashfully and quickly whisked her hand out of Connor's. 'Sorry, I thought you were someone else.'

Connor wanted to laugh. 'Oh, and here I was thinking you were concerned about me.'

Deana nudged him on the arm.

'Ow!'

'Serves you right,' she grinned.

'K. Use a bushy tail to erase our footprints from this dusty soil,' Sparkie said. 'I broke Tookar's ancient broom last week. The one he bought several hundred years ago. After all we don't want to lead any unwanted strays after us, do we? With our footprints gone anyone following us will be trapped and lost down here forever,' Sparkie grinned wickedly.

Connor dreaded to think what he would do if he were ever to become lost in a place like this. Determined not to think about it he turned to watch K transform shape. To his surprise, K maintained his human form. The only thing that was different was the long bushy tail, which had sprouted out from his behind, falling heavily to the ground.

'This should do the trick,' K smiled broadly.

Sparkie proceeded to take charge. He led the way down the sloping tunnel. All the while, K was brushing his tail behind him. They continued walking through narrow tunnels, passing many other routes branching off in various directions. Every now and again, Sparkie took another path. The walls were made mainly from red rock but tree roots were seen twisting here and there – their strength having broken the hard stone years ago. The roof was arched inches above their heads and a soft red soil scattered the ground. Their footsteps were silent as they moved warily along, through the corridors filled with a strong musty, earthy odour.

To Connor, it brought back the memories of when Tookar had come into his home. He'd smelt like this passageway. Surely, he hadn't been living down here. Deana's nose was also twitching as if remembering Tookar too. The lights had quickly dimmed behind them. K remained at the back, religiously sweeping their footprints away.

It grew surprisingly warm in the tunnel. It wasn't long before everyone started taking off their coats and jackets – except for Sparkie, who was already strutting about in shorts and T-shirt. K volunteered to carry Deana's thick winter coat. She blushed when she handed it over. When Connor asked if K would like to carry his jacket as well, K mumbled, 'No way. Carry it yourself.'

They had been descending for almost fifteen minutes, when suddenly the tunnel journeyed upward. Connor was close to feeling claustrophobic. He hadn't felt that way since Uncle Dorcus had locked him in a cupboard for the afternoon. Connor hastily buried that particular memory.

During their time in the tunnels, there was one thing Connor thought he'd never forget – the earthy smell, which lay gritty in his mouth. It reminded him of a room full of mushrooms. It reminded him of Tookar.

It wasn't long before the tunnel opened up into a circular section. They had a choice of ten other darkened paths. Connor glanced from one to the other. He didn't have a clue which one to pick. Luckily for him he didn't have to.

But before Sparkie made the choice, he suddenly stopped in front of them. Kneeling down, he scanned the ground with his eyes. With his fingers he reached down to touch the soil. Connor knew something was terribly wrong.

'Oh no!' Sparkie said in a whisper. 'It can't be!'

The others exchanged troubled looks – not daring to speak. Connor walked to the other side of Sparkie. He peered down at the ground and saw strange blue patches soaked into the dusty soil, creating damp clumps of mud. A pile of ashen remains also lay a few feet away. Near one particular passageway, something deep had scratched into the soil, indicating for certain that something had been dragged along the ground.

'Good grief! There's been a struggle here. Tookar's been injured,' Sparkie rambled. 'We must hurry on our way – increase our pace!'

So the pace quickened. K was whisking his tail so fast they were soon overcome with red dust. It reared up and pursued them along their trail.

Gradually the tunnels decreased in width and height. They had to bend either their heads or their knees – K, who was a lot taller than the rest of them, did both.

Tension grew in Connor's neck, eventually creating an uncomfortable ache. Soon he too had to bend his knees like everyone else as the burrow decreased in height. His under-used muscles quivered with effort, causing him to hobble like an old man.

After winding through further complicated networks of passageways, where at times it felt as if they were going round in circles, the dragging imprint in the soil vanished. But something else was stamped into the dirt – small footprints from a creature with only three toes on each foot. One footprint still continued to drag along the ground. Connor nervously wondered what it belonged to: a small prehistoric dinosaur or perhaps something more terrifying? He couldn't understand why they pursued this creature. Shouldn't they be running in the opposite direction?

At this point, more blue spots stained the ground. They appeared prominently along the last stretch of passageway.

The air had become stuffier. Connor felt dizzy. The huffing from laboured breathing became more noticeable. Connor didn't know how far they had travelled but he wanted to rest. He needed to stop. The dust was also beginning to affect everyone and they were constantly coughing and clearing their throats.

Sparkie was mumbling in a world of his own, not talking to anyone in particular. Connor envied his nimble feet as he walked skilfully in front. Minutes later, although it felt more like hours, they came to a small wooden door, designed for a tiny person – possibly a child.

Sparkie rapped with a rhythmic tapping and waited. When there was no reply he turned the handle and opened the door. A ray of sunlight greeted them.

'What the?' Connor gasped, peering through the doorway.

CHAPTER TEN

The Guardian of the Starstone

They crawled through the doorway on all fours, entering into another world, one so colourful and beautiful it was hard to imagine such a place could exist on earth.

'Close the door behind you,' Sparkie ordered.

'How is this possible?' Connor gasped in delight.

'This room we have entered is a hologram of the world from which Tookar has come,' Sparkie explained. 'He takes it to anywhere he travels. It helps him feel at home.'

Connor wrinkled his eyebrows in disbelief. 'You mean he can just pack up and go?'

'Exactly,' Sparkie answered. 'The technology on his planet goes far beyond ours.'

The first thing Connor noticed was the sunlight warming his skin. Fresh air filled his lungs as he stood in bewilderment. How was it possible to be deep underground and see the sun? It defied all logic. Where Connor expected one sun to be shining, he was overwhelmed to see two above their heads. The tunnel with all its restrictions had vanished behind the little magical door. They were free in a place full of wonder and mystery, on a typical warm summer's day.

'But before we go any further, stand still for me,' Sparkie said.

He pulled out a small device from his pocket, which looked similar to a peashooter. Very quickly, giving the group no time to react, he fired at each individual in turn. An electric blue light rippled through the air at lightning speed, striking each person. It delivered a shock so powerful that they fell to their knees. Then Sparkie turned it on himself and fired.

'What did you do that for?' Connor groaned, his leg twitching from the after effect.

'I've made us visible again,' he explained hastily. 'It's a new method that I've been working on and it seems to have worked.'

They looked at one another, shaking their heads. But it was impossible to stay angry with Sparkie for long. Besides, there was far too much to explore.

Bizarre insects with massive stings buzzed busily in the air, travelling from one flower to the next, creating an impressive pile of nectar. The insects weren't the ordinary insects Connor had seen in his back garden; some of them were the size of his hand. But the largest one, which frightened him silly, was the ugly one the size of his head. It had a long beak, a massive wing span and several wriggly, black hairy arms with small hands on the end. A large pointed needle stuck out from under its bottom. It had huge reflective black eyes and a habit of staring rudely at them, whilst hovering in mid-air. The next thing they knew it was making an angry buzzing sound, turning round and waggling its bottom at them in an insulting manner.

'Bill-Chew. Where is Tookar?' asked Sparkie sternly. 'Is he still alive?'

Bill pouted and then shrugged.

'Answer me, Bill-Chew!' Sparkie demanded. 'It's important we get to him. He could die!'

Pointing his beak towards a large tree, he immediately flew off with his beak high in the air, wiggling his sting in a show-off manner. But Bill-Chew didn't go far; he remained forever near but out of sight.

'Don't worry about him. He's got an attitude problem,' Sparkie explained.

'What is it?' Connor exclaimed. 'I've never seen anything like it.'

'No, I don't suppose you have. Think yourself lucky. He's from Tookar's planet. He's a right little mischief-maker if you ask me. But he's loyal to Tookar,' Sparkie told them. 'He tends to be a bit sensitive at times as you'll probably find out.'

Deana stood gasping in delight. She helplessly began immersing herself in the different kinds of flowers surrounding them. She was in awe of the gigantic petals, especially one particular flower with pink and white petals. She stroked it with her fingers and sniffed it. Luckily for her, K pulled her away just in time. A head, from the harmless looking flower she'd been sniffing, suddenly sprung out from the plant, baring fierce green fangs towards her.

Deana screamed and fell into K's arms.

'It's a guard plant,' K explained. 'Keep your hands to yourself while we're here.'

She lifted herself out of his arms and fluttered her eyelashes. 'So, does that rule apply to you as well?'

'Come on,' K said, looking too concerned about Tookar to appreciate her humour.

He grasped her hand and pulled her in the direction Sparkie had gone with Connor.

'I hope we're not too late,' Sparkie was mumbling.

A large tree, resembling a willow with long dangling branches, stood proudly before them. Covered completely with thin yellow leaves, it seemed magnificent yet ordinary at the same time.

Taking them quite by surprise, overhanging vines suddenly fell down from the massive tree. In seconds the vines entangled their bodies like muscular snakes. Bound tightly around their legs and arms, the group found that they were powerless to break free. No matter how hard they struggled they ended up getting more tangled. The vines continued to squeeze tighter, lifting them off the ground.

Connor was whisked off his feet and held helplessly upside down. Blood rushed to his head, turning his cheeks bright red. An uncomfortable pressure built up in his nose. The tree creaked loudly as the vines parted for a brief instance. Connor caught sight of two large eyes that had suddenly appeared on the tree trunk. The large brown eyes frowned while studying the wriggling bunch. The vines immediately returned to their previous position covering them once more.

'What now, Sparkie?' asked Connor, ignoring Deana's squeals of fright.

'For goodness sake Jomkim – put us down!' Sparkie demanded. 'This is no way to treat visitors. I thought I taught you better than that.'

'Sparkie!' spoke a joyous voice. 'Bill-Chew told me you were strangers.'

'I should have known,' grumbled Sparkie, 'perhaps we can continue our conversation with our feet on the ground.'

'Oh... yes... sorry about that,' Jomkim apologised.

The hanging vines lowered the group but, to their horror, it released them a couple of feet above the ground. With a thud, they landed ungracefully in a heap.

'Jomkim – you could have put us back on the floor before you let go!' Sparkie scolded.

'Oh, I am sorry!' Jomkim said bashfully. 'There's been so much happening today. I'm not thinking straight. Tookar is wounded and I'm at my wits' end!'

The fact that this tree could talk and move, let alone think for itself, impressed Connor greatly. He'd never seen anything like this in his life.

As they rubbed their aching limbs and sore heads, the friends watched the vines open gracefully like cinema curtains to reveal the source of the deep resonating voice. A large friendly face appeared on the bark of the trunk. The same golden brown eyes that Connor had seen previously were now staring straight at them. The facial features protruded beneath the bark, almost as if the bark were made of cling film.

'Tookar is hiding in the cave below me. You'll have to move further back!' Jomkim warned them.

His face quickly disappeared, sucked back into the trunk. The group did as they were told, moving several feet back from where they had previously stood. Deana, who was looking anxious, held on to K's arm. A moment later the ground quivered, the soil shifted and rising up on the roots of the tree was the strangest creature Connor had ever seen: a creature with a small blue body no bigger than that of a toddler. It was lying on its back with its eyes closed. Feeble rasping sounds came from its throat.

'Oh, Tookar – what happened to you, my friend?' Sparkie knelt down to lift Tookar off Jomkim. As soon as Tookar was free, Jomkim immediately withdrew his roots and slid them back beneath the ground, sealing the ground once more.

'Sparkie, is that you?' Tookar whispered in a croaky voice. Peering through swollen eyelids, he caught sight of Sparkie and tried to raise his frail arm towards him. 'My friend, I knew you'd come.'

Sparkie grasped hold of Tookar's hand.

'Definastine himself couldn't keep me away!' replied Sparkie, a slight quiver in his voice.

Tookar forced a smile but his pain got the better of him. He opened his mouth to let out a cry. His breath quickened as he turned his head.

'You've got… Connor with you,' he managed to say, before gritting his teeth and wincing.

It was hard not to be affected by the state Tookar was in. Deana's cheeks were soaked with tears. Tookar's eyes were badly swollen and purple. A trickle of blood was gently seeping from the corner of his mouth. His nose consisted of two small holes in the side of his neck with two flaps of thick skin protecting it. His two long pointed ears were torn at the top of his head and flopped over like two long rabbit's ears. He also had two short antennae which curled upwards at the highest point of his forehead. Although they were bright orange, at times they seemed to change to a more yellowy hue.

'Raider… caught up… with me,' croaked Tookar. 'He won't… bother anyone… again. He's dead… now.'

'You old fool,' Sparkie smiled solemnly. 'You never could get enough action.'

'I'm dying… my life is… draining away. I have so much…' Tookar cried out in pain, 'to tell young Connor.'

'Shhh,' Sparkie soothed. 'You're not going to die. Connor has the Starstone inside of him. Perhaps he can heal you.'

Tookar attempted to laugh. He was finding it difficult to speak without taking several deep breaths. 'He doesn't… know how to… control his powers yet.'

Connor was listening intently; he wasn't going to be told he didn't know how to do something.

'Let me try,' Connor pleaded. He looked at Sparkie. 'You believe it'll work, don't you?'

'Yes, I do.'

'Well then, let me try!'

Without wasting more time, Connor knelt beside Tookar, feeling extremely self-conscious under the watchful presence of so many eyes. He managed to ignore the gazes as he rested his hand on Tookar's body. What happened next was completely unpredicted.

Connor gave a cry of surprise. He never expected an electric shock to bolt up his arm making him feel weak. His first instinct was to pull away but deep down inside, he knew this was part of the healing. Although it was uncomfortable, he knew he would have to put up with it to save Tookar's life. His arm started shaking powerfully. Connor couldn't control it. At the same time, little specks of colour suddenly flickered in the air, like tiny silvery stars only visible to Connor. Swirling above Tookar's body they gathered speed until they were circling like a miniature tornado. They were spinning so fast. Eventually they merged into one great twisting beam of light.

Then, there was a blinding flash of light in front of Connor's eyes. He suddenly found himself back inside the tunnel, scared and alone.

It took him several seconds to realise he wasn't really there. Somehow his mind had travelled, leaving his body behind. This made the situation slightly less terrifying.

He became aware of shouting. Connor cautiously walked forward towards the din. Entering a circular chamber he saw a violent scuffle had broken out. He wanted to turn and run but curiosity made him remain. Two creatures were fighting one another. He recognised Tookar in his human form, but the other – well, it was the ugliest creature Connor had ever seen.

'It must be Raider,' Connor suddenly thought.

It was worse than a horror film. For starters, Connor felt he was taking part. It was all too close for comfort.

Huge black eyes were firmly fixed on Tookar. He didn't stand a chance, not when the creature was twice his body size. It was hunched and covered in thick black hair. It moved with frightening speed, as its tail whipped through the air. The hood had fallen back from Raider's head, revealing taut grey skin, stretching tightly over a skeletal face.

'You don't want to do this!' Tookar rasped helplessly as Raider pounced on to his body. 'This isn't you.'

'You pitiful, puny creature!' Raider mocked. 'With the help of that consulting mirror, I knew exactly where to find you. At last my master will get the Starstone!' he laughed heartlessly.

Snarling like a vicious animal, Raider clawed at Tookar, ripping his skin like paper. He brutally dug his claws deep into Tookar's body. Tookar screamed in agony. Just then, a flurry of wings was fast approaching.

Bill-Chew flew speedily round the corner, almost crashing into the wall. His eyes widened in horror. Pointing his beak he aimed directly at Raider. Moving swiftly, Bill-Chew dodged Raider's fists. Darting rapidly, he avoided every blow. Twisting his body adeptly he came up from behind Raider to sink his poisonous sting deep into his back. Raider flung his tail up in the air striking Bill-Chew. It sent him reeling through the air – his body slammed heavily against the cave wall. But it was too late. The damage had been done. The venom was taking hold.

Raider bent forward and began to breathe heavily.

'What have you done to me!' he screamed, turning desperately to look at Bill-Chew.

But before he could say anything else or cause any more damage, he collapsed to his knees, screaming in agony. As the poisonous venom took hold, his body convulsed violently, falling to the ground, where it crumpled into a heap of black dust.

Bill-Chew limped towards Tookar, spitting on the pile of Raider's remains as he passed. Apart from the heap of ashes, nothing else remained of Raider, except perhaps for the lasting impression of his cruel eyes. Connor knew it would be a long time before he forgot them.

Bill-Chew snuggled close to Tookar, nudging him and stroking his face.

'Don't die!' Bill-Chew cried. 'Don't leave me!'

Tookar was groaning helplessly as he lay in a pool of his own blood. A desperate urge to heal Tookar overwhelmed Connor.

As if by magic, a light blasted out of his body towards Tookar. Connor's spine arched violently backwards, as light surged freely from the centre of his chest. There was so much light surrounding him that he became impossible to see. Then, when Connor finally opened his eyes, he found himself lying next to Tookar on the ground, in the cooling shadow of Jomkim, surrounded by his friends. To his joy he noticed Tookar's wounds were disappearing before his eyes. Tookar was staring at him with a mixture of astonishment and deepest respect.

'I've never been so glad to see someone in my whole life!' he smiled weakly.

CHAPTER ELEVEN

The Starstone Explained

It was late in the evening on Thursday, four hours after the hospital episode, that Connor found himself being held in the highest regard possible. The air had silenced around him and he knew what he had done was something very special.

He didn't feel very special though, not now he'd experienced the after effects of his powers. A migraine had appeared out of nowhere, throbbing seriously inside his skull, causing intense feelings of nausea. The concept that he had saved someone or to be more exact, an alien, hadn't truly sunk in yet.

It had taken Connor a while to familiarise himself with seeing Tookar as an alien. After all Connor had never seen an alien body before, except in science fiction programmes on television where they were no more than people in rubbery costumes.

'Oh, Connor,' he heard Deana say softly. 'You did it!'

Sparkie's face had changed dramatically. His gloomy expression previously filled with melancholy was now replaced with an overexcited happiness. Holding Tookar's hand tightly, he was now shaking it up and down and jabbering so fast it was hard to understand what he was saying.

'Tookar! I can't pretend I know what's just happened here but you've been miraculously healed.'

Connor, however, fixed his eyes on Tookar, whose silvery pupils shone brightly towards him.

'I didn't believe it was possible for you to do that,' Tookar remarked. 'The Starstone chose wisely for you are the child with a pure heart. Thank you Connor, for healing me.'

Connor was lost for words. When he did speak it was barely louder than a whisper.

'Perhaps you can help me. There's so much I need to know.'

'Don't worry. All your questions will be answered. Perhaps we should celebrate and talk over a bite to eat. I'll get a table prepared for us.'

Tookar clicked his fingers and watched as several different insects flew to him. Communicating in a strange language, the insects hovered and listened. When he had finished speaking, the insects squeaked ecstatically and quickly flew off together.

'Now, I've made our dinner arrangements, you must please excuse me while I change.' Tookar walked behind Jomkin and a second later transformed into his familiar human appearance, wearing a smart silvery grey suit and tie for the occasion.

'Well – what do you all think? I bet you didn't realise I could scrub up so well.'

'I must admit, I've never seen you look quite so... how should I say it... I believe smart is the word,' grinned Sparkie.

'It's hard not to go over the top when you have just been given the gift of life,' Tookar beamed at Connor.

Connor bit his lips nervously, trying hard not to stare at Tookar. He remembered how rude he'd been to him, when he'd appeared in his house. Embarrassed by his previous lack of manners, he flushed scarlet.

It was midnight by the time they all sat down around a grand wooden table, so yellowy in hue it was as if it were made of solid gold. Dark grains swirled in patterns across the wood. They were feasting in a clearing in the middle of a forest where beautifully coloured birds, much like parrots, made soft sounds like wooden panpipes. The sun was still shining brightly in this strange world, which should by natural law, have been pitch black. Surrounding the table they each sat on massive blue mushrooms with purple stalks, as soft as velvety cushions.

Tookar insisted Connor sat next to him. Connor soon found that he was repeatedly slapped on the back after every joke Tookar made. Bill-Chew, who was pouting and busily spitting his tongue out at Connor from the shadows of a nearby tree where no one could see him, deliberately kept his distance from the group.

Many large insects entertained the group by politely serving them fruits during their feast. The smaller insects, on the other hand, did just the opposite. Secretly diving into bowls they nibbled the fruits and occasionally got eaten by accident. But since the fruits were delicious, no one noticed the odd taste of a straying insect.

'Come on, Bill-Chew! Join us in our celebration. You helped to save my life after all!' shouted Tookar, spying him in the tree. 'Without you, Raider would have finished me off once and for all.'

Bill-Chew joined them reluctantly. Puffing out his red furry chest he hovered close to Tookar. He didn't take well to strangers and wanted to play no part in their discussions. Humans were ugly creatures, especially the boy with the scruffy hair. The one with the pure heart… humph! What an idiot, thought Bill-Chew, sticking his head in the air and blowing a quiet raspberry at Connor.

The table was abundant with bright colours and juicy fruits. The guests couldn't help dribbling the juices from their mouths and occasionally spraying the person sitting next to them. Sweet berry fruits overflowed wooden bowls, each with delicious tastes, except for the one Bill-Chew sneakily dropped into Connor's bowl before flying off again. That one tasted foul, like a stinky sweaty armpit. Bill-Chew giggled as Connor spluttered it out of his mouth.

Tookar scolded Bill-Chew, having seen what he'd done. Embarrassed, he flew off with his sting between his legs, blaming Connor for his master's firm words.

'I apologise for Bill-Chew's behaviour,' said Tookar, shaking his head. 'He's suffering from a bout of jealousy.'

'He's jealous?' quizzed Deana.

'Yes, ever since the Starstone has chosen Connor for his host, he's been quite put out. He likes to be Mr Popular you see, and now Connor is here, he doesn't like it much. It's difficult to make Bill-Chew understand when he's in a mood like this.'

Connor was used to people not liking him. He accepted that Bill-Chew had problems like everyone else. Swiftly forgetting the incident he attempted to rid his mouth of the foul taste by devouring more fresh fruits.

Pink-looking bananas tasting like strawberries did the job quite nicely, followed by a turquoise toffee-tasting melon that could be scooped out like ice cream and spiky oranges that reminded Connor of kiwis. Small fruits resembling necklace beads burst in his mouth with a loud popping sound as soon as they touched his tongue.

Tookar waited until he had finished eating before explaining anything. This was fine as far as Connor was concerned. He'd almost forgotten his problems when faced with so much delicious food in front of him. He'd eaten so much, his stomach felt uncomfortably tight.

'I realise that when you first met me, Connor, I frightened you out of your mind, but it is in my best interest to dress shabbily at times. As you have learnt previously, I am an alien. My race of people is called the Tinxshian, and I am otherwise known as the Guardian of the Starstone. I readily adopt different disguises to hide my true identity. Acting as a wandering hobo has served its purpose nicely. Mind you, over the years I've played different parts just to survive and stay alive.'

'You wouldn't believe what he's had to become in order to survive,' Sparkie grinned. 'Tell them about the time when you became the Pope, or the time you became King, or what about the time when you...'

'None of that is relevant here,' Tookar said gently. 'All that can be told another time. Anyway, where was I?' Tookar paused for a brief moment to gather his thoughts. 'Ah… yes, that's right… it has been my longstanding duty to protect the Starstone religiously until a certain child would reach the age of twelve and become its host. That child was you Connor.'

'Why me?'

'I'm not entirely sure. It may have something to do with you being in a certain place at a certain time,' shrugged Tookar. 'Perhaps in time you will be able to answer that question yourself. I ask myself why I had been chosen to be the Guardian of the

Starstone for this length of time too. Why me out of all the other Tinxshians?'

To everyone's surprise, Tookar raised his hands in the air and a small misty globe appeared in front of him. He closed his eyes briefly and then opened them. He blew hard on the misty sphere, as if it was a birthday cake with a hundred candles to blow out. Immediately faded images appeared in the middle of the table, images that came straight from Tookar's own memories.

Speaking with clarity, Tookar's voice changed subtly, sounding softer. Everyone hushed. They ceased eating. Tookar began to tell his personal story with the images accompanying his voice.

'My people came across the Starstone purely by accident. We were forced to abandon our planet when a great meteorite struck, leaving us homeless. It caused a magnitude of destruction making our planet uninhabitable. Luckily, we were able to flee in our ships before it collided. Otherwise we'd all be dead.

'Our search for another home proved difficult at first. We were almost running out of food, when we were snatched into a dimensional portal and thrown out the other side.'

Connor gasped as he saw a fleet of magnificent circular spaceships, speeding through space. But suddenly, they were sucked into a shimmering, black glassy dimensional gateway.

'Call it luck or something else. I certainly can't explain our good fortune that day. But we came across another galaxy filled with uninhabited planets. On our quest for a new home we only found one planet abundant with life and early life forms, mainly small unnoticeable creatures… it was there we agreed to set up our new home.

'We didn't realise it at the time but there was something else living on the planet with us. Something so magnificent, I believe it gave the planet energy to grow and transform.

'At first we couldn't understand why the planet we found was brimming with wondrous life, when all other neighbouring planets were completely barren. It was only by accident that I came across a hidden cave, deep beneath the ground. It was there, through a complex maze of tunnels, riddled with dangerous booby traps, that I came across the Starstone. Don't ask me how I found it or why I didn't get killed but something was directing me to that place, guiding me so I wouldn't be harmed. I was able to foresee the traps and avoid them. It was almost as if that same something wanted me to find the Starstone.

'I first saw the Starstone positioned on top of a gigantic plinth, pulsating and circulating with a will of its own. I never tried to touch it. I simply left it alone. It looked so beautiful and peaceful. I hadn't realised, but whilst I was observing the Starstone several hours had passed in a blur.

'There was another duplicate plinth next to it, which looked dull in comparison. It looked to me as if something was missing. And as if to confirm my findings, the pictures I found drawn on the walls depicted two balls of light, instead of the one I saw before me.

'It was an intriguing place with many beautiful paintings decorating the walls. Strange creatures I can only describe as blue kangaroos occupied the main diagrams. They were obviously an incredible race of star-spirits that once thrived on the planet, but whatever happened to them is unclear. They had vanished without trace.

'More cave dwellings were found amidst the rainforest. Our only guess was they were once homes. But their mysterious abandonment left behind a disturbing impression. We wondered if the same fate that had obviously befallen those creatures would also befall us.

'We remained for hundreds of years, making the planet our home, before we encountered any other star-spirits. After the sun had set one evening, I went for my usual walk.

'I arrived close to where the cave dwellings were when I first heard the droning of many spacecraft humming above the planet. At first I was confused but my curiosity overcame my fear and, transforming my shape into the fastest creature I knew, I ran to where the spaceships landed.'

An image appeared in the sphere of a black creature with a long narrow nose, four long skinny legs and a slim body. It was running fast through the forest, stopping every now and then, before raising its two front legs. Its long pointed ears were twitching as it listened intently. Connor thought it looked like a child's drawing of a stick horse.

'I had no idea what had arrived on the planet but when I got close I transformed back into my true form to become invisible, remaining out of the way. There was shouting and screaming in the distance which left me feeling cold and sick.

'I couldn't stand the tortuous cries, so eventually I went towards the commotion to find out what was happening. That's when I first caught sight of Definastine.

'He was standing dressed in a black cloak, towering above a cowering figure kneeling on the floor. There seemed to be hundreds of other shadows moving among the trees, surrounding them. I moved closer. I realised the figure shrinking in fear was similar to the blue kangaroos in the drawings on the walls. She was a female called Lairia.

'So the Starstone is here somewhere is it, Lairia?' Definastine had said, his voice cold.

Kneeling with her head hung low, she refused to answer him.

'Just tell me where it is and I'll let you go!' Definastine growled.

'You have killed my children... my family... my people. What use to me is my freedom now? I will never give you the Starstone. It will remain free, as it has always been,' she hissed, struggling to her feet. Her courage was returning, although her body was weak. I believe she knew she would die, no matter what Definastine promised. But I will never forget the strength I saw in her beautiful eyes.

'Definastine,' she spat, *'you will spend your entire life searching for something that will never be yours. It will always remain out of your reach! Only the true ancestor of Kimcara will eventually claim the Starstone.'*

Definastine had been amused by her words. He retreated slightly as she raised her hands in the air. Her weak voice gathered strength as she spoke.

'I call upon the Starstone,

To fight back when the time is right,
And when our King is on the throne,
Fight with all your might!'

'King? There is only a handful of your kind left!' he mocked. Definastine's laughter erupted into the night and as his servants joined in, the noise became deafening.

'I wanted to help her, but it was impossible. When Definastine stopped laughing. The noise from his followers subdued at once. Lifting his hand he struck her repeatedly, until she fell back towards the ground. Eventually he knelt down beside her and then with his hands, he reached out towards her head. It was the most monstrous thing I had ever seen…' Tookar paused and took a deep breath. No one interrupted or made a sound. 'And the worse thing was I couldn't do anything to stop it. I was outnumbered on all sides.'

Deana moved closer to him and gave him a hug, still saying nothing. It was hard to know if Tookar had noticed her reassurance as he stared blankly ahead. When he spoke again his voice was full of hatred.

'Thin black wires came out from the fingertips of Definastine. They moved towards Lairia and entered into her head. She was screaming for mercy. I looked away and when he had finished with her, she was lying on the ground dead. He'd murdered and tortured her before her soul was freed.

'I have taken the information that I need. The Starstone is in the caves to our west. I shall send troops in there to retrieve the Starstone and bring it back to me!' said Definastine.

'I don't know what came over me. But I saw a misty apparition forming in front of me. It was Lairia's ghostly form. She wanted my help. She was worried. She beckoned me to follow her. I did. It was the least I could do. She led me to a secret entrance to a cave. She touched her hand on the rock. She beckoned me to do the same. I did. To my surprise the stone wall parted leading me into a passageway that appeared to be blocked. Again she touched an area of the facing rock. I did the same and watched as the rock disappeared before my eyes. I repeated her actions several more times until I found myself in the chamber with the Starstone. She had led me along another concealed route instead of the path I had once walked along which was riddled with trips. Lairia raised her hands up above her and to my amazement the Starstone floated down towards her. She appeared to be holding and stroking it, like a loving pet, before handing it to me.

'Take this and hide,' she told me. *'When the time is right, it shall be called upon.'*

'That was all she ever said. She led me safely out of the cave and I ran as fast as I could back to my people. I explained to them what had happened and told them I must leave immediately with the Starstone. With their help I managed to leave the planet unseen. I had no idea where I was going or what I was going to do. I didn't even know how long it would be before the Starstone would be called upon.

'That was the last I ever saw of my people. To remain undetected I crawled into the smallest spacecraft we had and fled the planet. Throughout that lonely time I felt the constant presence of Lairia with me. She took control of the spacecraft and directed me here, on earth, where I have been ever since.'

'That's the first time you have ever spoken to me about the truth behind the Starstone,' Sparkie said, nodding slowly. 'And now I understand why.'

'I've come to understand over the years the reason Definastine wanted the Starstone so badly. He wanted to use it to destroy other galaxies. He wants to be almighty and powerful,' Tookar explained. 'I have no doubt that if he'd found the Starstone before now, he'd have even destroyed earth.'

Connor fell silent. The story Tookar had told him was still full of mystery and unsolved questions. He tried to unravel the information.

'Do you think Lairia came from that planet you were living on?' asked Connor.

'I do,' Tookar replied.

'Did you see any others?'

'No, she was the only one,' said Tookar, looking at Connor with interest. 'And if I'm not mistaken your next question will be, where did she come from.'

'How did you know that?' gasped Connor.

'Because you have just asked my exact questions, that I had asked two thousand years ago when I witnessed the terrible fate of Lairia. I'm afraid I can't tell you. It would seem as if Definastine had kept her prisoner but I can't be sure. She may've been hiding on another planet until he discovered her.'

Connor was looking very nervous. 'If Definastine catches me again, will I be killed?'

'What do you mean by *again*?' Tookar frowned.

'He almost killed me and Deana at the hospital!' Connor explained.

'What!' Tookar's voice boomed.

Sparkie quickly informed Tookar what had happened to Connor.

'So, he sent Razor to sniff you out,' Tookar grumbled, not taking the news very well. 'We'll have to leave here soon. This is worse than I thought. How could Definastine be here on this planet? I thought the AAA was tracking him. I can't believe this!'

'I've got a bad feeling about this too!' said Connor. 'I could die!'

'You're not going to die,' Tookar told him calmly. 'I haven't been stranded for two thousand years to watch Definastine triumphant in his quest for absolute power.'

'He's learning of Connor's whereabouts through the consulting mirror,' Deana explained.

'And if he can create a doorway into any world anywhere, then none of us are safe,' mumbled K. 'Not even here.'

'I'm going to get some fresh air.' Connor stood up from the table.

'I'll come with you,' said Deana, rising up from her comfortable seat.

'No, I'd rather be on my own, thanks,' said Connor. 'I need some time to think, that's all.'

'Well, okay. But don't go off too far,' Tookar replied, worried.

There were many things Connor wanted to ask Tookar, especially about his parents, but he couldn't think straight. He needed time to be alone. He continued walking out of sight, following a narrow path.

CHAPTER TWELVE

The Gift

After walking for twenty minutes, Connor came to a small stream trickling peacefully past the roots of a tall tree. The sunlight's reflection was glittering peacefully on the water. For the first time in ages, Connor felt his tension easing. There was something about this place that seemed to reassure him.

Massive roots, stemming from a thick trunk, entrenched beside the stream. Tilting his head, Connor watched some birds, with incredibly long tails, sweep across the sky. Meanwhile, insects busily flew in the air, humming as they passed.

He sat down by the stream, relieved no one had tried to follow him. Taking off his trainers and socks he began dangling his feet in the water, gently lowering them in. The water was so clear that every now and then, Connor caught sight of a miniature fish the size of his thumbnail. Surprisingly, the water wasn't the usual shocking cold but was warm and pleasant. Connor felt exhausted. Sitting by the stream he was reminded how much he needed a decent night sleep. Leaning back on his elbows, he closed his eyes. It was so relaxing he was almost about to fall asleep.

But his peace was soon to be shattered as a large insect flew unexpectedly down from the sky, swiftly changing direction before twisting and tumbling out of control.

'Aahhhh!' it yelled. 'It's too heavy! I can't stop!'

Connor was too tired to respond fast enough. The plump insect landed right on top of him, winding him in the stomach. Choking, Connor pushed the creature off.

'What the–?' he said, coming face to face with Bill-Chew, who was smiling nervously, squirming under Connor's gaze. 'You could have killed me!'

'Sorry – that wasn't supposed to… um… happen!' Bill-Chew

was obviously horrified. He almost froze in shock, staring at Connor. In a small squeaky voice, he pleaded. 'Please don't tell Tookar what happened! I don't seem to be able to do anything right just lately.'

Connor frowned and rubbed his stomach. 'You need some flying lessons!'

'Tookar gave me this box to give to you. It's from your parents. He thought you might want it.' Bill-Chew began searching the area.

'I've heard of air mail but that's taking things too far and I don't see any box,' Connor calmly commented, in direct contrast to Bill-Chew's expression.

'It's probably sunk in the water,' he gasped, waddling to the edge of the riverbank and stretching his neck as far as he could so that his head reached in the water. Repeatedly, he ducked his head in the water, until he was out of breath. 'I can't see it!' he squeaked. 'I've lost it!'

'Is this it?' Connor rolled over and accidentally felt something hard beneath him. He lifted up a strange little wooden box. He was curious to see what was inside it but out of pure stubbornness, he refused to look.

'Brilliant, you found it. I could kiss you!'

'Well don't!' Connor snapped, holding the curious box.

Bill-Chew began to test his small transparent wings, fluttering them so fast that they became invisible. 'Good, they still work! I'll be seeing you around.'

'No, don't go!' Connor called. 'I don't mind you staying.'

'Really?' Bill-Chew looked surprised. 'I haven't been very nice to you. Why would you want me to stay?'

'Because I like you,' Connor replied. 'I think you're funny.'

'Well, stranger things have happened I suppose.'

Connor sat back down on the riverbank still holding the box in his hands as Bill-Chew came and plonked his plump body next to him, shaking his wet head.

'Urgh!' groaned Connor, wiping his face. 'Did you have to do that right next to me?'

'Sorry,' said Bill-Chew. Then muttering quietly he went on to say, 'But a little water never harmed anybody.'

Connor ignored him. He was looking at the box and stroking his fingers over the smooth wood.

'What's inside it?' Bill-Chew asked, after an awkward silence.

'Don't know,' Connor whispered.

Still holding the box, Connor examined it more closely. It had a small catch. All he had to do was click it open and flip up the lid. It was a simple motion requiring little thought but Connor was nervous. What had his parents sent him? Why couldn't they give it to him personally? He couldn't help but feel despondent. How long would it be before he finally saw his parents? Did they know what he was going through?

A trembling in his hands seized Connor's attention. The tremor had been so slight that Connor hadn't been sure if it had been his imagination.

'I think it just moved,' he gasped, lifting the box towards Bill-Chew.

'It's a box. A box can't move,' Bill-Chew replied tonelessly. He thumped the lid with his small fist. 'It's made out of wood. Wood doesn't move!'

'Jomkim does. He's a tree with a personality,' Connor added.

'True, but if you don't mind me saying so – I think you're nuts!'

Connor frowned at Bill-Chew but his eyes immediately switched back to the box when it started changing from the dark chestnut to a lighter auburn colour.

'Fly out of here!' screamed Bill-Chew, who was flapping his wings and dancing on the spot as if he were jumping on hot coal. 'It's going to explode. It's a bomb destined to blow you up!'

White-faced, Connor threw the box down on the ground. He jumped back several feet with his heart lunging. The box suddenly sprouted thick little legs with knobbly knees and began running towards Connor along the grass. Screeching madly, Bill-Chew flew higher, eventually landing on a branch of a neighbouring tree. Connor clambered after him.

With eight chunky legs moving frantically, the bizarre wooden box flipped open its lid and catapulted a small object, which landed neatly on Connor's lap. Then, once its work was done, it fled for cover beneath the dense vegetation.

'I've never seen anything like it!' Connor marvelled.

'You're not the only one!' screeched Bill-Chew.

So, instead of a wooden box, Connor now had a harmless glass marble in his lap, with a chain attached to it. He scooped it up in his hands to realise it was sliced in half.

'My parents have sent me half a marble! They haven't seen me for years and they sent me a stupid necklace!' Connor tried not to be disappointed but he couldn't help it. His disappointment soon turned to anger. 'They could have sent me something more interesting – like an apology for leaving me!' He suddenly remembered the shrouded letter he'd received from his parents and felt his cheeks burning. His parents had already apologised.

Connor's first thought had been to throw the necklace away but having second thoughts he placed it in his pocket. Climbing roughly back down the tree and scratching his knees, Connor noticed Tookar walking into the clearing.

'I see you received the gift from your parents.'

'Yeah, it's great,' Connor replied sarcastically, straightening his clothes. He strolled to the riverbank to retrieve his shoes and socks. His feet were slightly damp as he struggled to pull his socks over them.

'You don't seem very happy about it,' Tookar observed.

'Why should I be? A stupid necklace isn't something I generally get excited about,' he replied.

Tookar was chuckling gently. 'Yes, I can see why you would think that. Your parents thought it was exactly the same thing when they first saw it. They couldn't understand how it could be a communication device.'

Connor brightened considerably. 'A what device?'

'It's a communication device. It will allow you to speak to your parents,' Tookar explained. 'Just hold the flat surface in your hands for a few seconds. If your parents are wearing the other half you will have direct communication with them.'

'Are you kidding me?'

'No.' Tookar was deadly serious.

'Why would my parents have something like this? Why didn't they come and see me themselves?'

Tookar raised his eyebrows. 'Let me explain some things to you. Your parents are not here on this planet. Dangerous times threaten to overshadow us. They are needed elsewhere at this present time.'

'I need them here!' cried Connor.

'Yes, I know you do,' smiled Tookar gently. 'But it's quite impossible. I've known your parents for years, Connor. I was the one who helped train them when they first came to the academy. As soon as I saw them I sensed they were gifted. They worked extremely well as a team, you see, and were star pupils in the making. It was only natural they became the best we have. You remind me of your parents a great deal. You possess qualities from both of them.'

'I do?' murmured Connor, shyly.

'Strong willed, stubborn and determined; all, I must add, are great qualities. I became more than just a teacher to your parents. I became a close confidant to them both – a very close friend indeed. I witnessed your birth and the tears of joy in your parents' eyes when they first set eyes on you and I was there to see their grieving tears when they made the hardest decision in their life – to give you up. Believe me when I say, no day passes without them thinking of you.'

'Why did they never try to see me?' Connor asked quietly.

'They did, from a distance,' Tookar confessed. 'They would mingle with a crowd and watch you from afar. So many times your mother wanted to run over and tell you they were all right and loved you dearly, but she couldn't. She didn't want her visions coming true. She desperately wanted to protect you –'

'What visions?' Connor interrupted.

'Now is not the time to tell you,' said Tookar with regret. 'Right now your mum and dad have been called away in an attempt to prevent another war. They're protecting a fragile planet from Definastine's servants.'

'If they spend time protecting other planets, how can they be desperate to protect me, their own son?' Connor grunted bitterly.

'They believed they were protecting you by keeping your identity a secret.'

'Well, they should have stuck around and found out. They certainly didn't stop my uncle from beating me when I accidentally spilt his coffee and they weren't there to stop him shoving me in a cupboard for an afternoon when I'd been ill in bed and was late preparing his breakfast!'

Tookar's face turned deadly pale. In a whisper he said, 'I didn't realise it had been so bad for you.'

'Well it was. And it was much worse living it, believe me,' cried Connor, fighting back the burning tears accumulating behind his eyes. His emotions threatened to overwhelm him. This was the first time he'd ever told anyone about his uncle's treatment. 'So tell me – who were they protecting me from, because it certainly wasn't from my aunt and uncle.'

'Definastine,' said Tookar gently. 'They have been seeking to destroy him ever since they have become involved with the AAA.'

'I know,' Connor growled impatiently, feeling annoyed and confused. He was surprised by the strength of his bitterness surging through his body after lying dormant for many years.

'Whatever has happened in the past cannot be changed. Your parents love you very much. Use the necklace to talk to them. You'll feel much better when you do.'

Connor nodded and asked quietly. 'Can you tell me a bit about them?'

'Like I said before, they were both extremely gifted individuals. The AAA was very glad to snap them up for recruitment. Your parents, being incredibly hardworking, made their way to the highest rank and are now the best detectives we have. But they wanted to break free from the AAA when they discovered your mum was pregnant with your sister. They wanted to give her the best chance they could. When your sister was born your mum went through a terrible time. The doctors told her she wouldn't be able to have any more children. She was devastated.

It took months for her to get over that. She'd always wanted two children. They eventually moved into a lovely house, a hundred miles north of here, where I used to visit regularly with K.' Tookar smiled at what was obviously a happy memory. 'Then to her surprise, ten years after giving birth to her first child she gave birth to you. You should have seen your mum's face. She was ecstatic. You were her little miracle. Your parents were overjoyed and your sister was pleased not to be an only child.

For twelve years your parents didn't work with the AAA. Your mum was simply pleased to be a mother and your dad was self-employed running his own shop. But things started to get worse. Definastine was becoming increasingly powerful and was secretly creating large armies. More children were going missing and it was only when several disappeared at once we began to suspect Definastine. Finally, when a close friend confided in your parents about his missing child, your parents returned to work.

They felt they had no choice. They had to try and find a way to stop the children disappearing. After all, they had children of their own and they didn't want the same fate befalling you or your sister.

But they didn't leave you entirely alone. The asked me to watch over you from time to time. I did. Even if it meant sleeping on the ground outside your house, disguised as an insect.'

As Connor's anger slowly dissolved, hot tears began flowing down his cheeks. Tookar grabbed him and held him close, allowing him the space to feel reassured.

If it weren't for Sparkie calling their names, perhaps they would have remained there all day. Connor couldn't remember a time when a father figure had ever given him a hug. It was the best feeling in the world. Although he couldn't remember his parents, he felt he knew them a little better. He also felt closer to Tookar, who was obviously looking after his welfare and had been for years. Feeling a hundred times better Connor released Tookar.

'So now you understand why I won't let anything harm you again,' smiled Tookar. 'I've known you all your life. Never again will your relatives lay a finger on you. Never again, do you hear me? Come on dry your eyes. Sparkie sounds as if he's got a dracline running after him.'

'A dracline?' sniffed Connor. 'What's that?'

'A small green pig with two bottoms instead of one and smells worse than sewage,' replied Bill-Chew, coming to join them.

Rubbing his eyes, Connor tried to mask the fact he'd been crying. He needn't have worried for Sparkie was far too anxious to notice the state of his face.

Rushing into the clearing and breathing heavily, Sparkie was clearly upset. He pulled Tookar to one side, wanting to speak to him in private. Connor and Bill-Chew pretended not to listen but it was hard not to overhear.

'There's been a message from the AAA,' Sparkie wheezed. 'There's been an accident... Jeremy's dead.'

'Dead!' Tookar exclaimed. 'Good grief – this is terrible news, such terrible news. What happened?'

'Two UFOs were spotted an hour ago on the outskirts of Wislington Town. They collided with each other. The AAA have already retrieved the two spaceships and have taken the prisoners to the AAA establishment. Jeremy died a few minutes ago but Marion doesn't yet know.'

'Need I ask who was on the other spacecraft?'

'A crew of Armatripe. They've been captured, but all the dark hounds on board managed to slip away unnoticed. There are fifty of them by all accounts – all on the loose,' Sparkie informed him.

Tookar's expression swiftly changed from concern to distress. His voice lowered to a bare whisper. 'Go and be with Marion. You must let her know. How is K coping?'

'Not very well.'

Tookar nodded and reassuringly squeezed Sparkie's shoulder. 'Be careful. Look after yourselves. Wait for me at Marion's. I have a few things to finish up here before I join you.'

Puzzled, Connor left Tookar and followed after Sparkie, who was mumbling and blowing his large nose on a handkerchief, until it turned bright red.

CHAPTER THIRTEEN

Jeremy

Following the conversation, Connor was keen to discover who Jeremy was. By the time he was reunited with Deana and K, the table of food had been cleared. Deana, red faced and teary eyed, was sitting close to K. At this point it was hard to tell who was comforting whom, but Deana, in between loud sobs, quickly explained to Connor what had happened and who in fact had died.

Fifteen minutes later they arrived outside K's home in Sparkie's van. Lights were shining brightly from within the house. Knowing his mum would be waiting for them, K looked at Deana and forced a smile.

'It'll be okay,' she reassured him, lightly brushing K's cheek with her fingers. 'I'll be with you every step of the way.'

K nodded with appreciation, unable to speak. Deana's large eyes were watching him sadly. Connor could see how much they meant to each other, especially at this time of sadness. But feeling he was intruding, Connor quickly averted his gaze.

What an awful night this had turned out to be. Not only did Connor have his own problems to contend with, but amidst the maze of events, K's father had also been killed. At this stage it was unclear whether or not it had been an accident. But K had hinted more than once that his father was the best navigator on earth.

'Thunderbolt must've been damaged!' he kept repeating.

'Thunderbolt?' Connor quizzed.

'Dads spaceship,' replied K. 'Its defence mechanism was able to deliver a bolt of electricity so powerful it could blast other spacecraft out of the sky.' His voice was subdued and he continued staring blankly ahead. His thoughts had wandered and for a brief moment he became lost in them.

Connor said little else. He suspected his tongue would only tie up in knots and all his words would come out back to front.

Sparkie left the van. A second later he clambered back in, shivering.

'Brrrr!' he said, wrapping his arms around him. 'So cold out there tonight. I wouldn't be surprised if it snowed soon. Would someone please pass me my coat in the back of the van?'

K blinked his eyes with a start. Looking dazed he reached over his seat to the dark depths behind, tugging heavily at what first appeared to be a dead animal over the seat. Grunting with effort, he finally hauled a dark grisly fur coat into the light.

'Urgh!' said Deana, making a face. 'What is it? It looks as if it's been dead for years.'

'My coat!' snapped Sparkie, looking hurt. 'Don't worry. It's not a real fur coat. I made it myself. It's just an imitation.'

'Hope you didn't make any more,' mumbled Deana, looking down her nose at the shabby coat, covered in grey bald patches.

Sparkie left a second time, while the others braced themselves for the cold wind.

K's face had paled considerably. No longer looking like the gallant fighter, K walked nervously to the door, his legs stiff and heavy. The idea of breaking the news to his mum was suffocating. He was hardly aware of Deana stroking his back in support. In the last fifteen minutes he'd aged ten years and for the first time in his life suddenly took to biting his fingers nervously.

'I don't know how to tell her,' he said anxiously, stepping back.

'Don't worry, you'll know what to say when you see her,' Deana soothed. 'Just remember we're here with you.'

K's home was a detached cottage covered in overgrown ivy and rested on the top of a sloped driveway. Only the lights from the windows and front door were visible. Two smaller buildings were seen next to the cottage where evergreen trees and shrubs gave the cottage shelter, giving it absolute privacy from the road. Something uneven beneath Connor's feet made him glance down. He was standing on a cobblestone pathway that led straight to the front door.

In the night sky several small black bats were swooping past the outdoor light and circling hypnotically before returning.

Heavy hearted, the group made their way to the cottage.

'I can't do this!' K panicked at the last moment. 'I can't tell her. It'll break her heart!'

'Calm down K. Listen to me,' Sparkie said firmly, grabbing hold of K's shoulders. 'You have to tell your mum. You're going to have to be strong for her. She needs you right now. You are all she has left.'

Like a frightened rabbit's, K's eyes were open wide. Nodding slowly, he faced the door a second time, his expression more apprehensive than ever. Sparkie's words had done little more than increase his panic.

Sadly K ran his fingers across a wooden plaque next to the front door. Engraved were the words, 'Castaway Cottage.'

'Dad made it,' K told them, a lump forming in his throat. 'He told me he'd been a castaway landing on this planet. He'd been here a hundred years before he finally met mum. He used to call himself Robinson Crusoe.'

He pulled a key out from his pocket and breathed in deeply. This was the hardest thing he'd ever done in his life. He was about to put the key in the lock when the door unexpectedly flew open.

Connor remained hidden behind the group, peering between the bodies in front of him. With butterflies in his stomach, he watched nervously as a cuddly old woman appeared at the door with outstretched arms.

'K. I've been so worried about you!' she cried. 'I thought something terrible had happened. You were meant to ring me an hour ago but you never!'

Her rosy coloured cheeks and warm smile openly displayed a mother's love. Connor couldn't help but wonder if his own mum had been so caring. A plain blue apron, covered in flour stains, was tightly tied around her waist. Her grey blue eyes had been full of concern but seeing K washed her worries away. Wispy grey hair fell softly about her face, highlighting its roundness, and her speech took on an excited tone.

'Where is young Connor? You did bring him here to see me as planned, I hope,' she said, on the verge of looking disappointed.

Shyly Connor stepped forward into the light.

'I'm here,' he croaked, his mouth as dry as sandpaper.

'I can't tell you how pleased I am to see you, young man. Come up here so I can give you a big hug.' Up on the doorstep, Connor was immediately wrapped in her plump arms and lifted off the ground. She winked at Deana. 'My, oh my – how you've changed. You're so handsome. You look a combination of your parents, don't you? You must break a lot of hearts now,' she said smiling and pinching his cheek. 'Come in, my dear child, you'll be safe here for a while.'

Connor found he couldn't speak. He tried to say thank you but it came out more as a grunt.

'Well, come on in,' she said again, opening the door wider and stepping inside. 'It's too cold to be talking on the doorstep. Whatever is that you're wearing, Sparkie?' she said catching a glimpse of his coat and wrinkling her nose in distaste. 'It won't bite, will it?'

Sparkie rested his hand on her shoulder. 'No, but if you're not careful, I will.'

Chuckling happily, Marion led them into her large homely kitchen. She walked to the far end and placed the kettle on the stove. A smell of freshly baked sponge wafted through the hallway, but no one paid it much attention. Burdened with terrible news their appetites had long since disappeared. A large stove occupied the far end of the kitchen, with hanging herbs situated about the room. Chairs squeaked loudly as they were dragged across the tiled floor from under a large wooden table, where they all sat down.

Marion continued chatting easily in her cheery voice. Connor glanced at K, his face ghostly white, his mouth tongue-tied.

'So how did it all go? Was it a straightforward rescue from the hospital?' she asked breezily. 'I must admit when you hadn't called me, I thought the worse, but seeing you all here, it must've gone better than I expected. I can't say I wasn't worried but I knew my nerves must have been playing up. I expect you'd all love to have a hot drink inside you. It can't be easy running about in this weather. Can't tell you how glad I am to see you come home, K,' she pinched her son's cheek affectionately and immediately turned back to the cupboards, bringing out her best china cups and saucers. Placing them on the side, she began humming a bright tune whilst filling a teapot with several teabags.

'I hope you like your tea strong,' she called, turning round briefly giving Deana a smile of appreciation. 'You all right love, you look a bit upset, although I understand completely how you feel given the circumstances. I mean – what with Connor's rescue and knowing that he's safe with us now. And I should have known K would be all right if you were with him. You're a good influence on him. I only told my Jeremy yesterday that you and K are meant to be together.'

Deana blushed uncomfortably, any other time she'd have laughed, but not today.

'Why, you're a quiet bunch, aren't you,' Marion chirped. 'It's the weather. Makes people feel gloomy. My sponge will soon sort that out. Just give it another ten minutes. It's your favourite, K – you know, the one with the chocolate filling.'

While Marion was preoccupied with making the tea, Sparkie grabbed K's arm urgently. 'You've got to tell her. It's her right to know.'

K nodded shakily.

'Mum –' he began but broke off.

Marion's gentle eyes were watching him curiously. As if sensing something was wrong a furrow appeared between her brows.

'What is it dear? – Are you all right? You don't look it,' she walked towards him and touched his forehead. 'Well, it's not a temperature that's good. I hope you're not coming down with something.'

'It's not me, mum – it's dad!' K blurted out.

Marion fell silent, her bubbly mannerisms vanishing in a fraction of a second. The spark in her eyes disappeared instantly and was swiftly replaced with a troubled look.

'What is it? What's happened to your dad? He's all right, isn't he?'

'You'd better sit down, Marion,' Sparkie stood up from his chair and gently guided her to sit down.

'Something's happened, hasn't it?' she said, flitting her gaze from one person to another.

'He's been in an accident, mum,' K whispered, placing his hand on top of hers, pausing briefly before speaking again. 'He died an hour ago.'

'Tell me it's not true,' she said, clutching K's hand and searching his distressed face. 'Perhaps there has been some kind of mistake. Mistakes happen all the time. What about that security guard – what's his name?'

'Arnold,' said Sparkie.

'That's right, Arnold. He was diagnosed as dead, wasn't he? He was paralysed for two weeks by the hideous alien that got loose,' Marion said. 'And no one knew – prepared his funeral and everything – nailed him in a coffin. Luckily for him, he started banging on the lid as they were lowering him into the ground.'

K began shaking his head, his eyes filling with tears. 'I only found out a short while ago myself.'

Marion's face drained of colour. She began comforting K, much to his surprise. 'There, there, don't cry, darling. There has to be some mistake. I'd feel it in my bones if your father were dead now, wouldn't I?'

'Marion, I'm sorry but there's been no mistake,' said Sparkie. 'His body has been taken to the AAA, and a car will shortly be here to take you there.'

Marion shook her head adamantly. 'No – he can't be dead. He can't be.' She tightened her lips in disbelief. Gradually as the shock took its toil, she began staring at the kitchen wall, her body shivering. She began speaking tonelessly. 'Didn't think for one moment that your father was in danger. He's always so careful. It doesn't make sense that he's dead. I told him not to go out tonight, but you know what he's like – so insistent.'

'Before he left did he tell you where he was going?' asked Sparkie.

'You know Jeremy. Doesn't speak to me much about his work – says he doesn't want to involve me – thinks I need wrapping up in cotton wool. But I must admit he wasn't his usual self lately – kept quite distant from me – I even had to ask for a kiss before he left tonight. Most strange, I thought. I know something has been troubling him ever since he heard about that portal to Dramian being discovered. He's been quite edgy – kept saying sorry all the time. I haven't a clue why. I know it seems odd but I can't help thinking he knew he was going to die or something.'

'He was acting rather shifty the other day,' mentioned Sparkie. 'He hasn't let me see his work in the cellar for weeks now.'

'When he left, he kept saying he'd be all right and that he was just going to check the area. I told him not to, because Connor was coming over. I knew how much he wanted to see this young fellow, but he went in the cellar like he always does and came out looking apprehensive. He told me it was just a routine check. I should have known he was up to something. I can't understand what happened out there tonight.'

'He collided with another spaceship operated by the Armatripe,' K explained as best he could, another lump forming in his throat making it difficult to swallow.

'Your father has never crashed Thunderbolt in his entire life. He knows that spaceship as well as the back of his hand. It just doesn't make sense at all,' said Marion, her face beginning to redden. 'Do you think he suffered before he died?' she whispered. Tears began streaming down her face as the news finally sank in.

'Shhh,' soothed Sparkie. 'No, he died instantly by all accounts.'

'Is that meant to make me feel better!' Marion snapped, bringing her hand to her throat as a look of horror appeared on her face. 'I'm sorry… I…'

Understanding her raw emotions, Sparkie nodded but remained quiet. Several times her expression changed as she stared helplessly at Sparkie. Finally as the words truly made their impact, her body started shuddering in shock.

'NO!' she cried, shaking her head jerkily. 'No – not my Jeremy! He can't be dead! He can't be!'

Sobbing, she repeated her husband's name. K sprung from his seat and protectively wrapped his arms around her. During that time, the small group bonded together. No one was unaffected by the displays of grief in the room.

Through teary eyes, Deana looked at Connor and slowly pulled him out of the room with her.

'Let's leave them alone for a while,' she whispered gently.

If Connor had ever met Jeremy he couldn't remember him. He felt awkward and was grateful for Deana's interruption. He followed her through the hallway into a small cosy living room, where a blazing fire greeted them.

'It's probably best we sit in here for a while,' she said, stoking the fire. A firework of sparks escaped the boundary of the fireguard, which was meant to protect the carpet. Deana, leaping like a frog from her seat, caught them before they singed the carpet.

She sat in the armchair next to Connor, looking emotionally exhausted. She sniffed several times and wiped her eyes on the sleeve of her fur trimmed denim coat. Spotting a box of tissues on top of a piano, Connor retrieved them for her.

'Thanks,' she said, blowing her red nose loudly. 'Marion's right, you know. I saw Jeremy yesterday. He was acting really bizarre. Thinking about it, he gave me this ring – told me that if I were to marry K, it was with his blessing. Why would he say that he if hadn't sensed something was going to happen to him? I wonder what Jeremy was doing in his cellar. He must've been working on something really important.'

'Perhaps he was,' said Connor.

'I'm going to take a look,' she decided, springing from her seat to catch another flying ember. 'That's the trouble with open fires, you can't really leave them alone... not if you want to avoid another fire. Connor, stay here while I go and check the cellar. It might give us a clue as to what prompted Jeremy to go out tonight. I won't be long.'

'Can't I come?' he asked.

'No. Keep an eye on the fire and tell the others where I am in case they come looking for me.'

'All right,' grumbled Connor. He couldn't help thinking he was missing out on something important. 'But why don't you tell K about what you're going to do? He might want to come with you.'

'What? In his state? I don't think playing detective is going to be on his mind right now.'

Deana buttoned up her coat. Giving Connor the thumbs up, she darted out the back door.

Connor relaxed back in the chair, opposite the fireplace. Watching the captivating flames, he thought about everything that had transpired that evening. The events whizzed by in a blur and his eyes soon began to feel heavy as if someone was pulling his eyelids down. He sank deep into the soft armchair. Feeling snug he stretched his legs out in front of him.

A tall brass lamp stood in the corner warming the room gently in a soft light. Creamy lace cloths were draped over every chair and a much larger one was positioned neatly on a two-seated sofa, occupying one edge of the room. A bold brass frame enclosed a magnificently painted picture of a landscape, which hung over the fireplace, showing a world where trees were blue and the sky as a mixture of pale oranges and reds.

The house was alive with different sounds, the hissing and crackling firewood, the dimmed voices from the kitchen and an annoyingly squeaky sound on the window as a branch scraped against the pane. The wind had increased tenfold, causing havoc outside.

Deana returned ten minutes later, with scraggly windswept hair. Her face was more agitated than before. She scrapped her loose hair back off her pallid face, breathing raggedly. She was clearly disturbed by something.

'What's wrong?' asked Connor. 'What did you see?'

'It was awful!' she cried.

'What is it? Tell me!'

'I'm not sure,' she replied, flinging her arms up in the air, looking totally confused. 'It was horrendous. There were bodies everywhere. Bits of bodies just lying around. I couldn't stay in there – I thought I was going to be sick.'

'You've got to tell someone!' urged Connor.

Her voice turned to a whisper as she glanced nervously at the door.

'I'll tell Sparkie – he'll know what to do,' she decided, just as the door creaked opened.

Sparkie was standing in the doorway, looking much smaller now he'd taken his coat off. His expression was strained with tension.

'A car has just arrived to take K and his mother to the AAA headquarters. If you're going with them, Deana, it's now time to leave. Young Connor and myself will wait here for Tookar.'

'Okay, I won't be a minute,' she said, watching Sparkie leave the room.

'Connor, I'm going to have a quick chat with Sparkie before I go to the hospital. Are you okay about me going?' she asked tentatively.

'Of course I am,' Connor replied, though suddenly feeling an overwhelming gloom at the idea of her leaving.

She ruffled his hair affectionately, giving him a hug before darting out of the room. He went to the window, watching solemnly as K and his mother hastily left the house. There had been no goodbyes but Connor understood their minds were otherwise occupied.

A short time later Deana ran outside to the black car. Her hair was flapping wildly across her face. Connor saw her holding it down. She glanced towards the window where he stood. She waved before disappearing into the back of the car with K, who then looked up and waved as well. Connor waved back. K had saved his life but at this moment there was nothing that he could do to return that gesture. Even though he had amazing powers he couldn't bring people back from the dead. No one could do that.

Soon the car roared into the night taking his friends away. As Connor entered the hallway he noticed Sparkie closing the front door, bolting it securely.

'I've just been speaking to Deana,' he said frowning.

'She was really freaked out,' Connor said.

'Yes, she was clearly upset about something – almost hysterical I'd say. Not like her to lose her head. Seems to think she saw body parts lying around in Jeremy's cellar. Well, I can't believe that Jeremy has been murdering people for a hobby. Still – I'd better go and check.'

'Can I come?' Connor asked hopefully.

Sparkie shook his head.

'Why don't you go and make sure that all the windows are shut upstairs for me.'

'Why? Are we expecting trouble?'

'We could be in trouble before Tookar meets up with us. I'll place the van ready in the master bedroom just in case we need to make a speedy getaway. We'll be all right if we keep our wits about us.'

Sparkie entered the hallway and proceeded to check every window on the ground level. When he'd finished he left the house by the back door, closing it with a loud click.

Connor slowly climbed the wooden staircase. He looked up at the darkness. With no light on the upstairs landing, Connor half expected someone to spring from a hiding place and scare the pants off him. Luckily his hands came across the light switch and with a soft click he flicked it on. A delicate light immediately surrounded him.

The house, old fashioned but practical, was decorated with creamy coloured, flowery wallpaper. Connor proceeded to go from one room to another, trying not to be too nosy as he checked the windows. There was one master bedroom with a sink in the corner, two smaller bedrooms, a bathroom and a separate toilet. Connor came to the last room and went inside. There was enough light in the hallway to see inside the room.

It was the smallest bedroom of all but looked the cosiest. A single bed had been prepared with layers of blankets neatly tucked under the mattress. Connor strolled across the old carpet and closed a small window, which had been left open to give the room some air. He closed the curtains and looked about the room, wondering whose bedroom it was.

The furniture, consisting of a bed, wardrobe, dressing table, chair and side cabinet, all made from antique oak, shone with polish. A bronze patterned frame bordering an oval mirror hung proudly on the wall. Connor observed his shadowed reflection and noticed it was slightly distorted.

'Now this is what I call an antique,' he muttered to himself.

He took note of the photographs hanging next to the mirror and beside that stood a huge wooden wardrobe with two cardboard boxes on top.

Connor switched on the light. The room filled with a soft golden glow revealing more photographs positioned about the room. He was drawn to the photograph beside the mirror. Instantly recognising Marion, he decided the young child with her must be K. A tall man stood next to her, with his arm affectionately around her shoulders.

'Must be Jeremy,' He looked more closely. He didn't look like a murderer with eyes shining with kindness.

Another couple sat with a young child on a bench eating ice cream. There was something very familiar about them but before he investigated it further, a disturbance on the landing made him jump. Peering round the door, he was just in time to see Sparkie dashing into one of the rooms.

Sparkie had entered the master bedroom. To Connor's surprise, he was on his knees, pulling up a rug and tugging a floorboard up with a screwdriver. As the wood splinted and lifted, a secret drawer was revealed under the floorboards. A large padlock barred it from opening. Sparkie started striking it with the screwdriver, a hungry desire in his eyes.

'What are you doing?' Connor asked, walking further into the room.

'Trying to get this locked drawer open.'

'Why? Has it got something to do with what you saw in Jeremy's cellar?'

'Yes. Deana was right, absolutely right. She saw bodies in the cellar,' Sparkie gabbled excitedly. 'Poor thing. She got the wrong end of the stick. Jeremy hasn't killed anyone. He's been making body parts of himself. He made another Jeremy, someone that looks exactly like him.'

'Huh?' replied Connor.

'He's been working towards making a replica of himself.'

'Why?'

'I have an idea but I need to get this drawer open first,' said Sparkie, passing Connor a photograph from his pocket. Again he tugged desperately at the drawer, which was now seriously chipped and dented.

Connor glanced at the photograph. It was a picture of K, or at least he thought it was. On the back was another name – Daven.

'I know! I bet you could do it!' Sparkie declared, replacing his frustrated expression with one of hope.

'What me?' Connor said, pointing to his chest and looking very doubtful. 'I don't know anything about locks.'

'You know more than you realise. Will you try something for me?'

'As long as it won't hurt.' Connor passed Sparkie a funny look.

'Come. Put your hand on this lock for me.' Sparkie was looking more excited than ever. 'Close your eyes and think about the drawer opening. Visualise the drawer opening. Imagine the lock releasing.'

'Sparkie, are you feeling all right?' Connor asked carefully. 'You're acting a bit crazy, you know.'

'Forget how ridiculous this seems, just get on and do it, will you,' he said anxiously.

'All right,' Connor grumbled reluctantly. 'I don't know what you expect to happen, though.'

'I expect that drawer to open, Connor,' Sparkie replied, his face beaming. 'That's what I expect. And I believe the Starstone is going to help you do it.'

Connor mumbled something under his breath that sounded very much like, 'You're mad,' and closed his eyes tight.

'You're not trying to trick me, are you?' he asked, peering through a small gap.

'Not at all, dear fellow.'

Connor again closed his eyes and imagined the drawer opening, just as Sparkie asked. He didn't give it much thought but after a short while he heard something click and the drawer began pushing against the palm of his hand. He pulled his hand away sharply.

'What the –'

'By Jove! Jumping butterflies! You did it!' Sparkie congratulated him, thumping him on the back over excitedly. 'It's opened!'

Connor stared uneasily at the drawer. How could he really do something like that? Shaking his head, he began to suspect that Sparkie must've opened it up with a key or something.

Sparkie wasted no time at all. Rummaging on his knees, he pulled the drawer upwards, tipping the entire contents on to the floor. It was filled with hundreds of photographs and documents of some kind or other. After a manic five minutes hunched over the floor, Sparkie sat up straight, waving a piece of paper in his hands.

'Here it is!' he cried out. 'Look at this!'

Connor leaned over Sparkie's shoulder and saw that he was holding a birth certificate.

'What's so special about that?' asked Connor.

'This birth certificate isn't K's,' Sparkie remarked. 'It belongs to his brother Daven.'

'I didn't know K had a brother.'

'Nor does he!'

Sparkie searched for further evidence and came across an envelope full of photographs of Daven, pictures of a young boy who looked remarkably like K. His name was on the back of every single one.

'By Jove. Jeremy has planned a rescue all of his own!' whispered Sparkie. 'The old devil!'

'What are you talking about? Jeremy's dead!' Connor reminded him.

Sparkie was shaking his head. Gathering his things together he placed them back into the drawer.

'It all makes sense now,' he said.

'Not to me,' Connor grunted. 'What's going on?'

'I'll explain later. There are things I need to do.' With that, Sparkie covered the secret drawer with a heavy patterned rug and left the room, leaving Connor more puzzled than before. He returned a moment later looking sheepish. 'Oh, I nearly forgot. Marion wanted me to show you something.'

Intrigued, Connor followed Sparkie out of the room and back to the small bedroom he'd been in previously.

'Your life is like the missing pieces of a jigsaw,' said Sparkie. He folded the birth certificate and placed it in his pocket. 'Marion thought it would be a good idea to show you some photographs of when you were little to try and help you remember your past.'

'She's got some photos of me?' Flabbergasted, Connor's mouth fell wide.

'Yes, and since you can't remember the time when you were a little mischief-maker, I've been asked to show you where the photographs are kept. We all suffer from memory loss over time. Look at me, I'm getting old now and my memory isn't always my best asset. One day I'd love to meet a generous woman who makes good pies, even if I can't remember her name.'

'I can think of one,' Connor grinned, picturing Mrs Rosebud and Sparkie walking arm in arm up the road, with him wearing that ridiculous metal hat.

'Well, perhaps you can introduce us one day,' Sparkie nodded, looking amused.

'Have you ever been married?'

'No. I've always followed my heart and pursued knowledge. I love knowledge more than I love eating wholesome pies,' Sparkie smiled. 'But times change and I won't be working for the AAA forever. Time to settle down soon before I wear out for good. Can't work forever, you know. Travelling to other galaxies takes its toll on a man.'

'I can't imagine what it's like travelling to other galaxies.'

'You'll find out soon enough,' Sparkie said. 'By the way, just in case you're wondering, this used to be the bedroom you stayed in when you were younger whenever Marion and Jeremy babysat for your parents. Obviously they had to get rid of the cot, but other than that, everything else is the same. Marion thought it would be nice if you slept in this room again. She had hoped to be able to go through the boxes on top of the wardrobe with you. They're filled with photographs of your family.'

'Really!' Connor said. With an excited expression he hurried across the room to drag a wonky old chair from a dressing table to the wardrobe. Sparkie stopped him.

'Why make life difficult for yourself?'

'But I'm not,' Connor said, itching to get the boxes down.

'How about finding out how strong your powers truly are. Use your mind to try and get them down without using force.'

'Use my mind? I'm not sure what you mean,' Connor frowned, raising his eyebrows. 'Isn't it easier just to lift them down?'

'Maybe. But let's try this first. If you can't, don't worry. Call it a trial experiment. It's all about using the power of your mind,' Sparkie explained. He lifted his head and looked down the end of his nose, whilst adopting a very matter-of-fact voice. 'That's something you'll learn more about at the AAA. They have good training courses you will find most useful. All you have to do is focus and believe in yourself. Concentrate clearly on what you want to do and it will happen. Visualise the boxes floating across the room and landing on the bed and it will happen.'

'You make it sound so easy.'

Although Connor wasn't a hundred per cent convinced he opened the drawer, he had; after all, managed to heal Tookar, not to mention a hospital ward full of children.

'Quickly lad!' urged Sparkie.

Connor looked at the two boxes. He tried to remember what they looked like as he closed his eyes. He tried to visualise them in his mind's eye. It took a while before this happened. Once he could picture them in his mind, he willed them to lift off the wardrobe to fly in the air and land on the bed. It seemed so simple that Connor didn't think it was possible. At some point between the boxes leaving the wardrobe and travelling to the bed, Connor opened his eyes a fraction. Perhaps if his eyes had remained shut, the boxes would have landed safely. But as he looked at the boxes floating in the air, he gasped in surprise, lost his concentration and watched helplessly as they fell with a thud right on top of Sparkie.

'OW!' yelled Sparkie, raising his hands above his head in defence. He slumped to the floor, disappearing beneath a pile of photographs.

'Sparkie!' Connor called urgently, pulling the boxes off him. 'Are you all right? I'm sorry. I didn't mean that to happen – they just fell – I couldn't stop them from falling. I'm so sorry. Are you all right?'

Groaning loudly, Sparkie slowly sat up, a drunken grin on his face. He blinked his eyes several times.

'Don't fuss lad. It's my fault. First time I've seen stars whiz by my head, though. I should never have made you try something so big for a first attempt. Don't look so horrified. I'll live. It's nothing a cup of tea can't sort out.' Connor helped Sparkie to stand. 'But I must admit, I wasn't really expecting you to do that. I know the Starstone contains many powers but you seem to be coming along in leaps and bounds already.'

'I'm a complete jerk!' Connor said angrily. 'I could've killed you.'

'Let's just say, a few lessons wouldn't go amiss at this stage,' Sparkie chuckled, looking surprisingly happy. 'I'm going downstairs. Would you like a drink?'

'No, thanks,' Connor replied. Just as Sparkie was about to leave the room, Connor called out to him. 'I'm really sorry!'

'I know you are,' Sparkie replied, a mischievous glint in his eye. 'The Starstone would never had chosen someone who wouldn't be!'

Connor watched the door close, leaving him alone in the room. Sparkie's words rang loud and clear. There must be something good inside him the Starstone liked, but what it was exactly Connor couldn't say. He was just an ordinary boy – at least he used to be.

He picked up one of the boxes and started tidying the photographs. Then, when that was done, he hauled the boxes on to the soft bed, searching for more clues to his past. Rummaging inside the boxes he began to find the missing pieces of his early childhood, where he was only exposed to love and security. Somewhere over the past nine years he'd lost both. Now he had a chance to recapture some traces of his past and he wasn't about to waste the opportunity.

CHAPTER FOURTEEN

Dark Hounds

Connor spent the best part of an hour exploring the impressive pile of photographs. He was so excited, he simply lost track of time. Dusty photographs emerged of Connor as a cute baby and a daring toddler. Many were highly embarrassing. Connor was grateful that Marion hadn't felt the need to enlarge any of them and place them on show like so many other pictures.

The photographs had snapped moments in time. Connor was flabbergasted. They'd caught him running in the nude with food smudged round his mouth. Another one showed him peeing on the flowers in the garden. The best thing was of course discovering what his sister looked liked.

Her face was speckled with freckles and her long blonde hair swept down the length of her back. Her favourite clothes appeared to be jeans or blue dungarees. She seemed oddly familiar, as if he'd seen her before. Then he gave a laugh. Of course, he suddenly remembered, he'd seen her in his dreams.

Lying on the bed quietly, he could hear Sparkie moving about downstairs. The unmistakable sound of the kettle boiling on the stove for the umpteenth time made a roar like a low-flying aeroplane. Connor came to the conclusion that Sparkie was nervous. K had previously told him Sparkie always drank tea when he was worried about something. Connor prayed he was worrying unnecessarily.

Hoping that Marion wouldn't mind, since he wanted some photographs of his family, he kept four of them and placed them safely in his pocket. The first one he'd chosen was of his parents' wedding. They were pictured together outside a quaint flint church, smiling happily for the world to see. Judging by the amount of flowers in bloom, Connor presumed they must have married in the summertime.

The second picture was of his big sister cradling him, smiling proudly like a Cheshire cat with him in her arms. The third photograph he'd wanted was a typical family portrait of his mum and dad, sister and himself, standing together like a real family.

Near the bottom of the cardboard box, he later discovered a small creamy coloured photo album, full of snapshots of him with various animals. He could be seen riding a horse, stroking a Great Dane, patting a crocodile, cuddling a python, being picked up by an elephant's trunk and cleaning the teeth of a Tyrannosaurus Rex.

At first Connor assumed the photographs had been taken in a place filled with various models of different animals but he later discovered the photographs were genuine. On the back of every picture was a description of who was in the picture and whereabouts it was taken.

Much to Connor's surprise, he discovered K was the animal in each photograph, having shape-shifted into the form of different animals to interact with him.

'Every summer, you all used to go up north to a secluded holiday camp managed by the AAA. Harlingfield had been purpose built for human families and stranded aliens, who were all connected in some way to the establishment. Perfect place to enjoy the countryside whilst being safe, if you ask me,' Sparkie had explained to him. 'Since you were K's favourite playmate he'd change into an animal just to see you chuckle. Then, you'd beg for him to do it over and over again.'

The fourth picture he desperately wanted was the one where he had fallen asleep between the massive paws of a lion, the lion licking his face. Written on the back were the words, 'K and Connor, friends forever!'

It was two o'clock in the morning before Connor climbed sleepily into the bed Marion had prepared for him. Surprisingly, since his bottom sank in the middle of the soft mattress while his feet poked up in the air in an undignified manner, he fell asleep quite easily with a smile on his face. Dreaming of all the good times he'd had when he was younger, even though he couldn't remember them.

Two hours later, Connor woke with a start and for some reason he was wide-awake. He shuddered, wondering what could have woken him, then crawling out of bed he dressed quickly.

The wind continued to cause havoc outside. Windows throughout the house were rattling with a vengeance. Connor wondered if that was what had disrupted his sleep. It was possible.

It was four o'clock in the morning and, feeling surprisingly thirsty, he decided to go downstairs to make some hot chocolate. How his life had changed in the last few days. A week ago, while living with his aunt and uncle, he was living the life of a slave. He smiled as a tingling sensation raced through his body, knowing he was free and now being cared for.

Trees creaked and groaned, casting ferocious black shadows across the walls, fighting with one another like angry black monsters and with the radiators clumping and banging every five minutes, it was enough to put Connor on edge.

The television was still on downstairs. Lying in front of it was Sparkie snoozing and snoring loudly. Connor smiled and went into the kitchen, which now looked like a bombsite. Sparkie had used a clean mug every time he made another drink.

He boiled the kettle, found a nice sized mug, which happened to be the only one left since Sparkie had used the others, and heaped an extra spoonful of hot chocolate powder inside it so it tasted really chocolatey.

He went into the living room, spotting more empty cups on the table beside Sparkie. Sitting down in the empty armchair he decided to concentrate his mind on changing the channel. Focussing his thoughts he stared at the television without blinking. The screen flickered slightly before an interesting film appeared concerning good cops trying to expose the corrupt ones. For several minutes it grabbed Connor's attention, whilst he finished his drink.

He felt slightly guilty having enjoyed his evening looking at photographs. He only wished Deana had been with him to share those special moments. He was convinced she'd have been just as pleased for him. And there was another reason. He was beginning to miss her. He gave a thought to how K and his mum were getting on. And wondered what the significance was of the birth certificate that Sparkie had found earlier. Connor couldn't understand why K didn't know he had a brother. Why would his parents keep that information from him? It didn't make sense. And Sparkie had been acting really weird since finding out about Daven. He'd been chuckling throughout the entire evening, even when there was nothing apparently funny happening.

Connor added another log to the fire and listened to it hissing before warming to a reddish glow. A large lump of soot collapsed down the chimney. Connor jumped nervously, spilling what little drink he had left on his trousers. He sprang to his feet, making sure no embers had fallen on to the carpet. Wrinkling his nose, he then watched as a large red ant scuttled from the flames on to the rug.

Connor watched it darting hastily under the fire screen. He lifted his foot and was about to squash it when it rapidly started changing shape.

'Ahhh!' yelled Connor, falling back in the chair.

Sparkie slept on.

The ant increased in size, distorting its shape until Tookar stood in its place, his face aghast. Connor looked just as horrified.

'You were going to kill me!' Tookar exclaimed rubbing his head where Connor's foot had made contact. His face crumpled in disbelief. 'You almost had me. Your foot was on top of me –'

'I'm s… s… sorry, I thought you w… w… were an ant!' Connor stammered.

'I was!' Tookar replied sharply, 'but that's no excuse. A fire ant seemed the only safe way into this place, but I was very much mistaken. What are you doing down here at this time of night, anyway? It's not safe!' He looked across at Sparkie and tutted loudly.

'Not safe?' Connor quizzed, following Tookar like a shadow, into the kitchen.

Tookar promptly filled a dirty mug with water. Returning to the living room, Connor watched as Tookar threw the entire contents over Sparkie's face. He woke up instantly, spluttering and cursing. Before there was a chance to demand an explanation, Tookar was already speaking.

'We've got to leave immediately. Fifty dark hounds are outside the house at this very moment.'

Hairs prickled uneasily down Connor's spine. He peered through a small gap in the curtains. Trees were blowing forcibly and rain drummed loudly on the single glass pane. He couldn't see anything except dark silhouettes.

Then, as his eyes adjusted to the darkness, a movement caught his eye. At first it looked like a blanket of low black cloud. There were darker shadows creeping across the lawn towards the cottage. Connor gasped. The ground was moving in a thick mass of bodies. Or was it dogs? It was hard to tell the difference.

'Keep away from there!' Tookar growled, dragging Connor away from the window.

'Upstairs! Quick!' Sparkie shouted, leaping from the seat.

They raced into the hallway and caught sight of a long thin black snout poking through the small gap in the cat flap, sniffing frantically.

'Smell my foot!' Tookar yelled, kicking it hard.

A high pitched wail screamed into the night. They sprinted upstairs as fast as they could.

'I hope your van is ready to move out!' Tookar cried.

'Yes, it's in here!' Sparkie panted, adding in a mutter, 'I'm getting far too old for this!'

As they entered the master bedroom, glass was heard shattering downstairs.

Tookar slammed the door shut and turned the key. 'This won't keep them out for long.'

Many paws were clamouring up the staircase, scratching and slipping on the wooden floor in the hallway. Seconds later, howling cries were heard on the other side of the door.

The door banged heavily from the other side. Something had thrown itself against it. The hinges shifted slightly in the wooden frame. Desperate clawing started splintering the door. Gathering immense pressure more dark hounds began charging and battering it. The house was quickly filled with disturbing sounds: thumping bodies slamming into the door and vicious growling.

Huge powerful claws appeared through the door, ripping it to shreds as if it were made of cardboard. Connor was terrified. Through a splintered gap in the door he'd glimpsed a dark hound. It was enough to freeze him to the spot, paralysing him with fear. Tookar, seeing his state, pushed him inside the van, swinging the door shut.

Connor closed his eyes tight. Even then he couldn't escape the horror he had seen. The lasting memory of four huge fangs, drooling with saliva, remained with him, locked in his consciousness. Slanted black eyes had stared through into his soul.

Connor had seen a monster. Dark hounds seemed too kind a word to describe the beasts. They had thin long snouts and wide snarling mouths, filled to the brim with dagger-like teeth. Matted black manes and raised hackles ran along the length of their hunched spines. Bald patches were most apparent as if they were suffering from a horrible disease.

Sparkie hastily put on his metal hat. He pressed a button and pulled back a lever. A dark hound twice the size of the biggest dog tore into the room. It pounced six feet into the air towards them. The van gave a jolt and suddenly vanished.

Hearing the sighs of relief, Connor opened his eyes.

'Phew! That was a close shave. Where are we?' Tookar asked, breathing shakily.

'We're a hundred miles north from K's home and a hundred yards above an empty field in the middle of nowhere,' Sparkie told him, pulling out a handkerchief from his pocket and wiping his forehead. His breathing was erratic after the manic escape.

'What did those things want?' Connor asked, trying to stop his legs from shaking.

'You,' Sparkie said solemnly.

'I thought so.' Connor hugged his knees to his chest. Was this nightmare ever going to end? 'Those dark hounds were so scary.

I've never seen anything like them before. Where did they come from?'

'Definastine's home planet, Dramian,' Sparkie explained.

'Definastine has a lot to answer for. He found a way to snare animal souls keeping them prisoner for eternity,' Tookar said gruffly.

'Never underestimate Definastine, Connor. His mind is so corrupt and evil,' Sparkie warned. 'His dark hounds are vicious and callous and wouldn't think twice about killing you. You saw how strong they were. They could rip a human to shreds in seconds...'

'Yes, thank you for scaring the living daylights out of him,' Tookar broke in. 'Most of Definastine's servants have a weakness though. They can't survive daylight. So between dawn and dusk they will have to stay hidden somewhere.'

'Oh, that's good, isn't it? How does a person get to Dramian anyway?' Connor asked.

'Why? Are you thinking of going?' Tookar laughed. 'Well, you can't take a bus. Since it's in another dimension the only way to get there is through a dimensional gateway.'

'A dimensional gateway?' Connor gasped. 'You mean some kind of magic hole?'

'That's right,' Tookar smiled warmly.

'The gateway is hidden. You can only travel there on the night of a full moon. For thousands of years it has remained concealed but recently we learned of its existence. And now for the first time we'll be able to rescue the lost children – if there are any survivors.'

'The lost children?' Connor gasped.

'There's a rescue party leaving for Dramian tomorrow night,' Tookar mentioned.

'Oh, I didn't know,' Sparkie replied, looking upset. 'No one told me.'

'No one thought you'd be interested. You've been bending my ear just lately on how you're getting too old for this type of thing. Thought you'd want to take the opportunity to put your feet up and rest. Don't want you overdoing it now, do we,' Tookar grinned, enjoying himself.

'Yes… but… well, it would have been nice to have been asked,' Sparkie grunted.

'Are you going?' Connor asked Tookar.

'I hope to,' he replied thoughtfully.

'Well, I won't be,' Sparkie said bluntly. 'I was thinking of retiring anyway. I can't handle all the stresses like I used to. I don't care what you say. I *am* getting older every day. My bones seize up too quickly nowadays.'

'See what I mean. He's turning into a goose!' Tookar laughed and nudged Connor's arm.

'I'm not!' snapped Sparkie. 'I'll have you know my nerves are still as strong as ever. It's my body that's letting me down, that's all.'

'Keep your hair on, old man,' Tookar grinned. 'You don't want to lose that as well, do you!'

'Old man! Pah! Anyway if we're talking of age you were born a few thousand years before me,' said Sparkie peevishly.

'Maybe so, but I still look and feel young.'

'I'm not doing too badly either for someone born in 1831,' Sparkie remarked, raising his eyebrow slightly.

'1831?' quizzed Connor, not believing it for one moment. 'That's impossible!'

'He speaks the truth,' Tookar told him.

'But he's human! Humans don't live that long.'

'No, you're right. But I did spend some time in another galaxy where time slows down,' Sparkie explained. 'I was born in the Victorian era when Queen Victoria was on the throne. During my early thirties I met a fantastic young man who changed the course of my life.'

'Me,' Tookar said.

'You!' Connor gasped.

'Yes. Tookar found a way to mend his crashed spaceship. It allowed him to travel so fast it sliced through the dimensional fields to other worlds. He took me with him once. Even though it seemed only a few days had passed the actual time on earth had whizzed by. It was 1961 by the time we came back and Queen Elizabeth was on the throne then. I still looked the same as ever but a hundred years had passed.'

'What about your family and friends?' Connor whispered.

'They had all died,' Sparkie remarked sadly. 'Every single person I'd known had died.'

'That's awful!' Connor shook his head in disbelief.

'But that's life, Connor,' Sparkie replied, springing back. 'Things can happen to us everyday that may change the course of our lives. Meeting Tookar was the greatest thing I have ever done. We've been damn good friends ever since. I'll tell you all about my first space adventure one day.'

Connor, finding it hard to swallow Sparkie's story, glanced solemnly out of the window, coming face to face with a view misted with condensation. It looked as cloudy as his thoughts.

'Where are we heading now?' Connor asked quietly. He was trying not to ponder on what would have happened if the dark hounds had managed to pounce on him and trying not to think of them chewing on his head like a nice bone.

'Not sure,' Sparkie confessed.

'To be honest, nowhere seems truly safe, not if Definastine has the consulting mirror in his clutches,' Tookar reminded them. 'Ask it the right questions and it'll tell him everything that's happened in the past to this present moment. He could be watching us this very instance.'

'The best thing we could do is destroy it so it never gets in the wrong hands again,' Sparkie added, wrinkling his head in puzzlement. His voice took on a new edge. 'I've begun to pick up a distress signal somewhere. Here – I'll see if I can share it with you.'

He pulled out a loose wire from underneath the dashboard and connected it to his hat. A concealed speaker in the van began to transfer the message. It wasn't clear at first but crackled with interference. Sparkie twisted the wires on top of his hat and a distressed female voice came through.

'Help me!' she cried weakly. 'Please help me!'

'Good grief!' Tookar gasped.

'If there is anyone out there who can hear me, please come and help me!' the voice continued. 'I haven't got much time. I'm being held prisoner. Please, someone help me!'

According to his tracking device, the person in distress should be twenty miles north. Sparkie immediately instructed his van to take them there. In no time at all, they found themselves in an area of dense forest. There was no sign of life, no lights, no movement, no nothing. It confirmed his darkest thoughts.

'The signal is coming from underground,' Sparkie announced.

'You don't think it could be a trap, do you?' warned Tookar. 'Don't do anything rash.'

Sparkie nodded his head. 'I agree. It seems a little strange, especially after our recent episode with the dark hounds. But what if it really is someone who needs our help? Anyway, there's no telling how long she's been calling. Remember we could only hear her with this transmitter on.'

Connor listened quietly to the two men talking, but he wasn't feeling very well. Nausea stirred in the pit of his stomach and his head began to throb.

'I'm not feeling very good,' he whispered, looking down at the floor and clutching his stomach. Even his eyes began to play tricks with him. A white spiralling mist began swirling about his legs.

'Connor, what's wrong?' Tookar rested his arm about Connor's shoulders, looking deeply concerned.

'Do you see that?' Connor asked.

'See what?' Tookar frowned.

'That's answered my question,' Connor mumbled.

But before anyone else could speak, an opening appeared beneath his feet and a strong sucking force began pulling him towards the floor.

'Help!' cried Connor, sliding helplessly off his seat.

Then, screaming hysterically, he was suddenly drawn through the misty fog through the bottom of the van. Still screaming and kicking his feet, he expected to fall through the air straight to the ground but instead he was swept down a tunnel, sparkling like diamonds. His only companion was a constant popping sound in his ears.

He fell at a speed you would expect to reach if you were thrown from a helicopter a hundred feet above the ground. Anxious cries from Tookar and Sparkie could be heard from a distance. However, their voices gradually faded altogether, leaving Connor alone with his beating heart.

Eventually, and most unexpectedly, he was spat out from the glistening hole as if he were a foul tasting insect. With a thud he landed neatly in a heap on the other side of the chamber. Very shakily, and much to his alarm, he glanced about, seeing two of everything.

'Huh?' he groaned.

Connor stood up and dusted his behind. He wondered where he was. The dreadful feeling inside him had been replaced with something more adventurous. Perhaps knowing that he wasn't really alone helped. In fact, he hadn't been truly lonely ever since the Starstone had nested deep inside of him.

Glancing around the box shaped chamber; metal walls, metal floors and a thick metal door greeted him coldly.

A thick, green blanket was draped over a large object one side of the wall. Connor wondered what was beneath it. But thinking he probably shouldn't look, he tried to avoid thinking about it. The temptation proved too great, however, and seconds later Connor decided, after a brief battle with his conscience, to take a peep. So very gently he lifted the coarse material. He was hoping to replace it easily but it loosened and fell on top of him.

Finding his way out from the thick claustrophobic fabric, Connor staggered backwards as a large magnificent mirror was now exposed. It was of oval shape, being five feet high and three feet wide. The surface was moving delicately as if made of liquid. Connor caught sight of his distressed face staring back at him. He ran his fingers through his hair and watched it return to its upward position.

'Wow!' he gasped in delight, admiring the mirror. He ran his fingers over the smooth silver frame, decorated with the strangest symbols he'd ever seen. 'If only Sparkie and Tookar could see this, they'd be amazed. I wonder where they are.'

He jumped when his reflection suddenly vanished. Very slowly the mirror began shimmering and rippling in waves. The image changed dramatically. Very slowly, Connor retreated from the mysterious mirror only to see Sparkie and Tookar coming into focus, sitting with ashen faces in the van.

'Where's he gone?' Tookar cried.

'I don't know!' Sparkie flustered. 'He fell through the floor!'

'I'm here!' Connor called but it was hopeless. They couldn't hear him.

He looked with immense pleasure at the mirror and realised beyond doubt he was standing in front of the consulting mirror: the same mirror Definastine had been using to his advantage to find him and the Starstone.

The consulting mirror was dazzling. Made from a special grey, silvery liquid compressed between two panes of transparent glass like material, it hung on the wall where the liquid continued moving with a will of it own. Connor tried to recollect everything he had heard about it. It could only reveal events that have already taken place. It was not a device for seeing the future. Connor was so excited by his discovery that he momentarily forgot about where he was or finding a way out. This was his chance to ask the mirror any questions about anything, anywhere and finally learning the answer.

But Sparkie's voice came to haunt him. *'The best thing we could do is destroy it so it never gets in the wrong hands again.'*

Surely it wouldn't hurt to ask a question or two, Connor thought.

A hundred questions began streaming through his mind at once, until one question began repeating itself above the others.

Facing the mirror, Connor took a deep breath.

'Please show me where my sister is,' he asked politely, as if speaking to a person of importance.

Suddenly a white room with four people sitting in it came into view. The mirror acted like some sort of window to that room.

Connor saw Marion, K and Deana talking to a young nurse with long blonde hair.

Connor was stunned. His sister was comforting his friends. His sister was a nurse. She looked so much like the photographs he had of her, or at least her hair did anyway.

'Please show me a close up of the nurse,' he asked, walking closer to the mirror. He reached out to touch the face of his sister. Her face was flawless and beautiful with no freckles to be seen. She must've grown out of them, he thought, and her eyes weren't the same colour either. Must be wearing contact lenses, he decided.

'There must be some mistake, Jenny,' Marion was saying. 'What are you trying to say?'

'The man that was brought in here isn't your husband, Mrs Fallow,' the nurse informed them.

'Well, who is he then?' K asked, looking puzzled.

'It's hard to say at this stage. It certainly looks like Jeremy but the DNA samples don't match at all. We'll have to run more tests. But don't worry, we'll keep you informed,' Jenny answered truthfully.

'But if my dad isn't here, where is he?'

'I have no idea, but it's definitely not him lying next door on that table,' said Jenny.

'But it doesn't make any sense,' Deana remarked, a faint tremor in her voice.

'I must admit, it is very strange,' Jenny added.

Connor frowned heavily.

'If Jeremy isn't dead, where is he?' he asked the mirror.

An image, revealing a small boy huddled on the ground with his face resting on bent knees, came quickly into focus. He seemed to be in a small dark room.

'Is that Jeremy? What is this place?'

The mirror revealed a dark planet, surrounded by stars.

'I don't understand,' mumbled Connor. 'How do I get there?'

Directions immediately appeared. Flashing scenes of passing countryside were moving at least a hundred miles an hour. It was so confusing it made Connor feel light-headed.

'Stop!' he called out. 'You're going too fast. Show me where to go on a map.'

Then, a map came into view. An arrow was travelling towards a great expanse of water and didn't stop until it reached the middle of what was obviously an immense lake.

'He must be on a boat,' Connor murmured.

'I don't want to destroy you mirror, but what should I do? I can't leave you here, otherwise Definastine will use you to hurt people.'

The mirror didn't react. It couldn't answer his question.

'If only you were smaller,' Connor said. 'I could sneak you out easily then.'

Connor sat on the floor with his fingers running through his hair, giving some thought to the problem. Closing his eyes briefly, he suddenly snapped them open as he came to realise what he must do.

'I might be able to turn you into a watch of some kind,' he said.

He closed his eyes and pointed at the mirror.

The thought is the deed, he remembered. Just imagine it turning into a watch and it will. For several long minutes he stood concentrating with all his might. His arms, outstretched and pointing towards the mirror, soon began to feel heavy. As he lowered them, his thoughts turned to the discomfort in his body. This was no good; he had to concentrate harder.

'Come on!' he urged, eyes still closed. 'Transform!'

Then, eventually he felt something slipping around his wrist.

He opened his eyes to see the wall was bare and the mirror had gone. Touching the strange little watch he could see it wasn't a watch to tell the time but a watch to tell all things past. Its face had become the smallest of mirrors.

'I did it!' Connor was astounded. 'Now what? Why else am I here?'

The door across the room seemed the only way out. Connor went to open it but discovered it was locked. Where were his friends when he needed them most? In the van looking frantic, he recalled. It wasn't their fault he was stuck in this room, but he didn't think it was his either.

He had no clue what had happened in the van or why he was there.

'I could try to unlock it,' he thought, but was scared at the prospect of what he might find on the other side.

He stood helplessly, deep in thought, until he realised something wasn't quite right. He could have sworn he was getting shorter by the minute. He glanced around the room. The ceiling seemed higher than before, the ground closer. He peered down at his feet and stifled a cry. At first he thought his feet had disappeared through the floor, but he soon came to realise in actual truth he was melting. His body was dissolving on the spot into a blob of nothingness.

He was paralysed with terror. He couldn't move even if he wanted to, for at this moment his legs had almost vanished. His heart was thumping heavily and his pulse was tripling in speed.

He hardly noticed the warm sensations engulfing his body. At the same time a light began shining from his stomach. Connor struggled hopelessly. His navel continued dissolving. He tried desperately to stop himself from completely disappearing by supporting the rest of his body on his arms. His hands touched the floor. This seemed to help for a short time, until they too began to disappear, leaving him more helpless than ever.

'I'm too young to die!' he wailed, his voice echoing round the chamber.

Something deep inside him was taking over his body. His mind fought wildly but his body surrendered without a fight. He had no choice. The Starstone, more powerful than Connor, was suddenly feeling active and started to take control of the situation.

Drunkenly, Connor gazed down at his chest, watching it shrink before his eyes. He wanted to scream as he tried to struggle with the nightmare he found himself in, but no words came out. But there was no pain as his chin faded from sight followed by his mouth and finally his eyes.

Connor was now an invisible sludge of nothingness, yet he was still very much alive. A gentle voice started speaking to him. It was a silent communication from the Starstone.

We have work to do. We must save the girl and your aunt and uncle. I'll lead the way. Don't be afraid. I will not let any harm befall you.

The words were soothing and comforting. For the present time, Connor's emotions were put on hold. They did not exist. The invisible slime started moving and trickling beneath the smallest of gaps in the thickened door, leading out into a darkened corridor.

It entered the next room occupied by two hooded creatures.

Connor continued soaking up information like a sponge. Through a blue transparent lens he maintained vision and hearing. Resting a safe distance away from two gruesome figures, he was close enough to sense the tension between them.

'I was meant to get the boy and I failed!' the tall muscular figure raged, his powerful torso dwarfing his companion. As he shook his head with annoyance his hood fell back. A grey, bony skeletal face covered in deep ugly scars with purple tendons sticking out on each side of his neck could plainly be seen. Connor instantly recognised him as the same creature who had chased him across the hospital car park.

'Don't lose sleep over this, Razor,' the shorter one replied gruffly. 'We can't change the past. Those other two will be our bait to draw the child closer.'

'And what good are they to us? Tell me, Ruben – I'd be enlightened to know how your brain works. That puny child won't be able to find them. Can't you understand that Definastine wants the child… and why… because he has the Starstone you dimwit!' Razor seethed, losing his patience and denting the strong metal wall with his fist. An angry echo vibrated round the room. 'Time is running out!'

Ruben pulled back his hood. His face was very similar to Razor's, but broader with higher cheekbones. He frowned deeply, narrowing his eyes whilst staring coldly towards Razor. 'Definastine has others looking for the boy. We are not the only ones searching for the Starstone.'

'But it is us he counts on!' Razor growled fiercely. 'Not those hair balls.'

'Don't ridicule his pets. His dark hounds are well known for getting the job done,' Ruben replied coldly.

'Pets!' laughed Razor mockingly. 'They're not his pets! They're his snacks. He eats them when he's feeling peckish. And he cares for them little more than he cares for you!'

'Don't sneer at me!' Ruben glowered. 'I'm just as good as you are and you know it! You're the one who's slipping, Razor… you're not as good as you once were. You let your emotions get the better of you. In fact, it probably won't be long before Definastine chooses me to take command. What was it he said I had… a level head. He told me I could keep my cool and that's exactly what he needs in charge of the group.'

Growling angrily, Razor leaped forward, placing his hands around Ruben's neck and squeezing tightly. Ruben began choking. 'Don't count on it, you imbecile! You couldn't find your way out of this room without me helping you.'

A deep growl erupted from Ruben's throat. He brought both his hands up in the air, knocking them down hard on each side of Razor's neck. The force made Razor loosen his grip.

'Don't ever try to intimidate me again!' Ruben snarled. 'You're no match for me and you know it!'

Razor was breathing fast, his fists clenched so tightly they turned white. They stood opposing one another before Razor allowed a thin smile to spread across his face.

'So you think you are better than me, do you? Prove it. Go on. See if you can find that child before I do. Since those mutts have failed tonight, it's up to you, and me,' Razor grunted, turning sharply. Slamming his hand against the wall for a second time he tore it like a crisp packet.

'I believe my plan will work. The boy will not want those other two humans harmed,' Ruben replied indifferently. 'They will be our insurance. At some point he'll have to come for them and when he does, we'll be prepared for him.'

Razor was laughing coldly. 'You are so sure that your feeble plan will work. You stay and wait but I'm going to search for the boy.'

Just as Razor opened the door, Ruben called after him. 'Those men from the ACE must be reported to Definastine. We don't want them interfering with our plans. They were a little too close for comfort for my liking.'

'Getting scared are you? They were no threat. Weren't they outside all the time when we entered the boy's house through our portal gateway? We were in and out with those two humans before anyone saw us.'

Ruben, who was second in command to Razor, couldn't do much without his permission.

'There's no need to tell Definastine anything about them,' Razor smirked.

'As you wish,' Ruben replied, doubting Razor's decision. 'And what about Raider? He hasn't yet been in contact with us.'

'Oh, didn't you know? He's dead,' Razor announced coldly. 'He was murdered. There's just three of us left now.'

'What?' Ruben hissed.

'I saw it in the consulting mirror. It showed me what happened. A slight tussle with Tookar and he died. We're better off without him. I'm going there now to ask where the boy is. Care to join me?'

Connor was listening non-judgementally. In his present form, all emotions were non-existent.

'Does Definastine or Raven know that Raider is dead?' asked Ruben horrified.

'Definastine knows, I told him shortly before we had this chat.'

'Yet, you didn't think it important enough to tell me!' Ruben glared angrily. 'Raider is our brother, for pity's sake.'

'And now he is dead!' Razor glowered.

'I must speak to Raven and inform him of what has transpired!'

'Do what you must!' Razor turned on his heel and left the room, slamming the door hard behind him.

Connor followed, squeezing through the gap beneath the door, leaving Ruben alone in the room. He turned in the opposite direction to Razor. Like a fast moving snail he slithered down a wide corridor, up the walls and upside down along the ceiling. It was quiet with no other signs of life. The occasional lamp dangled prehistorically from the ceiling with loose wires dangerously poking out from it. Several light bulbs flickered annoyingly; others refused to work at all.

Through the gloomy, smooth walled corridors he journeyed, until he turned a corner and came across a strong metal door being barred securely by two strange creatures. They looked like huge oversized insects that had refused to stop growing. Black shiny armour covered their backs reflecting what little light there was. They stood seven feet tall like statues, wax models almost, but extremely ugly. A malevolent glint in their eyes and a permanent surly smile added to their hideous appearance.

Unnoticed, Connor seeped between their feet into the forbidden room. A nasty odour greeted him in this pitch-black room. But it didn't affect Connor, for he had no nose. Seeing in the dark, through his blue tinted window, was no problem. Two familiar looking people sat unconscious on a sofa. It was his aunt and uncle. There was no mistaking these two.

He also saw a slender girl, bound to the wall with heavy metal chains cruelly clasping her wrists and ankles. Her body was slumped forward, unconscious. Her locks of long hair hung loosely, covering her face.

Suddenly Connor's body returned to him. He grew like a plant from the invisible ooze. His body was twisting and jerking, stretching upwards until he appeared quite normal again.

His breath quickened. All the things he'd seen and heard at last made their impression on his consciousness. He was terrified and utterly confused. He had an idea what had happened to him and it left him quivering in fear.

For a short time he remained rigid with his arms hanging lifeless beside him. Everything was dark. But he knew he couldn't stay in that place forever. He had to do something. He had to think hard. He had to think of a way to get out of there, taking his aunt and uncle with him.

'If only I could find a way back to Sparkie's van,' Connor thought, wishing for a miracle.

A sudden idea came to him. He closed his eyes and concentrated with all his might. A bright circular door appeared in the darkness, shimmering like liquid. He opened his eyes just in time to see his aunt and uncle floating off the floor in a levitating sofa. It hovered towards the portal, where they disappeared without delay.

Spellbound by the astonishing sight he'd conjured, he glanced nervously towards the girl currently confined in shackles. The portal gate was gently illuminating her body. She looked so vulnerable. Connor went closer to her and touched her arm. Her body gave a shudder and she immediately raised her head. A smile crept across her face as her eyes fluttered open.

'I knew you would come,' she said weakly, her lips motionless.

Feeling incredibly angry about the girl's fate, Connor snapped the binding chains as if they were made of paper. Her weak body collapsed to the floor. He lifted her dainty frame in his arms and without hesitating, leaped through the portal.

'No, not again!' he cried.

The same flutter of butterflies arrived in his stomach as he was sucked back through the rocketing passageway, clinging on to the girl for dear life.

He soon found himself back in the van with Mr and Mrs Piggot positioned in the back. With their extra weight, the van started shuddering and lowering towards the ground.

'Goodness gracious me. You did it, Connor!' Sparkie and Tookar cried together. 'You're back!'

Later, Ruben and Razor stood silhouetted in the doorway with two gruff Armatripe behind them. They were both sniffing the air as if they were dogs, frantically trying to find clues.

'The bodies have gone,' Razor observed, searching the empty room.

'But how?' Ruben was mystified.

Razor gave an impatient glance towards Ruben. 'I can sense some kind of portal dust in the air. Someone came to rescue them and not by the front door.'

'How the devil did they know where they were?' Ruben cursed.

'Perhaps someone told them. Someone like you!' accused Razor. 'How else would they know about the consulting mirror?' His tongue, several inches long, was stretching out from his mouth as if he was a snake, flickering threateningly towards Ruben. Many rows of brown stained, razor sharp teeth were now on show and his fingernails were stretching out like long knives. 'You were desperate to make sure my plan failed. Perhaps you sent them away somewhere.'

Ruben was furious. Two long tentacles appeared from two flaps in his cheek, encircling Razor's tongue and causing him to choke. His dark eyes turned bright orange.

'I don't like what you're implying,' Ruben hissed. 'Shall I squeeze you harder? Shall I yank out your tongue?'

Razor was choking this time and fell to his knees. Ruben released him. His strange alien tentacles slithered back into his face where a flap of skin covered them up.

'Enough talk!' Ruben scowled. 'We've got some explaining to do.'

CHAPTER FIFTEEN

The Rescued Princess

'Oh, my goodness!' exclaimed Sparkie, when Connor reappeared out of thin air. He was holding what at first appeared to be an unconscious young girl. 'What happened to you? Where did you go? Who is this girl? How did you find those two?' He pointed towards Connor's aunt and uncle.

Connor was exhausted. His body felt weak. Was he stuck in a nightmare unable to wake up? He had no answers to the probing questions being fired at him. Sparkie ceased questioning him when he saw how distraught he looked.

Connor had no control over what transpired next. Gradually the light faded from his eyes and allowing the darkness to shield him, Connor fell into a deep sleep.

Almost a day later, on Friday evening, Connor eventually stirred. His bed covers had fallen off the bed, leaving the cool air to chill his body. For a brief instance, Connor was perplexed, believing his recent experiences were nothing but a bad dream. In actual fact, he thought he was back in his old bed in Wislington, expecting his uncle to call him at any moment.

Opening his eyes with a start, he realised at once that he was far from home. A sudden excitement stirred inside him, knowing that he'd never return to his previous life. It was all in the past.

A heavy snore close beside his ear caused him to turn his head. Tookar, who had been keeping watch over him for the night, had slumped on to the bed and appeared to have shared Connor's pillow all night. His hair had fallen across his face.

'Hey, Tookar,' Connor smirked. 'Wake up!'

But Tookar began snoring louder if anything, so Connor began poking him gently and when that didn't work, he began slapping his back.

'What? – When? – Who?' Tookar grunted, opening his eyes and looking just as confused as Connor had been. His bloodshot eyes glanced fleetingly about before finally resting on Connor. 'Oh, it's you. I thought something serious was happening.'

'How long have I been asleep?' Connor asked.

'A day,' Tookar replied, stretching his arms above his head and yawning. 'How are you feeling?'

Connor's body felt sore. Slowly he sat up, feeling nauseous and disorientated.

'Awful,' he groaned. 'I feel as if I've been fighting a crocodile with two heads. Where are we?'

Tookar laughed gently, watching Connor with interest. 'It's a secret location deep inside a mountain, though I don't expect it to stay secret for long – not if Definastine consults that mirror,' Tookar breathed wearily. 'While he has it, he's got us running about like headless chickens. That mirror is powerful and in the wrong hands, totally destructive. I think if I were to see it now, I'd get a hammer and personally destroy it myself. Then we'd all feel a lot safer – especially you Connor. The AAA is totally out of control at the moment. We've had problems with portals opening all over the place, with Definastine's servants rushing in and causing chaos before fleeing again. That's why we haven't been able to take you there yet.' Tookar breathed in deeply and stretched his legs. 'Anyway, what happened to you back in the van? Didn't know what to do when you disappeared through the floor like that.' Tookar leant back in his chair, rolling his head to loosen his neck. 'All I know is that was one crazy exit you performed.'

Connor, not wishing to keep secrets from Tookar, wanted to tell him about the consulting mirror. He felt torn in two. If he mentioned he'd found it, Tookar might want to destroy it, on the other hand, Tookar's friendship was much more important. Trust is a difficult thing to gain and he wasn't prepared to lose it. The choice was easier than he thought. The truth always wins between friends. In a whisper he said, 'I found it.'

'Found what?' Tookar quizzed, running his fingers through his shoulder-length hair.

'I have it with me. Here. Look.' Connor rolled up his sleeve, lifting his wrist to show Tookar the smallest mirror he'd ever seen.

'But what is it?' he said, wrinkling his brow.

'The consulting mirror.'

'No! Of course it isn't. It's much bigger than that!'

'It was,' Connor continued. 'I thought about destroying it, but I couldn't. So I shrank it instead. So you see, you don't have to worry about anything now.'

Tookar gave the biggest laugh he'd ever heard before ruffling Connor's hair.

'You're one brave kid!' he beamed, delighted. 'It would probably be safer if we kept this knowledge to ourselves for now,' he said on a more serious note. 'But tell Sparkie by all means.'

'Okay,' replied Connor. He rolled down his sleeve, feeling grateful that Tookar hadn't ripped the mirror off his wrist, crushing it beneath his boot.

'Out of curiosity, did you discover anything? I mean, did you ask it any questions?'

Connor nodded fervently. 'I found out who my sister is.'

'Did you?' Tookar laughed. 'I bet that came as quite a surprise to you. I don't suppose there's any harm talking about her now, since you know.'

'She looked just like her photograph,' said Connor, pulling a picture from his pocket. 'This is her, look.' He pointed to the young girl cradling him when he was a baby.

Tookar frowned. 'Yes, that's her. Not much of a resemblance now though. Her freckles are the same but since she's been dying her hair to fool you, it's now a completely different colour.'

'What are you talking about?' said Connor. 'It's just the same. I saw it.'

Tookar frowned, looking deeply puzzled. He opened his eyes in surprise. 'Oh, perhaps she dyed it back again. Just exactly what did you see?'

'My sister, Jenny,' Connor told him.

'Stone the crows!' Tookar declared, laughing loudly, and almost choking. 'Your sister isn't called Jenny! Her name is...'

'How's the hero feeling then?' said Sparkie, bursting into the room and bringing with him a drink for Connor.

'A bit tired,' Connor confessed. 'But I'll live.' With suspicion, he surveyed the glass of green liquid bubbling in Sparkie's hand.

'Drink this. It'll get rid of any grogginess that you might be feeling,' Sparkie said brightly.

'It looks disgusting,' Connor said flatly, sitting up and sniffing the glass.

'Now, now, don't be so hasty to judge. Appearances can be deceiving. You should know that by now. Come on and drink up. It won't harm you,' Sparkie encouraged. He was looking very pleased with himself.

Doubtful, Connor reluctantly took a sip. He swished it about inside his mouth before swallowing with a loud gulp. Tookar and Sparkie were grinning at his hesitation. But it was lovely – delicious in fact. It was light and bubbly with a very sweet, fruity taste. Bubbles were still gently exploding inside his body a few seconds later. With each sip, immense strength came flooding back to him, easing his aches.

'That's the most amazing drink ever,' Connor said gratefully. 'What's it made from?'

'Can't tell you. It's my very own special secret formula,' Sparkie told him, tapping his large nose. 'Has the hero told you anything as yet?' Sparkie looked at Tookar.

'Not very much,' replied Tookar, still scratching his head.

'Then I've arrived just in time,' Sparkie grinned, pulling a chair closer to the bed.

'I suppose you want to hear what happened? You're probably not going to believe me...' Connor murmured. 'I don't really believe it myself.'

'All we know is, one minute you were with us and the next – poof – you'd gone!' Sparkie breathed excitedly, sitting on the edge of his seat in direct contrast to Tookar who had adopted a more relaxed posture, leaning back and listening carefully.

Connor began explaining everything in detail that had happened, from falling out of the van through a strange tunnel, to finding the consulting mirror. Knowing he was now safe he was able to speak excitedly about seeing his body dissolve and the conversation he'd overheard between Ruben and Razor, not to mention how he'd finally come across his aunt and uncle. All the while Sparkie and Tookar were listening intently, with astounded expressions on their faces.

'Recognised them at once,' said Connor, enjoying the attention. 'They were still sitting on the sofa. The place stank. It was awful. There were no windows at all in the room, so there was no fresh air. I felt sorry for the girl chained in the same room as them. It's bad enough being kept a prisoner but kept in the same room as my aunt and uncle... urgh! If that's not cruelty, I don't know what is.'

Connor went on to explain how a bizarre light entered the room, whisking his aunt and uncle away. 'So I tore the chains off the girl and jumped through the light too.'

'The Starstone is a consciousness,' smiled Tookar, standing up quickly, 'a living form with powers beyond our understanding. If you put your mind to it, you could probably do anything. You've been blessed with magical power!'

'But why did I feel so awful afterwards,' Connor reminded them. 'I'm only just beginning to feel better after that drink Sparkie gave me.'

'Using the Starstone the way you did – opening portals – turning into some kind of invisible form – rescuing three other people – it must've drained you,' said Tookar.

'I'm not a sink!' Connor grumbled.

'I meant to say it drained you of energy – not dirty water.'

'Sorry, I didn't mean to snap at you... it's just that I... I don't understand anything anymore. One day I'm just an ordinary boy and the next I've developed strength like Superman and I'm being hunted down like a... like an animal.'

'Don't worry, my lad,' Sparkie said, tapping his hand a little too enthusiastically for Connor's liking. 'It's amazing – absolutely amazing. What a gift you have – can't believe it, really. A boy with super strength and powers – can't believe your luck. The possibilities opened to you are immense – absolutely mind blowing, I must say! Glad you're on our side!'

Mildly amused by Sparkie's ecstatic response, Tookar switched his attention back to Connor, leaving Sparkie, who was now so excited that he bounced round the room and began talking to the walls.

'Believe me, this will be nothing more than a memory one day, something to tell your grandchildren,' Tookar said calmly.

'I don't know about that,' said Connor. 'I might not live that long. By the way, what happened to my aunt and uncle?'

'They've been taken to the AAA and will be treated and cured of their... err... weight problem.'

'That's good news. About time!' Connor smiled. 'What happened to the girl? Who was she?'

'Princess Kia is safe and well, thanks to you. Don't look so shocked. She's a lovely girl and very much down to earth. She was kidnapped a few days ago and brought to this planet, where none of her people would think of rescuing her. Didn't take you into consideration though, did they Connor? That was a big mistake. Definastine wanted her taken to Dramian tonight, to extract some important information from her mind,' Tookar told him.

Connor gulped loudly. Terrifying thoughts pierced his mind of mad men, grinning insanely and wearing white coats. In their hands they were waving sharp instruments: scalpels, knives and scissors. They were dancing round a table prepared for Kia's mind extracting operation.

Tookar continued: 'Needless to say, it's a process that would have eventually killed her. You're quite the hero in her eyes. She hasn't stopped talking about you ever since she arrived here. You saved her life like you did mine.'

'I'm glad I rescued her. Did she tell you about those hooded creeps, Ruben and Razor?'

'Yes, she told us quite a lot actually,' said Tookar on a more serious note, his eyes darkening.

'I found out something from the consulting mirror, concerning Jeremy,' Connor told them.

Sparkie's eyes widened. 'What is it lad?'

'He's not dead. He's alive. He's transformed himself into a child. I think he's on a boat somewhere.'

'I knew it!' Sparkie erupted happily. His arms were swinging everywhere. He looked at Tookar. 'I told you the old fool was up to something, didn't I. I knew he was planning a rescue of his own. He just couldn't wait.'

'What's going on?' asked Connor.

'The dimensional gateway to Dramian lies at the bottom of the Great Lake. Jeremy learnt that Definastine's spies wait close by for the portal to open. It's a full moon tonight. He's probably on Dramian now, trying to rescue his child.'

'K's all right, isn't he?' asked Connor, suddenly worried.

'It's not K he's gone to rescue, but Daven,' said Sparkie. 'Daven is Marion's and Jeremy's first born child. I've been doing a bit of digging about and it turns out their son was kidnapped years ago and taken there. Jeremy's gone to find him. He faked his death so no one would know what he's up to.'

A knock on the door startled them and a small elfin shaped face peered round the door.

'Hello,' said Kia. 'May I come in?'

'Of course you can, dear child,' said Sparkie, still grinning broadly. 'We'll leave you to have a little chat before we leave.'

'Leave? Leave where?' said Connor, looking anxious.

'We'll be leaving for Dramian in the next hour or so. The gateway is open. There's a full moon tonight. I've decided one more adventure won't hurt me before I retire,' Sparkie grinned.

'Am I coming with you?' gasped Connor, his chest tightening with anticipation.

'Of course,' Sparkie replied. 'It'll be your first proper trip to another dimension.'

'My only one,' Connor grumbled uncomfortably. He hadn't even travelled abroad, let alone a trip to another dimension.

'Hi,' said Kia, sitting down in the same chair Tookar had occupied seconds earlier.

Her long golden tresses shone brightly, sweeping past her waist, down to her knees. Then, as if by magic her hair began to change colour. Little lights sparkled delicately, like stars. There were also decorative flowers and jewels strung on to neat plaits. Connor found himself mesmerised by her appearance.

'You okay?'

'I think so,' Connor said, trying to unravel the amount of new information he'd received. He couldn't believe Jeremy was planning a rescue all of his own. 'How about you?'

'Much better,' she grinned.

Connor thought so too. Her face, previously drained of colour, was looking much rosier than when he'd last seen her, fastened to the wall by heavy metal chains.

'I hear you have a habit of saving lives,' Kia smiled. 'Thanks for rescuing me.'

Connor smiled awkwardly, feeling equally shy when he realised she wasn't human. Her smile revealed pale lilac teeth and lilac eyes, glowing bright blue from the centre. Connor stared rudely and gave a little gasp. 'You're not human!'

Kia giggled nervously. 'No, I'm a Stanchy.'

'Wow! I've never met a Stanchy before.'

'And I haven't met a human boy before, either, so I guess we're equal.'

There was an uncomfortable silence before they both spoke again.

'Do you live…?'

'Do you mind…?'

They began to laugh.

'You go first,' said Connor.

'I was just going to ask if you minded going to Dramian?' she asked. 'I hear that there's a huge rescue party travelling tonight, to help free the lost children. Sparkie's hoping to meet up with them after helping me rescue my ship.'

'To be honest, this is the first I've heard about it,' confessed Connor.

'You've been asleep for ages,' Kia reminded him.

'I've been doing a lot of that just lately. I seem to spend my days sleeping.'

Kia giggled. 'Sparkie's really nice. He said he could get my ship back for me. Without it I can't get home.'

'Can't he take you back in his van? It's really amazing!'

Kia giggled again. 'His van is very clever but I have a great distance to travel. I don't even know the way back home from here. My ship has a navigation map that I need to make it back safely. Otherwise I could easily get lost forever. It's my only chance to get home to my people... and my family. I can't stay stranded forever. Not when I have a chance to get home.'

There was a desperate plea to Kia's voice and Connor knew how important this was to her. Wouldn't he want someone to help him too, if he were in her shoes? He smiled. Given his present situation, he did have people helping him.

'You speak really good English,' Connor acknowledged.

'Thanks. Tookar allowed me to learn it.'

'You learnt it? But you haven't been here long enough to learn a new language!'

'For you maybe, but that's my gift. Stanchies have the power to learn any language they want. All I have to do is touch the part of your body where your brain is and I can absorb your language and understand it in seconds.'

'Wow!' gasped Connor. 'But how come we heard you calling for help, even before we met you?'

'I was using telepathy. Telepathy is a universal language, where everyone can communicate and understand one another, even if they speak different languages.'

Connor was amazed.

Kia laughed at his expression. 'You remind me of my brother!'

'Why, is he handsome like me?'

Kia raised her eyebrows and placed her hands on her hips. 'I was going to say you both have the knack of getting into trouble!'

'Ha, ha!' grunted Connor sarcastically. 'So why did Definastine have you kidnapped? What does he want from you?'

'Why does anyone ever want to take what doesn't belong to them! He's greedy. Dad says a mixture of greed and power drives a star-spirit mad. You don't know much about Definastine, do you?'

Connor shook his head.

'Well, I can tell you the little I know. He's thousands of years old and was born a good star-spirit, called Daa. But his problems began when he tried to befriend a greedy and destructive personality called Yamar. He truly believed that he could change his ways and make him a kinder star-spirit. But Dad says a star-spirit will only change when they want to, and not when someone else makes them. Yamar was too powerful and Daa's plan backfired. He slowly changed from being a peaceful and gentle giant into a hideous beast instead.

Dad says Yamar needed an apprentice to do his dirty work for him and Daa soon became known as Definastine. But Yamar's plan backfired as well. Dad says, those who live for the darkness will die by the darkness. Definastine recently killed Yamar in his search to become the ultimate master. If you ask me, I think Definastine is rapidly coming closer to fulfilling his dreams, of finally seeking to control the entire universe and every living star-spirit. Well, that's what dad says anyway.'

'Tell me about Yamar?'

'I can only tell you what others have told me. His race lived peacefully on a small planet. They lived a simple life and wanted for nothing. Dad says, Yamar was born a bad apple from the very beginning. I heard that wherever he walked, the ground would darken and plants instantly died in his presence. But his mum refused to believe he was evil. She helped him escape. On the day of judgement to decide his future, which meant certain death for Yamar, his mum sent him far away in her spaceship, so he could begin another life somewhere else. Her love for her son has caused many deaths to others. He came back one day to revenge his people, killing everyone including his own mum. He blamed his mother for the way he was,' Kia told him.

'He needed serious counselling!'

'Now Definastine is loose, with no reins to hold him back.'

As Kia shifted in her seat, Connor became aware of dainty wings behind her back, glittering with different pastel colours.

'Are those wings?' he breathed excitedly.

'Of course,' Kia replied. Her small fragile hands pulled a flower from her hair. 'Every female Stanchy can fly. Here. I want you to have this, for saving my life.'

'What is it? I'm not really a flower person,' he replied bashfully.

Kia looked hurt. Connor wished he hadn't said anything.

'It isn't an ordinary flower like the ones you have growing on your planet. I was given this one as a gift from my father. He said I was to have it, because it was my right as a princess. This flower takes many years to grow. It will never die… well not unless…' she paused.

'Not unless what?' Connor asked eagerly, opening his hand to receive the flower.

'It will only die if Definastine himself touches it, or comes close to it,' she told him. 'He's like Yamar. He has the power to destroy beauty wherever he walks.'

Connor wasn't sure where to put the flower, certainly not in his hair like Kia anyway. In the end he decided to put it in his T-shirt pocket. Speaking at great length, the two of them chatted happily away. Time has a habit of speeding when you are enjoying yourself and soon Tookar was knocking on the door and announcing they had ten minutes before they would be leaving for Dramian.

CHAPTER SIXTEEN

The Gateway to Dramian

Sparkie and Tookar had seen to the supplies. They'd filled the back of the van with numerous warm blankets and several large cardboard boxes of tinned food. A little gas cooker with an extra bottle of gas rested in the back next to Sparkie's woolly mammoth coat. There were other boxes filled with weapons, which Sparkie had retrieved from the AAA, during the time Connor had been sleeping.

'Your aunt and uncle are now being cared for at the AAA,' Sparkie told Connor as he placed another spare blanket in the back on the van. 'They were still unconscious when we arrived. Don't worry about them, they'll be fine.'

'How long are you planning to stay on Dramian?' asked Connor, not wanting to discuss his relatives.

'As little time as possible. But if we can't make it back before the gateway closes, we need to be able to survive,' Sparkie explained. 'We need to be prepared.'

Connor, nodding dumbly, went to sit in the back of the van with his new friend, Kia. His chest rose as he breathed in deeply, trying to steady his nerves. But the breathing technique wasn't working as well as he'd hoped. Although he tried to convince himself that everything was going to be all right, images of being pursued were constantly haunting him from the forefront of his mind.

Talking quietly between themselves, Sparkie and Tookar were discussing the various options. The distinct sounds of buttons being pressed increased Connor's anxiety. He wondered why he'd agreed to such a foolish idea. It hadn't seemed so bad when he'd felt safe in the hideout. But now, with the van positioned just above the immense water at the Great Lake, Connor tightened his grip on the edge of the seat and shook his head miserably.

'I can't believe I'm doing this,' he mumbled to himself.

'It'll be okay,' Kia said brightly, sounding a little too cheerful for Connor.

'The secret gateway to Dramian lies just below this massive lake,' Sparkie indicated, widening his eyes until Connor believed they were going to fall out of their sockets. 'Who would ever have guessed?'

The landscape appeared calm. Not even a breeze stirred the silver water on the lake. This area was a well-known attraction for campers, yet tonight no campfires were burning.

'It's almost as if people know to keep away from here during the light of a full moon,' breathed Sparkie.

In the distance, an orange glow from a nearby village lit the sky to the north and hundreds of stars sparkled like little diamonds. The trees, which were darkly silhouetted against the sky, had their images mirrored in the lake.

'It's massive,' noted Connor. 'Looks more like the sea.'

'Indeed it does. It's forty miles long and fifty miles across by all accounts,' Sparkie told him. 'We'll enter the lake close to the edge and work our way beneath the water. That way we won't miss the portal.'

The full moon peacefully watched them from above, showering the lake with its never-ending silvery light. Hovering inches above the surface, the van began to lower.

'Aren't you worried someone might see us?' asked Connor.

'No,' said Sparkie. 'And if anyone does, we'll become yet another statistic for an alien sighting. Ooh – someone looks happy.'

Connor followed Sparkie's gaze. The fish in the van were bustling with excitement. Tails and fins were flipping wildly, creating masses of bubbles. Connor closed his eyes for a time, trying to recollect his thoughts. The gentle swaying of the van was comforting at this stage. It was now completely submerged under the water, causing soft, noiseless ripples to spread wide across the lake. With a smooth motion the van continued to glide underwater, like a strange submarine.

'We'll each be wearing a bracelet on Dramian,' Sparkie called to the youngsters.

'Forget it!' Connor eyes snapped open with a start. 'I'm not wearing some girlie bracelet. No way!'

Sparkie was already smirking, as if predicting Connor's reaction. 'Thought you'd gone to sleep.'

'I was just resting my eyes. Why do you want us wearing stupid bracelets anyway?'

'Not so stupid, if you please. The atmosphere on Dramian may kill us. We have no idea what the air is like there and I'm not going to die finding out either. The bracelets will automatically shield us in an invisible force field when we exit the van, similar to huge bath bubbles.'

'Doesn't sound very safe to me. Bath bubbles pop easily,' Connor pointed out.

'Which is why I was about to say, they are much tougher than bath bubbles,' Sparkie continued. 'I personally guarantee them not to burst.'

'Is that meant to be reassuring?' Tookar smirked.

Sparkie ignored him. 'The invisible shield provides several days' worth of oxygen and will stick tightly on to Dramian's surface, allowing us to move in any direction. It'll be quite fun, I assure you. Don't look so worried Connor. You'll love it.'

Connor made a face and turned his gaze to the white screen on the dashboard, but there was not much to see. The screen showed a black and white picture with various tones of grey. There were no fish and no excitement. It was like watching a television without an aerial.

Sparkie switched the headlights on after passing a certain point beneath the water but they revealed little more. Still it was strangely peaceful down in the depths of expansive space and Connor began feeling more relaxed. He'd never done anything like this before and smiled as a solitary fish, looking quite lost, twisted and danced in front of the van, reflecting the lights off its scales.

Connor hugged his knees to his chest, resting his chin on them. He wished he could stay down in the water forever where he felt safe. No one could find him down here. It had to be better than going to Dramian.

He wondered how many children would give their right arm to experience this. Surely he should be feeling excited? But his future was unclear and he didn't know what to expect. How could anyone get excited about the possibility of death?

'Your planet isn't very big, is it?' Kia said suddenly.

'It's big enough,' Connor replied.

'Our planet is at least ten times the size of earth. And your trees look so puny to our huge trees and our lush lands are occupied with wonderful creatures roaming wild and free. Our lakes are hundreds of times bigger than this one.'

Connor stared at her in disbelief. 'Sounds massive.'

'It is,' she said.

The leather seat Tookar was sitting on squeaked as he turned to face them.

'Kia. Why were you travelling so close to Dramian, when you were caught?' he asked.

'I … I … was…' she broke off. 'I was doing something my father distinctively asked me not to,' she quickly blurted out, closing her eyes tight. Opening them a fraction, she smiled awkwardly.

'Why?' Connor asked.

'I had to. I didn't think I had a choice.'

'We all have choices,' Tookar said smoothly.

'I didn't. Or at least I thought I didn't. A star-spirit called the High Priestess Serena Iona shares our planet. All her people died after a terrible war with Definastine.'

'How did she survive?' asked Tookar.

'She was travelling at the time. My dad – the king – gave her sanctuary and in return she showered us with her gift of life, giving us wonderful crops in abundance, so we'll never starve. Serena Iona is truly wonderful. She helped to make our planet more colourful than ever before. She's part of our family now. But something awful is happening. Recently our crops have failed and Serena has become terribly ill. Her skin is peeling and all her light has faded. It's as if she is draining our own planet of life force. She secretly told me before I left that one of her people must still be alive. She believed Definastine must have captured one of them and is forcing that person to turn over to the dark side with him. If this continues... Serena Iona will die.'

'But why?' asked Connor.

'Her people are closely connected in bodies and minds. What happens to one is felt by the others,' Kia explained. 'So you see, I came close to Dramian to try and rescue the other Tria.'

'Tria?' said Tookar.

'Serena Iona is a Tria, as you are a Tinxshian,' she said facing Tookar. 'Please forgive me, but I need to try and find my ship. It will make it easier for us once we get to Dramian.'

'What are you talking about?' asked Connor.

'She's going to astral travel and find her spaceship for us, so we won't be running about like headless chickens,' Tookar grinned.

'Oh,' replied Connor, keenly watching Kia. He didn't know anything about astral travelling, but wasn't about to tell anyone else that.

Sitting cross-legged on the seat, Kia immediately closed her eyes. For a while her eyes appeared to be rolling beneath her eyelids, until they came to a rest. After a short while, Connor looked away, thinking Kia had fallen asleep.

'Found it!' she said briskly, startling Connor. From her bright expression, it was clear she was happy about something. 'When we enter the gateway you'll find my Hyas transporter ten kalameres away from it. It's still in one piece.'

Connor made another face and had no idea how she found out that information. 'Ten kalameres? What does that mean?'

'It's about three miles,' said Sparkie, checking his appearance in his mirror and wiping his nose with a tissue.

Kia carried on. 'There's a team of Armatripe waiting close to the portal. We'll be okay as long as we're in this van. We can fly to safety.'

'Now we know what to avoid, it shouldn't be so hard.' Sparkie adjusted his glasses and peered quizzically at Connor. 'What happened to your glasses?'

'I haven't been wearing them for ages,' laughed Connor. 'I found out I don't need them anymore.'

'Oh,' said Sparkie. 'Lucky you.'

'I can't believe this.' Connor was shaking his head as panic swelled from the pit of his stomach. 'I can't believe what we're going to do! We must be mad! I must be mad!'

'But that's what people do for one another. We risk our lives to help save others,' said Tookar.

Connor knew Tookar was right. In his heart he realised he was doing something that as a kid he could only dream about – being a hero and helping to save the world. He used to think he could fly like superman and help rid the world of evil people. Strange as it seemed, his dream was now coming true in an odd kind of way.

Travelling deeper into the heart of the Great Lake, Sparkie decreased the van's speed, being extra careful so as not to collide with any unexpected rocks. The depth of the lake was immense, and situated at its lowest point, three miles down, was the gateway.

'Who created the AAA?' Connor asked after a lengthy silence.

'Arbtu,' Tookar told him. 'He came from another galaxy and saw an opportunity of creating an organisation to bring star-spirits together across the galaxies.'

'I remember Deana mentioning that name,' Connor said wistfully, watching a long fish speed in front of the van. He hoped Deana was all right, wherever she was.

'Well Arbtu sought out humane people all over the world and brought them together. He could read people's minds, you see. No one could keep secrets from him. If someone had foolish plans to betray him, he would know before they did,' Tookar explained.

'Does the government know anything about the AAA?' Connor asked.

'They have their suspicions but nothing is concrete. Luckily for us they have never discovered our various secret hideouts.'

Sparkie became quite agitated at the mention of the word government. 'We are all star-spirits and should treat each other, as we ourselves would like to be treated, with respect. While there are many star-spirits who are harmless, others are not. But what horrifies me most of all is to have one set of morals for humans and another completely different set for aliens. To think that government officials experiment on aliens in their eagerness to know how their insides work. It's disgusting! They wouldn't treat humans like that.'

'Some do,' said Tookar.

Sparkie ignored that comment. 'They're sharks, that's what they are.'

'Oh, I'm beginning to feel queasy!' Tookar mumbled, looking slightly dazed.

'We're quite a way down. We're feeling the effects of compression. But don't worry, I'll adjust the settings in the van. We'll feel better in no time.'

The lights in the van dimmed. Connor shivered. He hated the dark. It was safe to say this was not his favourite place right now. When the van lights finally flickered on, Connor felt more reassured.

'Sorry about that. I pressed the wrong button!'

Sparkie reclined in his seat, placing his hands together behind his head. For now the van was on a course and for a while there was nothing more for him to do. As long as he kept an eye out for obstructions, they'd be fine.

'I might as well give you your bracelets now.' Sparkie reached into the glove compartment and pulled out some brightly coloured objects. He handed them out. 'Just pull the clasp open and fit them around your wrists.' He quickly demonstrated how to secure them.

'It's pretty,' Kia murmured, stroking it with her soft hands but she handed her bracelet back. 'I won't be needing this. My body adjusts to any planet's atmosphere.'

'Lucky you,' Connor replied, wrinkling his nose.

Kia started laughing at him. 'Is it really so bad for a boy on earth to wear a bracelet?'

'Definitely! Boys don't dress like girls. No way!'

'Some do,' said Tookar.

'That's so strange. Everyone, including boys, wears bracelets on my planet!' she giggled.

'Why doesn't that surprise me,' Connor muttered.

It took a while for Connor to open the clasp on his blue bracelet and in the end Kia helped him. Her dainty fingers unlocked the clasp instantly and much to Connor's pleasure she helped secure it to his wrist. As it was quite a large fit, Connor thought it would easily fall off. Yet, as soon as Kia had secured the fastener, it immediately began to shrink, eventually adjusting to fit his wrist perfectly.

'Wow!' he gasped, mesmerised by the glowing red stone in the centre. 'Is it magic?'

'Something like that!' Sparkie replied.

Keeping the yellow one for himself because it was his favourite, Sparkie had given Tookar the green bracelet. Although they were different colours, each bracelet contained the same magical pulsating red stone.

'When you want to move in any direction, simply touch the red gem and move it in the direction you want to go. It's as simple as that,' instructed Sparkie.

Connor ran his finger over the stone. It felt warm and rolled beneath his touch.

'Hang on! Prepare yourselves for a bumpy ride,' cried Sparkie. 'Land ahoy!'

The van was decreasing in speed and with a heavy thud, rebounded off the bottom of the lake, disturbing thick layers of mud. Everyone was holding on tightly. Pulling back a lever, Sparkie eased the impact by helping the van to levitate off the ground slightly. The van continued disrupting the grimy layers below as it swept passed, while floating a few inches above the bed of the lake. Yet it made little difference to the view, which was already dark and murky.

'The gateway is further to the north.' Eagerly, Kia pointed her finger ahead, almost poking Sparkie's eye out when he suddenly turned round. Luckily his glasses saved him. 'Oh, sorry,' she giggled nervously.

Wiping the mark off his glasses where Kia's finger had made contact, Sparkie turned to consult his compass. He changed their direction slightly, whilst pressing his nose close to the screen. It was like driving in thick fog. No one could see anything. A short while later Kia cried out:

'Stop the van!'

Sparkie jumped and instantly pulled back a lever before touching his heart. The van shuddered to a halt. Before anyone could ask what was wrong, Kia was pointing and looking ahead in distress.

'Look! Can't you see them?'

'Can't see anything!' Connor mumbled.

Squinting, they all stared dumbly at the white screen. As the murky water settled slightly, hazy movements could be seen. Gradually as their eyes adjusted to the dimness, large black creatures burst out from what appeared to be another large lake at the bottom of the Great Lake. It looked as if they were coming up from under the ground.

'It's the gateway!' Kia said. 'They're coming from Dramian. What are they doing? Are they coming after us?'

Sparkie shook his head solemnly. 'Those monstrous brutes! This is where those young children have been disappearing. Definastine's sending out those creatures to go after them.'

'What are those things?' Connor blinked hard.

'Atropertries.' Tookar's expression darkened. 'How many can you see, Kia?'

'Must be at least fifty,' Kia counted, watching the last one swim away. 'Luckily they didn't see us.'

'Thanks to you,' said Connor, gratefully. 'Have you got x-ray vision or something?'

'No. But it does seem to be better than yours.'

Sparkie was becoming frustrated. 'I'm trying to look for a gateway, but I still can't see anything.'

'You won't from here. The gateway is beneath that strange liquid,' Kia explained to him.

Sparkie pushed a lever forward. The van lowered and began to pass through the thick green liquid. It emerged on the other side in a pocketful of clear colourless water with a whirlpool of light illuminating the surrounding area. Like a large flat, round lollipop, the whirlpool shimmered with three swirling tones of yellow mixing together, creating a brilliant pattern. It was roughly fifteen feet wide and big enough for the van to enter. The water was sparkling like champagne.

'Isn't it beautiful!' Kia murmured.

'Yes, indeed!' Sparkie chuckled with excitement.

'It's totally amazing!' Connor whispered, forgetting his fears. 'So this is the gateway to Dramian. How can something this beautiful lead to a place so horrible?'

'That, my lad, is what we're about to find out. Strap yourselves in,' Sparkie ordered.

The clinking of seatbelts hastily filled the van. Connor passed a nervous glance over to Kia.

'Don't worry,' she told him. 'The sick feeling doesn't last long.'

Connor's eyes widened. 'What sick feeling?'

But before she could answer, Sparkie had already prepared their launch.

'Let's not waste any more time. Are we ready?' he cried.

'Yes,' said Tookar and Kia in chorus.

'No,' whispered Connor.

'Let's go!' Sparkie announced. 'Dramian, beware! Here we come!'

The van moved gradually, descending towards the swirling lights. Suddenly a force they couldn't control sucked them into the brilliant sphere. With a life of its own, the van tumbled and turned through the large dimensional avenue. Rocketing with speed, it soared into the unknown. Streaks of blue and white light enveloped the van as it passed through the twisting tunnel. At this point Connor realised what Kia had meant. He was feeling extremely nauseous by the time the journey ended.

Several seconds later they were spat out from a large circular ring. Sparkie immediately pressed a button and a huge rubber ring filled with air sprung out from under the van making it look like a strange little boat. It absorbed most of the impact but the van still crashed heavily, scraping several feet across the ground before grinding to a halt.

Squeals of terror were now replaced with silence. Sparkie recovered quicker than anyone and was the first to speak.

'Well – we're here!' he announced in a croaky voice, sounding like a tour guide.

The fish that had been happily swimming about instantly vanished when Sparkie flipped a switch.

'What have you done to them?' cried Connor aghast.

'They've been miniaturised, that's all,' Sparkie explained.

The van had turned into a greenhouse, or so Connor thought. A transparent material surrounded the van, leaving them no place to hide. It rested like a forgotten golf ball, in the middle of a terribly bleak landscape. The only source of light on this gloomy planet was a full moon, the twinkling stars and the headlights from the van. Sparkie switched them off immediately.

'Bit late for that,' whispered Tookar. 'They know we're here!'

Connor shivered and glanced through the windows. Unfamiliar plants with skeletal branches grew wild in the hostile environment. The ground was completely strewn with hard rocks and stone. High in the sky displays of shooting stars could be seen. Occasionally one exploded. The large full moon watched them peacefully, offering little comfort to the foreigners on foreign land.

'We'd better move on,' said Tookar grimly. 'It's not safe.'

Sparkie attempted to pull down a lever but it appeared to be jammed. 'I can't budge it!' he panicked.

'What now?' asked Connor, chewing his fingers nervously.

At that moment smoke and jets of steam began to pour out from the front of the van followed by a loud hissing sound.

CHAPTER SEVENTEEN

The World of Dramian

'This is all we need!' glared Tookar, frowning heavily towards the smoke and steam, which continued to rise from the engine along with sizzling sounds.

'I'll go outside and check the damage,' Sparkie growled, annoyed with himself rather than with Tookar. Reaching towards the door, he felt a strong pressure holding him back, preventing him from leaving.

'No, you won't!' Tookar said sharply, pulling him back down on the seat with a thud. 'You're staying here!'

But before Sparkie could argue, Kia was screaming, 'The Armatripes have surrounded us! We've got to get out of here fast!'

It was clear that Kia possessed powerful vision and was able to see further than any of them. She could see the Armatripes lining up in a circular snare, slowly advancing towards them. Marching footsteps began vibrating from the floor of the van. Great hulking bodies were moving stiffly through the darkness with glinting swords raised in mid air. The group was trapped with nowhere to run. Connor felt his legs melting like butter in a saucepan. He couldn't help but relive every moment leading up to this predicament they now faced.

In fact, no one escaped the intense feelings of despair and foreboding, swiftly mounting from this harsh situation.

Sparkie was clearly panicking. Acting like a half-crazed mad man, he was swinging his arms wildly, missing Tookar's face by an inch. Jabbering agitatedly, he continued pressing buttons and jiggling stubborn levers. But no matter how desperate he was for his van to respond, it remained locked in its rigid position like a stubborn mule.

Meanwhile, Tookar had scrambled into the back of the van. He was hastily rummaging about in one of the cardboard boxes when

Sparkie finally collapsed on the seat looking thoroughly exhausted.

'Oh, dearie me!' croaked Sparkie, his glasses lopsided on his face. 'Whatever have I done?'

'If we're stuck here we must...' Kia said thoughtfully, 'grab a weapon! Dad says, one mustn't give up until the battle is won.'

'Your dad is perfectly right, of course. Great minds think alike.' Tookar had already armed himself with a massive gun that needed to be supported on the shoulder. 'You two grab the smaller ones. While you're still alive, you might as well help.'

The Armatripe were closing in. Sparkie, sensing the change of mood, pulled out a black umbrella from the glove compartment. 'At least I've got this!'

'We're facing war... and you're concerned about... rain?' Tookar growled, shaking his head.

Sparkie passed him a puzzled look. 'What are you talking about? Who said anything about rain? This, my friend, is a weapon!'

Connor wrinkled his nose. It still didn't look like a weapon from any angle.

'Another one of your amazing creations, no doubt,' smiled Tookar.

Sparkie hastily pressed a small button on the roof. It slid open with ease. 'At least this still works!'

A soft gush of air rushed into the van, before an invisible shield, shaped like a dome, sealed shut across it. Connor breathed in deeply and welcomed the burst of fresh air, since the atmosphere in the van had turned stuffy. The air was refreshing and appeared to be harmless. Perhaps the planet had oxygen after all, he thought.

Standing shakily on the back seat and wearing his shaggy mammoth coat, Sparkie looked through the invisible domed shield, exposed from the waist up above the van roof.

'If you open the roof again, I can go out and shoot them.' Kia's eyes were blazing with excitement. In her hands were two small black guns.

'Are you sure you want to do this, Kia?' asked Tookar. She nodded.

'It'll be dangerous,' said Sparkie. He gave her a brief hug as if he'd never see her again.

'This material above us prevents anything coming in. You on the other hand can fly out of here without anything stopping you,' Sparkie explained, lifting up his hand and poking it through the strange matter to demonstrate his point.

With lightning speed, Kia flew out of the van and into the night sky, leaving her friends behind.

'Tookar, come and stand on this seat with me. I need you to fire from behind,' ordered Sparkie.

The Armatripe were now less than ten feet away. Every second was crucial.

'Be sure to point the weapon outside the bubble when you use it!' Sparkie warned.

Tookar positioned his heavy-duty weapon on to his shoulder. With a slurping sound he exposed the end of his weapon through the protective matter. Both the men were exposed from the waist up above the roof but protected within the shield.

Connor crouched into a tight ball with his weapon held tightly, until his palms became sweaty and his knuckles turned white.

'Don't aim too high!' shouted Sparkie. 'I don't want young Kia being struck down.'

They began firing the moment the first Armatripe made contact with the van. Huge pinchers slammed heavily against the van from all directions. The black armoured Armatripes glimmered in the light of the moon. Surly faces watched Connor from all angles. Their black eyes, as cold as ice, made him shiver. They reminded Connor of massive beetles. He huddled behind the back seat and closed his eyes, shuddering. The van was rocking back and forth, yet luckily for them it remained intact. He covered his ears to try and block out the awful sounds. But eventually curiosity overcame his fear.

Sparkie's unique umbrella was repeatedly blasting powerful lights. Every time it fired, it cracked loudly. One by one the Armatripe fell.

Tookar's weapon was noiseless. It fired as fast and ferociously as a machine gun and appeared to do little damage. Connor soon realised that each pellet acted like a small explosive device. Once it became embedded inside the enemy, it blew them to pieces seconds later.

'Gottcha!' yelled Sparkie.

The Armatripes' onslaught was slow but consistent. Their strength was clearly obvious, not to mention their strange grunting, indicating grave danger, for whenever a creature is enraged its strength is increased tenfold. There were boisterous war cries that sounded like grunting dinosaurs stampeding over the land.

Connor observed Tookar handling his weapon with natural ease as if it were part of him. In truth he'd killed twice as many Armatripe than Sparkie. At one point, Tookar ceased firing and was holding his hand out eagerly towards Connor.

'Quickly, pass me one of those small cardboard boxes!'

Connor made a grab for the closest one and swiftly passed it to Tookar, whose forehead was now dripping with sweat. He tugged the lid open, pulling out a small cartridge of ammunition from the box and placing it into a compartment at the side of the weapon.

The thick wall of Armatripe was clearing, like a dense fog. Although losing miserably the last remaining Armatripes still approached relentlessly.

'Why aren't they running away?' Connor whispered under his breath.

But the war wasn't over yet, no matter how much Connor wished it to be. The Armatripes continued to tread clumsily over the great wall of their dead comrades, with faces of fury and little black eyes full of menace.

Connor smiled in relief when at last he realised the enemy was losing and large obvious gaps appeared between their ranks as the last line of attack was being shot down. Soon not one Armatripe was left standing. Seconds later, Kia returned to the van, looking exhausted. The battle was over in minutes, yet it had felt much longer. Connor's heart still continued thumping fifteen minutes after the battle.

An odd silence had descended after the tremendous war cries and crackling gunfire. A dreamlike quality followed the aftermath of the battle. It left Connor wondering if a battle had really occurred. Needless to say the ground was strewn with dead bodies. Although this was proof in itself, Connor felt he'd entered into a nightmare and if he pinched himself hard enough he'd eventually wake up.

He was vaguely aware of voices celebrating above him. Tookar and Sparkie were still standing on the seats. Kia was sitting on the van roof throwing her head back and laughing. Connor tucked his weapon inside the waist of his jeans and zipped his jacket up to conceal it. Although he hadn't used it, he believed it might come in useful later.

'Kia, good tactic that!' Sparkie cried excitedly. 'Saw what you did! Took them quite by surprise, didn't you! Coming up from behind them like that was extremely clever – took them out one by one – fantastic work – they never even knew you were there!'

'Come on,' Tookar smirked. 'Miniaturise this van and let's get out of here.'

They departed the van by the doors rather than by the roof like Kia had done. Once outside, Connor was in for another surprise. After Sparkie told him to press the stone in the centre of his bracelet he was suddenly aware of a blue tinted giant bubble restricting his movements. Slowly, with a plop, the bubble bounced from the step of the van to the ground. Gravity didn't exist in the bubble and Connor found he had no control over his body. No matter what he did his feet wouldn't return to the ground. So he floated weightlessly inside the transparent bubble, which stuck to the ground like sticky toffee.

His legs continued to cause suffering when they insisted on floating apart in two separate directions – north and south. Levitating clumsily like a circus clown, he even had to endure Kia laughing at him. She couldn't fly for ages for the cramp in her stomach.

'You look so funny!' she squealed in delight.

Connor ignored her. Although he had a bad start, it didn't take him long to get the hang of it. Soon he was experimenting with various somersaults.

Meanwhile, Sparkie was floating face down and with his arms outstretched. He'd miniaturised his van to matchbox size and carefully rolled his bubble over towards the dinky vehicle. Once positioned on top, he gently, so as not to burst the bubble, reached through to pick the van up. Once he secured the van safely inside his pocket he then signalled everyone to follow him.

Kia flew above, looking like a decorative fairy. Her wings were gently humming with speed and her hair trailed long behind her as if she was immersed in water. Connor envied her. She looked so at ease. Her slender legs neatly kept together and her dainty arms were relaxed by her sides.

Although having improved slightly, Connor still looked all arms and legs. He floated facing forwards, even if it did mean sometimes rolling upside down. With a little help from his belt, which he tied securely round his legs, he was able to fly a touch more gracefully.

Tookar adopted a more practical position. He levitated cross-legged like a genie on a magic carpet.

'Okay, time to move out!' Sparkie indicated. 'Touch your bracelets and move forward!'

And thus, their journey began.

'Urgh!' Connor groaned. His stomach was feeling queasy as he travelled over the dead bodies of the Armatripe.

But to everyone's surprise, the dead bodies suddenly shrivelled up and vanished, leaving the ground bare with no trace of a battle having happened. Sparkie was looking perplexed as he shook his head.

'Armatripes don't vanish when they die,' Connor heard him mutter. Tookar's expression looked just as confused.

They cautiously progressed a short distance along a smooth matt path, which shone vividly in the light of the moon. On either side was a wild, jagged, unpredictable country. It was so tempting to continue their journey up the level path to a massive stronghold in the distance, given the other choice of the wilderness. But to take the path, although the easier option, would be like waving a flag and telling Definastine they were coming.

'Urgh!' Connor frowned when his hand accidentally touched the boundary of the invisible shield. It had felt like a bucketful of cold slugs. He sharply drew his hand away where it made a squelchy sound on removal.

They gingerly made their way through a rough path, barely wide enough for each of the bubbles to pass through. Kia navigated them through the winding routes, since she had the advantage of foreseeing their direction. She flew a short distance in front making sure she kept her friends within vision. To avoid the various obstacles, including dense skeletal plants and huge boulders of rock, they were forced to travel twice as far. Their movements were dramatically delayed, as the path they proceeded along proved hazardous. The spiky fingers of the reaching branches, grey and pale in the light of the moon, proved most difficult to pass.

The novelty of flying inside a bubble soon wore off and the journey grew wearisome. At first the air was crisp and fresh but Connor grew concerned it wouldn't remain like that. He didn't particularly like the idea of suffocating in the very thing that was meant to keep him alive. Confined like a prisoner, he wondered how long he could remain in the small enclosure before wanting to burst the bubble himself and escape. And if that wasn't bad enough his ears felt blocked because of the dampened sounds around him.

Deeply shadowing the land to the west was a range of mountains varying in height. The ground below was so dark it looked like a vast pit.

They soon learnt that the world of Dramian was a mixture of different temperatures varying from freezing to boiling point due to the presence of underground boiling larva. Boiling liquid at various points beneath the surface flowed continually. Bubbling eruptions threatened to spurt unexpectedly from the ground, taking the group by surprise. In other places it was so deep below, the crust was frozen hard in ice.

At various intervals through the rugged rocks, the smooth wide path could be seen. But they avoided the path as if it were a poisonous snake and opted reluctantly for the jagged land. It would take them longer but they had little choice. The huge boulders, often blocking their path, were a hindrance, but they also provided shelter from various groups of charging Armatripe who tore down the wide smooth strip towards the dimensional gateway. Luckily Kia would warn them of an approaching group and they all huddled out of sight until the enemy passed.

Apart from the Armatripe there weren't many other life forms to see. Occasionally a shy lizard wandered across their path, scuttling from sight into the undergrowth with its bottom wobbling furiously. To the east bubbling brooks could be seen spurting red-hot liquid high into the sky like fireworks varying in height. The piercing heat would be enough to destroy their bubbles and them. Connor shuddered.

'We need to go in that direction!' Kia shouted, pointing ahead.

After making their way through a network of large stones they found themselves standing at the edge of a large pit, fifty feet deep. It seemed to be a large defensive ditch of some sort. The only way forward was to cross a small path two feet wide, and Kia had led them directly to the small crossing.

'What now?' Tookar asked doubtfully.

'We don't have much choice,' Sparkie replied, taking the lead once more. 'We must go on.'

'Follow me, Connor, you'll be all right,' smiled Tookar.

I don't want to go anywhere! Connor wanted to scream. *Leave me here alone. Come back for me later!* But he knew he was being a coward and said nothing, because the thought of being left behind didn't appeal to him either.

They slowly progressed in single file along the narrow track above the gorge.

'Must be at least fifty yards,' Connor noted, trying to judge the distance he had left to travel before he could feel safe again.

Sparkie was skilful enough to maintain their previous pace, but Connor and Tookar were having difficulty keeping up. To make matters worse the narrow section was clearly visible from the main road.

Suddenly, Kia screamed. Connor looked up. He noticed that Sparkie had disappeared. Kia was still screaming. Tookar appeared to be struggling with something. His body was jerking. He was crying out. Then without any warning, Tookar vanished in front of him. Connor stared in disbelief when he noticed the path was disappearing. He tried to move backwards, but not quickly enough. The path beneath him vanished and like his friends before him, he plummeted down into the great ditch.

'Nooo!' Connor cried. He was tumbling over and over, and beyond the sound of his own terror erupting from his throat, he was vaguely aware of Kia calling their names.

CHAPTER EIGHTEEN

The Rock Dwellers

Falling weightless inside their bubbles was a dreamlike experience, mixed with a nightmare reality. Connor's only comfort came from knowing that Tookar and Sparkie were falling down in the pit with him. It all happened so fast. As he neared the ground the bubble continued to spin but Connor was suddenly on his back looking upwards.

Eventually his bubble slammed into the ground, rippling and shuddering lightly from the pressure before it popped with a squelchy sound. His back fell heavily on to the rocks from where he'd previously been floating three feet in the air. He tilted his head forward, to avoid banging it, allowing his back to absorb the majority of the impact. It wasn't a conscious decision, but more of a survival instinct. It hurt like mad but apart from serious bruising, nothing was broken. Now his shield had been destroyed, he lay for several seconds waiting to die – expecting a darkness to blanket his eyes. Inhaling a last desperate breath, Connor found he could breathe quite normally. The shields had been totally unnecessary after all.

Connor lay in shock, but not for long. A commotion was happening a short distance away from him. He struggled to lift his head up. Groaning uncomfortably, he lifted his upper body and rested on his elbows just in time to see Tookar, who was unconscious, being lifted away by some little grey men, who wore nothing but loincloths. They carried him into a darkened doorway inside the rocks.

Connor panicked. He'd seen these little grey men before, with their massive black eyes and wrinkly skin. It was the same creatures he'd fought in his bedroom. They'd sliced his skin with their small sharp daggers.

They were short compared to him, standing at just five feet in height and stooping gently. They were gentle with Tookar and carried him away carefully as if he were a prized possession.

'No!' Connor yelled, drawing unwanted attention.

Another group of little wrinkled men spun round and eyed him curiously. They scrambled towards him with bent knees. Wincing with pain, Connor immediately jumped up. Tugging the gun from the waistband in his jeans, he quickly armed himself. The adrenaline surging through his body was enough to put his pain on hold.

He walked backwards until his body slammed against the steep wall enclosure. The little bald men approached him cautiously, wobbling their elephant seal like noses.

'Come any closer and I'll shoot!' he threatened.

Strangely they didn't seem very dangerous but as soon as Connor waved the gun at them, their expressions transformed into sneers. The little creatures looked confused and communicated to one another in a gabbling alien language, creating an annoying whinnying sound. With suspicious faces they began to surround Connor, pulling the familiar shiny daggers out of their belts and pointing them at him.

'What do you want with us?' he shouted. 'Where have you taken my friend?'

There was more of their bizarre talk. One of them came closer, poking Connor in the chest with the sharp tip of his blade. Connor knocked it away with the gun and fired. The grey creature fell instantly and a second later it turned to dust and disappeared.

They stopped talking and watched him nervously. Then, in a frantic response, they scrambled away to distance themselves from Connor. Behind another rock came a faint whimper. The rock dwellers cocked their heads at the sound and looked round as Sparkie emerged from behind a great rock. The little grey men began dancing excitedly, temporarily forgetting about Connor.

'Ow!' Sparkie groaned, glancing towards Connor. Whatever else he was about to say died on his lips as soon as he caught a glimpse of the strange little men. He shook his head in fear as the creatures turned their attention to him.

The little grey creatures started running towards Sparkie. Soon they had lifted him up and were taking him through the same doorway into which Tookar had disappeared minutes earlier.

'No!' Sparkie screamed.

Connor was running after them as they all passed through the door. He fired his gun and shot another two creatures. He didn't dare shoot the others surrounding Sparkie, just in case he missed.

As the last creature disappeared, the doorway immediately vanished. What was once an opening inside the hard stone had now become solid rock, looking like nothing more than any other wall of stone. The red stone shone like coal and in some areas was as sharp as glass. Connor reached out to stroke it and sliced the tip of his finger, blood pouring freely from the wound.

'Ouch! What the –?' he mumbled. 'Sparkie! Tookar! Can you hear me?' He began thumping the hard stone with his fists. Questions of why he was left there alone confused him. Why didn't they want him too? What was wrong with him? Perhaps he should be glad they rejected him. 'Give me my friends back! Let them out!' he screamed. 'Let me in!'

He stood alone in the empty pit, looking upward. Where was Kia? He began screaming for her, until his voice went hoarse. But she never came. He was now alone wondering what to do next.

He paced around the edge of the pit like a caged animal, circling it until he was dizzy. In frustration and anger, Connor kicked the loose rocks beneath his feet, stubbing his toes on an extra large one that insisted on remaining where it was.

'Ouch!' he cried, hopping on the spot.

He stared hopelessly up at the stars, towards his only way out. He wasn't afraid to scale a fifty-foot wall but this was no ordinary wall. He held his finger tightly, trying to stop the flow of blood. This wall was spiked with rock that could slice his skin like the sharpest blade. What *was* he going to do?

He kicked at the ground again in frustration. Something cracked beneath his foot. He jumped backwards in surprise. Glancing down warily he saw something silvery and white flash beneath his feet. He bent down to take a closer look. He reached out to touch it. It felt rough towards the end but smooth along its length. Suddenly he gasped and jumped back, a lump forming in his mouth.

Was that what he thought it was?

A shiver extended down his body to his legs. He almost fell in shock. For what he now saw in reality, he'd only ever seen in books before. He stared in disbelief and fear when he realised the spot he was standing on was covered in – bones.

Human remains were scattered on the ground. Connor had stepped on a long bone with nodules at each end, roughly the size of a thighbone. The femur was cracked clean in half.

His breath quickened, his stomach tightened. Why hadn't he seen them before?

'Oh, no!' he gasped, afraid to move in case he stepped on more. His eyes scanned the area where the moon was shining down. There were so many lying about.

'It's not safe here,' a small voice whispered behind him.

Connor spun round fast, almost losing his balance. His heart pounded with adrenaline but he had nowhere to run and nowhere to hide or escape. He hadn't heard anyone approaching. It was as if the person had walked straight through the wall.

'Keep away… f … from me!' Connor stammered. 'Just keep away!'

'Shhh!' the boy whispered. 'They'll hear us. They don't know I'm here. You've got to go now. It's not safe.'

The young boy stood nervously, looking no older than Connor. Yet his skin was incredibly wrinkly in places. His body was wiry and thin with ribs poking out from his skin. He looked no more threatening than a wilting daffodil. His eyes however, though wide and scared, clearly held strength and shone an amazing colour blue. His nose was different too from the other rock dwellers. It wasn't huge and wobbly but small and very human looking.

'Who are you?' Connor asked warily, stepping backwards carefully to avoid standing on more bones.

'I'm a rock dweller,' said the boy, rubbing his hand over his smooth, hairless head. His eyes were neither hardened nor cruel but desperate. 'Come, you must leave now.'

'Not without my friends,' Connor replied stubbornly.

'There's no time to argue. Your friend Sparkie has already called for assistance. He wanted me to help you. Your friends are alive but you must go quickly. You are their last hope of escaping, but if you're caught then their hopes will be dashed.'

'You know Sparkie?'

The boy nodded. 'He and the other man have been taken to a cell together on level three. I've just been speaking to him. He's a great man. But for now you have a chance to escape and you must go while you can. I cannot bear to see you trapped here like this. You are just a boy like so many others here and I will not help my people capture you for anyone – not even for Definastine.' The boy's face saddened. 'I have to be cleansed tomorrow. My time has come for I have reached maturity. My fate has been decided but yours hasn't, you can still leave. Go now, while you still have the chance. You alone cannot fight the many rock dwellers here.'

'But my friends!' Connor whispered urgently. 'Will they be all right?' His words died on his lips as the boy looked away from him to touch the stone wall.

Suddenly it began to move and shift to form a ladder up the wall.

'Th… th… thanks,' stammered Connor, staring at the boy in awe. 'Thanks for helping me. Are you sure you can't help my friends?'

The boy shrugged. 'I'm doing what I can.' Clearly agitated, he kept glancing nervously behind his back every few seconds. He pointed upward and said in an urgent voice, 'Go!'

Connor wasted no more time. Forcing his legs to move, he slowly began climbing. He turned around and looked down just in time to see the boy vanish through the rock as if there was nothing there to hold him back.

With sheer determination and strength Connor made it halfway up the steep wall.

He stopped for breath. His arm muscles were aching badly, but he was going to get to the top if that was the last thing he ever did.

A commotion below startled him. The bottom of the pit was moving with angry rock dwellers swarming over the area below and screaming up at him in their strange language. He was ten feet from the top when a thick rope fell down beside him with a loop in the end.

'Put your foot in the loop and I'll pull you up,' a gruff male voice called down to him. 'Hurry!'

Connor couldn't see to whom the voice belonged. But with nowhere to run, he had little choice but to trust it. Still holding on to the stone ladder, he nervously placed his foot inside the loop. Then reaching out to grasp the rope with both hands he began praying that whoever was holding the other end wasn't going to deliberately let go of it and hurt him.

The rock dwellers below were placing their hands on the rock face and suddenly the ladder vanished in seconds. Connor gasped. He grabbed the rope for dear life, praying he wasn't going to be released to the hungry mob.

But whoever was holding the rope continued to heave him up. As soon as he was raised to safety, he collapsed on the ground. His mind was spinning with confusion, fear and guilt. It was as if all his strength had vanished. He couldn't even look up at the person who had just saved his life.

'My friends are down there!' he cried weakly. 'I must help them!'

His saviour didn't speak. Instead he walked towards the edge of the cliff and began firing. Many rock dwellers were scaling the rock surface like spiders but with a single shot they fell and died, turning to dust. The others on the ground scattered, vanishing quickly through the walls.

Then the stranger rested a large hand over Connor's shoulder. As he did so, Connor was engulfed with the strangest feeling. Fighting past the fear was something peaceful and calm, like a fire extinguisher calming a roaring fire. The hands of his saviour were communicating directly to his body, warming and reassuring him. For the first time since he'd arrived on the planet, Connor felt safe.

He lifted up his head and saw a huge beast kneeling on the ground beside him, with a length of rope slung over its shoulder. Its body was covered in a short layer of soft brown fur, which thinned on its face. Metal armour clung to its body, gleaming in the moonlight as if it were a mirror. Wearing black leather trousers with massive black boots it looked strangely human.

'You!' gasped Connor. 'Don't I know you?'

Reawakened memories were released to the surface of his mind. He knew this beast in front of him but the creature he had remembered as a hairy-faced man was now revealed not to be human at all.

'Hello, Connor,' said the beast, gently. 'Didn't expect you to recognise me. It's been a long time, aye, a very long time indeed.'

'You were the one who took me from my parents when I was small,' Connor blurted out.

'That I did, young man,' the beast smiled sadly. 'Seemed only right, since I was one of your Star-Lord fathers.'

'What?' gasped Connor.

'Explain later,' said the beast.

'Thanks for helping me,' said Connor, rubbing his face and leaving a trail of blood behind. He looked at the open wound on his finger.

The beast frowned, his eyes showing concern at the wound. He pulled from his pocket a piece of cloth and a small leather bag. Inside the leather bag was a thick white cream, which he began dabbing with the cloth. 'Keep still, this won't hurt.'

He tended to Connor's hands. The ointment had a cooling effect and seemed to penetrate deeper than just skin level, sinking into his sore muscles. The tip of his finger instantly stopped bleeding and the throbbing eased. He then wiped Connor's face gently to clean it.

'What is that stuff?' Connor asked, shyly.

'Flutis, it's a healing ointment,' the beast smiled in reply, replacing the ointment back in his pocket. 'Come. We've got work to do.'

'But I don't even know your name,' Connor pointed out.

'Bromie.'

'I'm Connor.'

'I know,' Bromie smiled, standing up.

Connor stared rudely. He'd never met anyone so tall: Bromie stood at least seven feet. 'Yeah, sorry,' he grinned, bashfully.

The beast gathered his rope and slung it over his shoulder. 'Sparkie told me to look out for a boy with scruffy blond hair.'

Connor was speechless for several seconds. 'You spoke to Sparkie?'

Bromie nodded. 'He's still got his corbee with him.'

'Corbee?' Connor wrinkled his face.

'It's a communication device, similar to a mobile phone but much more advanced,' Bromie explained. 'We've got others here from the AAA. They're working their way in through the tunnels trying to find the lost children. That's why I was able to help so quickly.'

'Oh! Is Sparkie all right? Did he mention Tookar?' Connor asked.

'They're together for now. But rock dwellers eat humans,' Bromie told him bluntly. 'Apparently Tookar and he are on the menu tomorrow, in aid of a cleansing ritual for a young rock dweller named De-ma.'

'I think I met him.' Connor explained how a young rock dweller had saved him and provided a ladder to escape the pit. 'He mentioned something about a cleansing ritual, he didn't look too happy about it either.'

'What's good about having someone interfere with your brain?' Bromie said. 'Tomorrow all the goodness from his soul will be stripped away, leaving him like the others you saw.'

Connor gulped. 'Then we must help him too, but why didn't the other rock dwellers take me away?'

'You're stronger than they are, and they could sense it. Besides you have a gun. Rock dwellers don't like a fight. They like to be able to kill their prey quickly and easily. Come. Enough talk. We're going to the stronghold. It's our only chance.'

Bromie helped Connor on to his feet. They began walking in the same direction Connor and his friends had earlier taken. Connor was following close behind Bromie, thinking of Kia.

'I don't suppose you saw a flying girl?' he asked. 'Another friend of mine went missing and I haven't a clue where she went.'

Bromie stopped and turned around, his face tense with worry. 'Kia's gone missing too?'

'You know her?'

He nodded. 'Sparkie mentioned her.'

'The last time I saw her was just before we fell into the pit,' Connor told him. 'So what are we going to do now?'

'To meet the rock dwellers and try to bargain with them.'

'Bargain with them? What with?'

'Their own lives,' Bromie grinned.

In the far distance magnificent mountains framed the horizon. A warm glow from a fire stood out like a beacon on the tip of a huge pointing monument, but it was too far away to see clearly. A few feet from where they walked, a bubbling pool peacefully spurted out thick muddy lumps making rude noises as it did so. The same type of small lizard creature spotted earlier, scampered close to the pool, sinking its bright orange skin beneath the soft muddy ooze. Another one followed closely behind, repeating the procedure of the first.

'Nice place, don't you think?' Bromie asked sarcastically.

'It reminds me of what planet earth will look like if we carry on destroying it with pollution, greed and power,' Connor mumbled.

'That's a serious discussion for a young man,' Bromie remarked, kicking with ease a stone similar in size to the one which Connor had painfully stubbed his toe.

'I read a book once at school. I feel as if I've stepped on to the page. The artist drew a world like Dramian.'

'Maybe he's been here before or possessed the power to visualise places without visiting them,' Bromie suggested.

'Maybe,' Connor whispered. After what he'd seen up to date, anything was possible.

They trudged for a mile and a quarter before they came to rest behind a cluster of leafless trees that offered temporary cover. Bromie squatted down, to spy through the large gaps between the branches.

He lowered his voice and pointed ahead. 'Can you see those creeps?'

A group of Armatripe guarded the only entrance to the stronghold. Their backs were covered in black armour and glistened as if they'd been polished for hours. Adding to their grotesque appearance were six crooked arms, with claws like a crab instead of hands. Powerful bodies rested on two skinny crooked legs with huge flat feet.

'I've seen them before. They look like deformed dung beetles,' Connor muttered.

Bromie grinned broadly and whispered, 'They're fried giant cockroaches if you ask me. Well, we're going to have to get past them before we can get into that place.'

'What?' said Connor feeling uncomfortable. 'You want us to go in there?'

'You want to rescue your friends don't you?'

'Yes but… do you have a plan?'

'Nope, do you?'

Suddenly the night sky buzzed with activity. From behind them a loud humming noise hovered overhead. Bromie pushed Connor further between the trees so as not to be seen. They remained crouched like hibernating animals, hidden from sight, yet seeing everything. The sky was teeming with streaks of colour from hundreds of flying aliens strongly resembling stingray fish, illuminated by an eerie blue light. The strange decorative lights passed overhead, shooting and zigzagging through the blackness towards the stronghold. The persistent humming noise continued until all the creatures had passed over. They were protectively guarding something in their group but what it was Connor couldn't see.

'What are those things?' Connor whispered.

'Whizzers.'

'They're fast.'

'Shhh! Keep still!'

They watched as the whizzers dropped something to the ground just in front of the entrance. The Armatripe picked the limp bundle up. Connor narrowed his eyes to focus. Only when an Armatripe heaved the object over its shoulder did Connor finally realise what they had been guarding.

'It's Kia!'

But Bromie placed his hand over Connor's hysterical mouth as the whizzers retreated the way they had come. The deafening low flying cloud flew straight above them, sounding like a truck revving its engine.

'I hope she's all right,' Connor mumbled, gritting his teeth in anger.

'At least we know where she is. I'm calling for help.'

He pulled out a small round metal disc-shaped object and flipped the lid. As he dialled some numbers into the device a three-dimensional hologram image sprouted out from it. A large transparent head appeared floating above the device, looking similar to Bromie but wearing a black eye patch over its right eye.

'Where the devil have you been?' the voice sounded worried.

'I'm about to rescue some of our men. But I need help.'

'Give me your co-ordinates and I'll be there in a jiffy. Do you have your bridge with you?'

'Yes.'

Bromie reeled off numbers that meant nothing to Connor and very soon their conversation ended.

'What was that all about?' Connor asked. 'What's a bridge?'

'It's a way of travelling from one place to another by using co-ordinates. Now we have the co-ordinates to this forsaken country we'll be able to come here any time without waiting for a full moon.'

'Is it like a spaceship?'

'No. A bridge is a small device that has the power to transport you in seconds to a place a million miles away.'

Connor gulped. And gulped even louder when he turned around to face a nine-foot giant who held weapons in both of his hands and wore a patch over his right eye. Connor slammed Bromie on the back in shock. The giant wore leather trousers, tied with a buckled belt, and a matching waistcoat. Connor watched nervously as Bromie stood up, warmly greeting the stranger.

'Connor, I'd like you to meet Obi, my brother.'

In a small squeaky voice Connor said, 'Pleased to meet you.'

The giant roared with laughter and swooped down to shake

Connor's hand. 'And I sir, am pleased to make your acquaintance. I hope my brother has been looking after you.'

Connor nodded shyly.

To Connor's surprise, Obi breathed in deeply and roared loudly. The Armatripe near the stronghold looked their way and couldn't fail to notice Obi's head sticking up from behind the tree. Obi didn't even try to hide.

'Cooeee!' he shouted and waved to the enemy.

Needless to say the whizzers returned almost at once. They immediately began attacking Obi who was now laughing with pleasure. Connor returned to his previous position, keeping out of sight.

Obi was bellowing louder than Mr Piggot ever could. He swiftly swatted one whizzer after another with a weapon resembling a tennis racket. At the same time he poked a large metal rod with a clear crystal at the end towards another whizzer. It was zapped and destroyed instantly.

The tennis racket knocked the whizzers out of the way and the metal rod made them vanish. One by one, they flicked their tails at the giant as if trying to sting him but although Obi was big, he moved with adept skill and speed. Fascinated, Connor huddled within the branches of the trees, watching him zap the creatures and make them disappear altogether. After a chaotic five minutes all whizzers had vanished from sight.

'Easy peasy!' Obi laughed victoriously.

Three Armatripe charged towards the commotion. Bromie gripped his massive sword in both hands and jumped over the tree to fight on the other side from where Connor lay hidden. He landed nimbly for someone his size and positioned his legs wide for combat. These Armatripe were armed with the same powerful looking swords as the ones that had ambushed Connor and his friends earlier. Connor hadn't realised how slow the Armatripes moved. By the time they were raising their swords, Bromie was already swinging his weapon high above his head and slicing the grotesque creatures as if they were nothing but fleas.

'What a party!' Obi laughed. 'I haven't caught so many

whizzers for a long time.' He looked down at Connor and extended his hand to help him up. 'Are you all right, sir?'

Connor nodded his head. He liked being called sir.

'One sting of their tail and you're paralysed for hours! Good job you stayed hidden,' he grinned. 'But they'd never sting me!'

'Why not?' asked Connor.

'Why not!' the giant howled. 'I'm too fast for them, that's why not!'

Connor found himself smiling and taking an instant liking to Obi.

Bromie cleared his throat. 'Thanks for helping, Obi, we'd be here for hours otherwise.'

'That's what brothers are for,' he grinned. 'Anyway, if it means destroying anything belonging to that over-sized pinkly-doodle-pop, I'm all for it.'

'He means Definastine,' Bromie explained.

'Why, that oversized pee pot brain!' Obi carried on, still referring to Definastine. 'He'll never get away with it!' He thrashed his rod in the air. 'I'll track him down and tear him limb from limb.'

'Would you?' Connor asked in awe.

'No – probably not. He'd turn me into a giant jam buttie before I'd be able to get anywhere near him. So where to now?'

'The stronghold,' Bromie replied.

Looking incredibly relaxed, Obi took the lead, strolling confidently with massive strides. Connor found himself having to run just to keep up.

CHAPTER NINETEEN

Screams of Despair

Confidence oozed from Obi like a running stream and seemed to be contagious. Connor found himself feeling calmer and more reassured. Having a nine-foot giant on your side in battle made him feel more optimistic. Bromie appeared more relaxed too. He relinquished his leadership role and was content to let Obi make the major decisions.

'He's my older brother,' Bromie explained, cutting down a thorn bush since Connor couldn't step over it as well as Obi could. 'Where I come from first born are always taller than the rest.'

'And he's the runt of the family,' Obi turned, grinning broadly and pointing his thumb over his shoulder towards his brother.

It was abnormally quiet when they reached the exterior of the fort. Obi slowed his pace and signalled for the other two to stop. The moon was situated high above them and was watching their every move. Its silvery light shone brightly above, revealing shadows shifting from behind the stone enclosure.

Obi shook his head and laughed aloud.

'Fools!' he sang out. 'We know you're there!'

The secret ambush preparing for them was suddenly exposed and in the short time Connor and his new friends were standing outside the stronghold, the place was in utter chaos. Whizzers charged with speed from around the corner. The noise was deafening. It sounded like a thousand bees trapped in a small metal container with a microphone pressed to it.

Obi was soon yelling insults at the enemy as he struck them down. Meanwhile, Bromie grasped hold of Connor, pulling him behind his body to protect him.

Whizzers flew everywhere, occupying every available space, but with his sword, Bromie sliced them in an instant as if they were nothing but apples, all lying dead on the ground like rotten fruit as the lights faded quickly from their bodies. Bromie acted fast, each action precise and deliberate, destroying anything that came close to them.

Connor was gaping in admiration at Bromie's skill. He pulled out the weapon he'd concealed earlier beneath his jacket and much to Bromie's surprise began shooting. A few shots went astray but Connor soon got the hang of it and was shooting like an expert. It was hard to miss when so many of them were in the sky.

Obi had since disappeared beneath a blanket of whizzers but a grunt and a deep hearty laugh reassured his comrades he was still alive. An occasional remark could be heard such as, 'Come here you little buzzies, I want to tickle your tummies!'

Obi was smothered in a thick blue sparkling cloud, continuously ducking and diving and spinning round quickly not to give the whizzers a chance to strike him. Whizzers were being whacked and zapped, flying out at different angles before darting back for more. Obi swatted them like gnats with accuracy and perfection. By his sheer skill alone the flock of whizzers decreased and Obi was again laughing victoriously. When the last one had been eradicated not a drip of sweat could be seen on his furry forehead.

But that wasn't all they had to fight against.

Several towering Armatripe were now rushing towards them with black ugly faces contorted in fury and bellowing with open mouths, showing their rotten brown teeth. Seeing their movements weren't too fast, Obi sat down, yawning cheekily. Only at the last moment, when they were almost upon him, did he jump up, engaging himself in battle. At this point the two brothers rushed forward, fighting side by side, leaving Connor safe behind them.

Obi was busily jumping and crashing his hefty weight down on the Armatripe he'd knocked over on the ground, squashing them flat as if he were a wrestler. Connor was shuddering at the sounds of cracking bones. More Armatripe followed the first group, then another and another.

Obi was knocking them down with his weapons; a swift bang to their heads was enough to bring them to their knees. And just to make sure they wouldn't get up again, Obi continued jumping in the air before sitting on them.

Bromie too, was dealing with them in his own way by slicing their heads off with a single motion of his sword. Strangely enough, Connor remained calm. The Armatripe resembled nothing human at all. They were hideous giant insects, as far as Connor was concerned.

Meanwhile Obi had thought of a new game. Picking up an Armatripe he threw it towards the others, knocking them over like skittles. The scene where Obi stood looked like the remains from a massive war. Armatripe laid sprawled everywhere. Some looked as if they were sleeping but others looked as flat as pancakes with eyes bulging out from their sockets. Some were headless.

Connor remained close to the wall, watching the last few remaining Armatripes get beaten.

While the brothers were preoccupied they failed to notice an Armatripe creeping up behind Connor. Connor sensed the creature before he saw it. The hairs on the back of his neck prickled uneasily and, spinning round fast, he came face to face with a creature suffering from really bad breath. It moved stiffly, appearing older than the Armatripe already engaged in battle.

The creature pulled him harshly, its voice deep and husky. Connor was only just able to make out the words. 'You! Come with me!' It sounded like someone talking on a radio with a lot of interference.

Connor reacted quickly, not allowing fear to take control. Holding his jacket securely with its pinchers, the foul creature was trying to pull him away. Connor was wriggling to free himself but was fighting against a strength that far outweighed his own.

'Get off me!' he screamed, lifting up the gun and pointing it at the Armatripe's face. 'I'll shoot!' The Armatripe gave a nasty grin and tightened its grip. 'I warned you!' snarled Connor, pressing his finger down on the trigger.

He fired immediately. The Armatripe's face blew up into thousands of pieces and a fountain of green grunge rained over him. The leftover debris of the evil alien ooze was trickling over his face.

'Urgh!' Connor cringed, feeling nauseous. It smelt worse than a stink bomb. 'That's so gross!'

'Connor!' Bromie was running towards him. 'You all right?'

Connor nodded slowly, his face turning green. Clutching his stomach, he leaned forward and gagged.

'You did really well. I saw what happened but I was too far away to do anything,' Bromie paused briefly. When he next spoke he sounded disappointed, though not with Connor but more with himself. 'I should've been watching you!'

Connor nodded, unable to say anything, being sick a second time.

'You did well, lad.'

Connor nodded, his lips quivering, and leant his body forward to heave for a third time.

'Let's get you cleaned up, mate.'

Bromie led Connor towards Obi. 'We've got a casualty.'

Obi was jumping on the spot from one foot to the other, full of energy, and completely revitalised after his battle. Waving his weapon in the air like a racket, he looked more like a tennis champion than a warrior. Next to him was a pile of dead Armatripe that were looking suspiciously squashed. He made a face when he saw the state Connor was in.

Smiling in sympathy, Obi was pulling out a large flask of water to pour over Connor's head. The freezing cold liquid immediately washed away the green gunge from his face. Connor felt instantly better.

Obi slapped his back a little harder than Connor would have liked. 'So, you killed your first Armatripe did you? You did well, sir. You're one of us now.'

Connor managed a small smile. Until today, he'd never killed anything in his whole life apart from the odd spider when he was too young to know better, now he'd killed a rock dweller and an Armatripe. He tried to make excuses for what he'd done. He tried to convince himself it was all right to have killed a cruel beast – a beast that constantly destroyed and harmed others. Surely that wasn't a bad thing. But deep down inside no matter how he tried to disguise the fact, he had killed and from experience he knew killing was meant to be wrong, even though it couldn't be avoided.

Whistling jovially, Obi stepped through the entrance to the stronghold where they came across a large, flat roofed building. Around its perimeter the building was square and made entirely from stone, except for the metal doors barring the entrance. Bromie appeared more attentive than Obi at this time but it wasn't really the case. Although he was whistling, Obi's senses were heightened to the constant threat of danger.

Rubbing his hands together, with his one good eye he eyed the massive doors.

'How come your brother has a patch over his eye?' Connor whispered quietly to Bromie.

'He lost it in battle a few years back,' Bromie explained.

'That's awful.' Connor wondered what it must look like beneath the patch.

'This is where I come in really handy,' Obi was saying. His muscular leg kicked the doors fiercely. Connor jumped. The echo of banging metal reverberated beyond the doors, enough to deafen anyone standing close behind it. Once he'd made a small gap big enough for his hands, he reached through, ripping the doors off their hinges and throwing them over the high stone wall as if they were paper aeroplanes. 'Ha, ha!' Obi roared happily.

'Wow!' Connor murmured. 'Nothing can stop him!'

Bromie grinned.

Deep inside the entrance a flurry of activity roared down below in the tunnels.

'More whizzers. Stay clear.' Obi braced himself for another onslaught. 'It's playtime again.'

He dashed inside the building without looking back.

'Be careful, brother,' Bromie called after him.

The passageway inside the entrance sloped downwards to where a tremendous racket soon erupted. Bellowing sounds echoed through the tunnel, filling the air. Connor covered his ears as the noise blasted out from the doorway. They waited in silence for Obi to emerge a few minutes later.

'Well, I think I got them all,' he told them, sounding breathless but satisfied.

'You're getting old, brother,' Bromie jibed.

'That I am,' he agreed. 'But there's still a lot of life in the old dog yet. Be careful where you step. There's a lot of mess inside and I didn't have time to clear it up.'

It was terribly dark and damp in the passageway. Connor shivered as he slipped on the remains of some dead creature but luckily remained on his feet. Obi led the way down the slope, stepping over the dead whizzers in his path. Further along the passageway green lamps glowed gently, lighting their way. The air in the massive corridor became stuffier and Connor started coughing to clear his throat. The smell was terrible too. Covering his nose with his jumper, he was relieved to have a whiff of the homely scent of Marion's home, sparking recent memories of his short time spent there. He wondered how they were all coping and whether or not they were aware of Sparkie's theories that Jeremy was still alive somewhere on Dramian trying to rescue his son, Daven. But what if Daven were already dead? What if they couldn't find Jeremy?

'There's a large room ahead!' Obi called, interrupting his thoughts.

They entered a circular room, filled with a mysterious blue light, with a magnificent domed ceiling beautifully carved from stone. Pale blue stone seats occupied the boundary of the room and in the middle of the floor, a pinhole of blue light was shining down from the ceiling.

'That's the moon,' Bromie told him. 'This room is positioned directly below it when the moon is at its highest.'

'Looks like a meeting place of sorts,' muttered Bromie, glancing at the seats.

Apart from a massive doorway there seemed no other way to proceed. Goosebumps spread across Connor's skin as his eyes fell on a magnificent stone carving of a massive bear, with huge teeth and thorns down its back, on the wall. Its eyes shone with a yellow stone and seemed to stare right through him.

'That bear,' said Bromie, 'must be some kind of protector to this place. There are references to it everywhere.'

It was true. On every wall was a carving of the bear, standing tall and mighty with a double row of thorns down the length of its spine.

'It's creepy down here,' Connor said. 'I wonder if this is where Kia's ship was taken. But there doesn't seem to be any other way out of this room apart from that door.'

Obi bent down and ran his fingers along a circular ridge in the ground. It was almost as round as the room. 'Ah huh! This level appears to be a lift. Look for something loose, like a button or lever of some kind. This lift is going to take us lower down.'

'I saw something sticking out of that wall as we came into the room,' Connor pointed to the wall and quickly regretted what he'd said. Was he mad? Did he really want to descend to a bottomless pit, which was possibly overrun with rock dwellers who enjoyed chewing the bones of humans?

Obi grabbed hold of the lever. 'This must be it! Good work, Connor! Stand in the middle of the floor.'

Connor was rooted to the spot. Bromie held his shoulders and pushed him forward.

'Don't freeze on us now,' he said gently. 'Just remember as long as you possess the Starstone no harm can come to you.'

Nodding, Connor firmly gripped his weapon. The Starstone might be powerful but he hadn't quite worked out how to use it. The gun, on the other hand, seemed a more reliable method of protecting himself.

'Here we go!' Obi warned and gripping the lever in both hands yanked it down in one fell swoop. A deep throbbing sound immediately came from within the walls. The ground seemed to tremble. Obi swiftly ran back to join the others, jumping surprisingly lightly towards the slowly descending floor.

Clanking metal on metal sounded somewhere around them, as the ground began to rumble. Connor was terrified. He'd never encountered an earthquake before, but he felt he was experiencing one now. Even the ground he stood on wasn't secure anymore.

The deep sound of a metal chain was rattling heavily in time with Connor's pulse as the ground began to lower slowly.

Soon they were fifteen feet below the room level and another minute later they were twenty feet further down.

At that moment, Connor became aware of a familiar grey creature leaning over the edge of the room above them, looking down curiously, with its dark eyes, staring wide.

'I think we have company,' Connor notified his friends. He looked upwards where several other rock dwellers had now joined the first.

'As long as they don't come down, we'll be all right,' Obi said frowning.

The contorted faces of the rock dwellers were filled with panic and their language filled with doubt. Unsure of what to do they threw down a couple of daggers, which narrowly missed Connor's feet. The blade caused a spark on the stone before breaking clean in half.

The others seemed less keen to lose their weapons. Suddenly their voices began to fill with excitement. Several disappeared from sight.

'They're going!' Connor said, cheering up.

'Doesn't sound very hopeful!' Bromie remarked.

'They've thought of a plan to stop us!' Obi growled. 'Let's hope they're too late.'

When the ground suddenly came to a standstill, it was all too clear what the rock dwellers had done. They had stopped the lift from progressing any further. For now they were stuck in-between levels in an enclosure with smooth slippery walls. Escape looked almost impossible.

'They're going to try and keep us here until we starve, aren't they?' panicked Connor, his mouth feeling dry and his stomach rumbling in neglect.

'Well, you know what they say – where there's a will, there's a way!' Obi immediately bent down to inspect a two-inch gap surrounding the lift on all sides. It was almost as if the wall had vanished. 'We're almost there! This is the level we were coming to. Stand back and watch out for any more flying daggers.'

He pulled out his sword from its sheath behind his back and lifted it high into the air. As he was about to bring it down on to the stone surface one of the rock dwellers had thrown a dagger.

'Look out!' Bromie cried out, leaping forward.

The dagger was thrown so fast that Bromie couldn't push his brother out of the way in time. It whizzed straight through the air and sliced through Obi's skin and muscle, embedding itself inside his shoulder.

'Ahhh!' Obi cried out, grabbing hold of the handle and ripping it out. He took in a deep breath as deep blood oozed freely from his wound. A cheer of victory erupted above them. Grimacing angrily he turned abruptly and flicked the blade with speed back from where it had come, slicing into the very heart of a rock dweller and causing it to fall below. Its body slammed heavily on to the huge stone slab, its bones snapping. Connor turned his head away and closed his eyes. The rock dweller was as cold as the slab of stone on which he lay and crumbled quickly into dust. Above, the others hushed, slowly retreating.

Bromie, standing by Obi, was urgently rubbing healing ointment over the deep gash. Obi was breathing heavily and remained still while his brother continued to nurse him. His clothes were soaked in blood but at least with the ointment the wound had stopped bleeding and very gently began to heal. The muscle fibres had already begun gently knitting together. In another hour the wound would be as good as new.

'You evil fiends!' Bromie snarled up at them.

The rock dwellers were frightened by the tone of Bromie's voice and retreated slightly. They were shrugging their shoulders, not understanding a word Bromie had said.

'Thanks brother. Let's get out of here!' Obi grumbled, lifting his sword once more and striking it hard at the stone slab on which they stood.

Connor gasped as the sword shimmered in the air and was more astounded to see the blade remaining intact as it crashed down hard over the bloodstained stone. What sword could possibly be stronger than a great chunk of rock? Slinking cowardly away the rock dwellers disappeared from sight. Connor grinned and wanted to laugh out loud. It felt good to see them flee with their tails between their legs.

A large crack had appeared in the surface of the rock. Obi stamped his foot at the edge and watched a chunk give way, falling in the chasm below. It seemed the lift could travel much further down than the level they had reached but for now that was where they were getting off. The hole in the floor was big enough for Obi to climb through. He sat on the edge of the hole with his legs dangling below. Reaching out, he struck his sword into the wall just above the level they were going to swing to.

'Hold my sword before lowering your body. Make sure you swing enough to make the jump. Otherwise you'll disappear below.'

Connor's jubilation had long since vanished. What they were doing was suicide. They could easily misplace their hands and plunge into the chasm below. What if the sword gave way? He tried not to think of it. Obi didn't seem to think it was difficult, but he was stronger. He was also heavier. If the sword could withstand his weight then Connor would certainly be okay, as long as he didn't release the sword.

Obi reached forward, grabbing his sword that would now act as a handgrip for them. Slowly he lowered his body down through the large gap. Lifting his legs forward he swung his body back once before making the jump.

'Hurry!' he urged the others.

'Go on, you can go next!' Bromie encouraged. 'You'll be all right.'

Connor was shaking. He sat on the edge of the hole and tried to reach forward but the sword seemed too far away.

'It's no good,' said Connor. 'I don't think I can reach it.'

'Hold my hands,' urged Bromie. Connor looked up at him, petrified. 'Hurry up.' Connor did as he was told. 'I'll lower you through the hole and swing you instead.'

Connor might have resisted this idea if he hadn't seen Bromie's earlier display of strength. He'd managed to lift him out of the crevice with ease. Trusting Bromie with all his heart he held on tightly to his large, powerful hands that were roughened by years of hard work. Bromie wrapped his hands around Connor's hands and wrists. The tops of his hands felt soft and furry, yet his palms were more like leather. His fingers held Connor securely and, strangely, despite such dangerous circumstances, Connor felt safe.

Connor was gently lowered down, until he was suspended above a bottomless shaft. Once his body was through the gap, Bromie began swinging him.

'I'll catch you!' Obi called out, his voice echoing. 'Swing him a little bit more. That's great. Now after three let him go. One... two... three! Go!'

Connor was flung like a dirty tea towel straight into Obi's arms. Obi was laughing hard as he released him. Connor stood ghostly white, shaking with relief. After the initial fear had faded, Connor was left feeling courageous. Never in his life had he faced so many trials and thankfully survived them all. He felt invigorated and strong. He believed after such an experience that he could face anything.

'Stand further back!' Obi urged Connor. 'Bromie's going to make his jump.'

Connor stood several feet away from the edge as Bromie prepared to come down.

'Hold on well, brother!' Obi called out.

Through the hole they watched Bromie's feet dangle before the rest of his body came into view. With a single kick, he swung with ease just like his brother before him and landed safely. Relief swept across Obi's face to see his brother safe. Then standing on tiptoes, Obi reached up to retrieve his sword from the rock.

The room in which they stood was an exact replica of the one they had been in previously but it looked different with the central ground raised leaving a gigantic gaping hole in the middle of the room. Looking around they spotted a small passageway leading from the room.

'I guess I'll just have to make it bigger,' Obi shrugged and, lifting his large sword, brought it crashing down into the rock. The huge chunks of collapsing rock broke on impact. He kicked the huge boulders away as if they were empty cans and continued to knock down the walls until he was able to pass through. The noise he was making was deafening yet something else could be heard above the racket.

The place came alive with shrieking screams of despair and hopelessness. They stopped dead in their tracks listening to the harrowing sounds coming from somewhere in front of them.

Obi frowned, his eyes darkening with concern. No one spoke. He elevated his magnificent sword high above his head and continued to sever the rock. It fell apart as if it were tree bark. Haunting cries rose above the racket of falling slabs crashing to the floor. Obi was sweating and looking uncomfortable. Screeches and wailing moans made Connor's blood curdle. He shivered and stood with a look of pure terror on his face.

Previously he'd come face to face with Definastine, his dark hounds and rock dwellers, all were equally scary yet these screams without a face were something else entirely, more terrifying and soul destroying. They had a way of entering your body uninvited, frightening every cell and atom in the process.

'What do you think is making that noise?' Connor asked in a small, quivering voice.

'The lost children!' Bromie whispered, appearing equally affected by the haunting din. He stared ahead with sympathetic eyes. 'We've got our work cut out for us.'

'The lost children?' Connor gulped and felt a shimmer of excitement. If they had found the lost children then surely they'd find Jeremy here too.

The smell around them was putrid and foul, like entering the heart of a sewage system. Connor almost gagged and tried to cover his nose and mouth at once. Pulling out a couple of sweet smelling handkerchiefs, Bromie tied one round Connor's nose and then tied one across his own. Obi did the same. Like bandits they entered through the widened doorway into a massive corridor lined with beautiful decorative pillars. Eerie green fungus shone dimly from the walls, lighting their way. Obi moved carefully along the strange passageway when something suddenly screamed next to them on the other side of the wall, causing them to turn round sharply.

No obvious doors could be seen but quite plainly behind each wall persistent cries of insanity could be heard screaming out. Banging sounds vibrated through the walls as if someone was thumping it from the other side.

They walked the entire length of the fifty-foot corridor but the way in to each cell was still obscured from sight. Every now and then Connor jumped as dampened wails erupted from behind the wall beside him. If it was terrifying for them to hear the screams, how much worse must it be for the prisoners themselves?

'These are cells!' said Obi. 'But there are no entrances to them.'

Connor suddenly had an idea. He explained to Obi how the rock dwellers were able to manipulate rock and move it in certain ways. He told him about how they had made a doorway disappear and how a young rock dweller had made a ladder appear in the rock so he could escape. Bromie confirmed his story, having witnessed it himself.

'So you see, the rock dwellers must have sealed them!' finished Connor.

'That explains it,' Obi said thoughtfully. 'We'd better let our troops know our position.'

He pulled out a small black device from his pocket and flipped the lid up. It gave a loud beep. 'Sampras, send our men in to these co-ordinates. We've found the lost children.' He went on to reel off several different numbers, which meant nothing to Connor. After ending his call he smiled at Connor and then at Bromie. 'There's only one way I can think of handling this situation.' He grinned as he pulled out his sword. It flashed in the green light. 'Stand back and watch the master at work.'

CHAPTER TWENTY

The Lost Children

After a lengthy pause, Obi hesitated and lowered his sword, his eyes revealing a thoughtful state.

'What is your worry, brother?' Bromie asked with concern. He rested his hand on Obi's shoulder.

'Perhaps we'd better wait for back up,' Obi said. 'We don't want to stir up a hornet's nest.'

'Huh?' Connor wrinkled his face. 'You think the noise might be coming from a hornet's nest.'

'No!' smiled Obi. 'But what if it's something else behind the walls, something evil. I don't want to release a demon alien species from here and have to fight them. I could do without that right now – we all could. We can't be one hundred per cent sure it is the missing children behind these walls.'

'Then deal with one cell at a time,' smiled Bromie, his cheeks lifting. 'Together we can deal with anything that might jump out.'

Obi nodded. 'Okay. It's agreed. Let's prepare ourselves.'

Bromie moved to the right of Obi, keeping his distance. With his sword in hand, he widened his stance. Returning his smile, Obi nodded slowly. They looked similar to each other at moments like this, when they were contemplating the next plan of action, but when it came to fighting they were like chalk and cheese. Bromie generally fought in silence with an occasional grunt due to effort, whereas Obi's voice fought alongside his sword, ridiculing everyone he killed.

With his mind made up, Obi went forward and pressed his ear to the wall. 'Stand back from the wall!' he shouted. He wasn't sure if he was understood or not, but it made him feel better warning whoever could be behind the wall.

The haunting shrieks subsided at once. Obi lifted his three-foot sword in the air as he'd done so many times before and brought it down with all his might onto the hard surface of stone. The blade sparkled as a large crack appeared in the wall. The crack continued down to the ground where the wall in front of them crumbled and collapsed into a heap of rubble. The noise was deafening as the bricks fell. Startled cries erupted once more, but this time they were full of panic.

Connor protectively positioned himself behind Bromie and nervously peeped so he could see. As the red dust began to settle the cries had completely diminished and the corridor became deadly silent. Connor did not know what was worse, cries of despair or an unsettling silence.

Bravely, Obi stood his ground ready for action if needed. He peered inquisitively at the hole he'd made. He blinked his eyes free from dust. There was movement on the other side of the wall. Slowly emerging into view were five frightened children, three boys and two girls, dirty and wearing nothing but smelly torn rags. Their eyes were filled with distrust and bewilderment. They came out looking wild with matted hair and their skin was torn in places like the rags they wore.

'The lost children!' gasped Bromie.

Obi immediately altered his warrior pose to one less threatening. He knelt down so as not to appear too intimidating and replaced his previous expression with one full of empathy. Connor came out from his hiding place.

The larger boy placed the smaller children behind him and looked at Obi with fire in his eyes. He muttered something in a language they didn't understand. He tried again but Obi shook his head.

'I'm sorry. It's no good. We don't understand.' Obi turned to Connor. 'I can speak several different languages but only English from this planet. Can you speak any other language?'

Connor shook his head.

'There must be someone here who can speak English,' muttered Bromie. In a slow drawn out tone he asked, 'Do any of you speak English?'

'I do,' said a small voice from the back of the cell. 'I can speak English.'

Obi's eyes began to blur with tears. It was all so heartbreaking: scared children kidnapped and torn away from their families to a place offering nothing but fear.

'Hello,' Obi said warmly. 'What's your name?'

A small girl stepped out of line and slowly moved towards him. 'Debbie,' she told him. 'Have you come to help us?'

Obi widened his eyes in pain. 'Yes, we've come to take you home.'

'Oh,' said the little girl. 'I can't remember where my home is. I've forgotten. My mummy will be angry with me for running away. I went after Scampi, my puppy. He ran away. I was only trying to find him. Then the birds took me away.'

'The birds?' quizzed Bromie.

'It's okay,' Obi said. 'Your mummy won't be angry. She'll be happy to see you again, trust me.'

The little girl smiled. Obi's voice had an instant calming effect and gradually the children walked over the rubble and out of the cells for the first time since they had arrived there. Connor raised his eyes in surprise. He'd never heard someone so big speak so gently. With a voice like that he'd be able to tame the wildest animal.

The children clutched each other desperately, having formed a close relationship with one another. They were able to communicate largely by a method of sign language they had developed. Whatever length of time they had been in there for had certainly made them a close knit clan.

'How long have you been here, Debbie?' asked Obi.

'Don't know.'

'Did you used to go to school?'

She nodded.

'Can you remember a date when you were last at school?'

She bit her lip and thought hard. She began to shake her head but stopped. 'I was going to watch some fireworks but I didn't because the birds took me away.'

So she'd been there for roughly three weeks, he worked out. Debbie's face was tearstained and muddy. 'Well, you'll be okay now. Don't worry. You're going home today and no harm will come to you. Do you understand?'

Debbie nodded, her dark brown eyes full of trust. She looked like she was going to cry so Obi scooped her in his arms where she began sobbing loudly, her little body shaking with relief. The other children came closer to Bromie and Obi, all wanting a cuddle too. Some of the other children began crying.

'We must let them go straight to the AAA,' Bromie said. 'These children have been taken from all over the world. They'll need medical help and besides the AAA will be able to track their families faster than the police can.'

'You're right,' said Obi. He gently released one of his arms from the children and reached inside his waistcoat for his corbee communication device. 'Don't be scared,' he told the children. He pressed a button and a second later a hologram image of a man's face appeared, looking somewhat concerned. His face was transparent with a blue light around him. The children screamed.

'A ghost!' Debbie cried, shaking. She tried to run away but Obi held her securely.

'No, don't be frightened,' Bromie smiled. 'He's on our side. He's going to help us, to help you.'

'Agent Obi, I've been worried about you,' came the voice. 'Is everything well?'

'Arbtu, we've found the lost children,' Obi explained. 'This corridor we're in is filled with them. We need a portal to the AAA hospital wing. These children are frightened and need help.'

'Straightaway,' Arbtu said proudly. 'Give me your co-ordinates.'

Again Obi reeled off various letters and numbers.

'Good work team,' Arbtu smiled. 'When your work is done make sure you get home safely. Any sign of Sparkie or Tookar?'

'Not yet, sir,' Obi said. 'But we're getting closer to them. I can feel it in my bones.'

'Hope you find them soon,' Arbtu said, instantly vanishing.

Obi replaced his corbee in his pocket. A slight breeze soon

began to fill the corridor. The children stiffened and tightened their grip on the adults, their knuckles turning white. A small pinprick of light magically appeared in front of them. Slowly it grew bigger and bigger until it was the size of a huge hula-hoop. It shone and shimmered dully, like liquid grey mercury.

'Wow!' gasped Connor. 'It's amazing.'

'You must go through now!' Obi urged. 'Don't be frightened. Kind people are waiting for you on the other side. They will give you clothes and food.'

Debbie made a face as she looked past the portal to the other side of the corridor. 'There's nothing on the other side,' she whispered disappointedly. 'I can't see anyone waiting for us.'

'You won't. This is a magic doorway,' Obi swiftly explained. 'It'll take you to a special place where you will be safe. From there they will begin to find your families. It will take you far from here.'

Debbie bit her lip.

'If you go first, you can help the others understand,' Bromie suggested. 'You'll be a heroine.'

'You're funny,' Debbie giggled.

Turning round to face her friends, she beckoned them to follow her. One by one the children held each other's hands to form a link. She was pointing to the portal and smiled. Then she pointed to her stomach and pretended to eat. The others were soon smiling. The idea of eating food was enough for any of them to take a leap through a magic doorway. As soon as Debbie reached the portal she turned round, a shimmering light reflecting on her cheeks.

'Thanks,' she said in a small voice.

It was the most amazing thing Connor had ever seen. The children were walking through the portal and one by one they vanished. As soon as the last child had left, Obi began smashing every wall connected to the small dirty cells.

The corridor became teeming with dust and rubble. The small hazy figures of children were emerging from their confined cells, all frightened and confused. Several of them were coughing as they struggled through the dust. For a second they looked like chimneysweepers. Their faces and ragged clothes were covered in dust and dirt. More children were appearing by the second.

Their voices were restrained at first. They didn't understand what was happening. Gradually, when they realised they were being rescued, their voices increased. Soon the corridor was filled with many different languages gabbling at once.

At the end of the corridor a group of strange looking men turned up, wearing black leather trousers and waistcoats. Obi ran to greet them. It occurred to Connor, after noticing the bizarre appearance of these men, that they couldn't possibly be human. It was too far to see properly but he could have sworn one looked like a rhinoceros. After their brief conversation the strangers charged down another corridor.

'This operation has turned out to be much bigger than what we first anticipated. It seems there are several more corridors housing imprisoned children. We have five other groups operating on different levels to empty the other cells,' Obi explained to them. 'If we don't find Tookar and Sparkie here, there's a good chance the others will find them.'

Wasting no time, Obi suddenly raised his voice. Connor jumped. When asking if anyone could understand him, he was pleased to discover twenty other children raising their hands, replying in English. It was these children who helped communicate to the others that there was a safe place waiting for them on the other side of the portal.

In one massive line the children held hands with one another and started walking towards the shimmering portal. The younger children looked hesitant, yet excited by the prospect of escaping. Fifteen minutes later, having watched hundred children pass through the portal, Obi breathed a sigh of relief.

Unfortunately, his satisfaction was short-lived. Not everyone had been so lucky. A group of elderly people and younger adults had been discovered huddling in their cells, refusing to come out. It was these people who had cried so insanely beforehand. Their eyes were blank from any expression – soulless and destroyed inside. Every now and again they would look up to the ceiling, open their mouths and cry desperately, like lonely animals. Moving like zombies, they had to be physically pushed through the portal. Otherwise they would have remained where they were, staring into space and banging on the nearest wall.

Connor kept out of the way of the older people who frightened him. He watched Obi and Bromie assisting them through the portal. The older people didn't have a clue where they were going. Connor's throat tightened. How long had those poor people been huddled and forgotten in this desolate world, turning them into shadows of their former selves?

With hunched backs and fragile movements, they shuffled through the portal like a herd of timid sheep. These were the last people to be sent through. Once the task was completed, Obi communicated with Arbtu again.

'Mission accomplished,' he smiled.

'You've done an excellent job,' Arbtu praised them. 'Terrible business, absolutely terrible – poor souls. They need complete rehabilitation. Thank goodness you found them in time. Ah – I see you found young Connor.' Arbtu's face turned and smiled directly at him. Connor tingled with pleasure. 'May the light guide you all home safely.'

With that the communication ceased and the portal disappeared.

'Come on. We'd better continue on the lower level,' said Bromie. 'I think we've exhausted every avenue here.'

Obi frowned heavily, before nodding his head in agreement. Connor sensed his anger and felt the same. How could anyone treat people like that? It was cruel. As they were leaving the corridor a small grey figure staggered round the corner. A deep growl rumbled from Obi's throat. He pointed his sword towards the creature and was about to charge towards it. Panicking, Connor placed his hand on Obi's arm.

'No, don't hurt him!' he urged. 'It's the rock dweller boy who helped me escape the steep crevice.'

Connor wrinkled his face in puzzlement and started running towards the young rock dweller.

'Careful. It might be a trap,' Bromie called after him.

But Connor threw caution to the wind. He ran towards the rock dweller. De-ma was gripping the wall with all his strength. His face, battered and bruised, showed signs of weariness. His shallow breathing was sounding raspy. His body bore the signs of torture. Deep whiplashes had cut across his back and shoulders, from where red blood poured freely. He staggered over to Connor and collapsed by his feet.

'They found out... I helped you,' he panted. 'They punished me. They know you are here. I've come to warn you. They are setting up a trap for you down on level five... There's a girl there... be careful... Sheena's there too... she's so powerful... she can control minds... don't look at her eyes... or she will control you.'

'Where are our friends?' Obi asked softly.

'Down on the next level. It's exactly... like this one. With just as many prisoners... I've been helping them... as best as... I could.... I've been secretly feeding the humans so they didn't starve... Definastine has destroyed my people... he made them cruel... he made them the way they now are.'

'Will you take us to our friends?' Bromie asked.

'I don't know if I can... I struggled to come this far.' De-ma's voice was fading. He pulled something out from his pocket. 'I stole this... it's a map of this place. Use it and find your friends – help as many people as you can.'

Bromie already had his ointment out and was soothing it over De-ma's back. 'You did a very brave thing helping us. Thank you De-ma.'

'I'm glad you're here... to save the children... I only did... what I felt... was right,' he whispered, his eyelids closing. He took his last breath before his body fell limp.

'No!' Connor cried. He ran his fingers over De-ma's forehead where it still felt warm.

'Come on, Connor. We have to go.' Bromie tried to pull Connor away but he refused to budge.

He shook his head. 'No, I want to save him,' he insisted. 'He saved me.'

Ignoring Bromie's words, Connor held De-ma's hand and closed his eyes, half expecting to feel an electric shock, similar to the one he'd felt when he began healing Tookar but there was no sensation at all. Instead in his mind's eye, he saw a bright light encircling De-ma's body encouraging his soul body to leave the physical one behind. Connor saw De-ma smiling. His ghostly image sat up and reached upward to the light shining above. Floating upwards like a weightless balloon, he turned and waved to Connor before vanishing peacefully into the blinding brilliance.

Connor opened his eyes. A single tear trickled over his cheek. He quickly wiped it away. He couldn't explain what he'd seen. There was certainly no visible light in the corridor. No one else had witnessed De-ma's soul departing his body.

Tears were in everyone's eyes for the child who lay before them. They barely knew him, but their grief wasn't lessened. This brave child had saved so many lives. He'd risked his own to save others. Connor was overcome with guilt. If De-ma hadn't helped him, he might still be alive. If only he'd been able to repay him in some way.

'He's a brave little warrior,' Obi smiled and gave a sniff. 'But he's gone to a better place now.'

'Better place?' Connor whispered. 'What do you mean?'

'He's gone back home to the place that connects every living being in the universe. To the land of the spirit.'

'You mean heaven,' Connor corrected him.

'People call it different names,' Bromie replied. 'We call it the land of the spirit. The funny thing is, we all fear death but it's our true home, from where we were born. We have nothing to fear and no one is excluded.'

Connor remembered seeing the huge smile on De-ma's face and felt strangely comforted knowing the land of the spirit existed. So there really was a place that people went to after death. Death wasn't the end. It was a process people went through to pass into another dimension. Connor brushed away his tears.

De-ma had inspired him in so many ways. With utter determination, De-ma had struggled despite his pain, to offer them help. Connor felt ashamed when he thought about how he had shrunk away from helping those old people – the same people De-ma had been secretly feeding.

Something stirred deep inside of Connor. The humble rock dweller boy lying dead on the ground had unknowingly provided Connor with an experience that would help him grow into a more mature person. His own example now shone inside Connor.

Obi whispered a short prayer. The others closed their eyes briefly in respect. He finished with saying, 'May his journey into the light be complete.'

Connor was still kneeling down as Obi examined De-ma's gift. It was a small red ball, with a yellow button. Obi pressed it and instantly a map was magnified to mammoth proportions in a hologram image in front of them. A red pointer flashed repeatedly, to mark their position.

'Let's not waste what precious time we have left,' he said.

'What about De-ma?' said Connor. 'Aren't we going to bury him or something, out of respect?'

'Do you think he'd want to be buried here?' Obi asked.

But even as they were speaking De-ma's body started decomposing. His body started wrinkling. He was growing older in the seconds they stood and watched. Soon his body crumpled like the walls had, leaving nothing but dust behind.

CHAPTER TWENTY-ONE

The Queen of the Palamores

Working their way down the steep stone spiralling staircase was especially awkward for Obi and Bromie, since their feet were so big. Cheering and jubilation sounded from various passageways, as Obi's comrades were helping other children escape.

Naturally alert for any further sign of trouble, their senses remained heightened to the environment. Ready for battle at any turn, they continued cautiously. Since the incident with De-ma, Connor had become more confident and sure of his abilities. He held in the forefront of his mind an attack that would turn their enemies into stone. He didn't enjoy seeing blood so it seemed a reasonable way of stopping any opponent. He'd never tried it before but believed it was certainly worth a go.

But much to their relief, nothing stopped them progressing down to the next level. Apart from their soft footsteps treading on the stone floor and an occasional grunt from Obi, as he slipped on the odd step, they journeyed in silence. Eventually they exited the stairs to another lengthy corridor.

Connor tightened the handkerchief around his face. The smell increased the further they descended and the odd whiff stabbed up his nose. It was disgusting. Connor was near the verge of vomiting several times but tried to control it by breathing and holding his breath. This meant becoming dizzy but Connor didn't think he had much choice.

Obi ran slightly ahead. He was shouting more warnings, giving people a chance to move back, before lifting his sword and slamming it into the hard stone. It was a repeated performance but this time he wasn't worried about what was behind the walls. De-ma had already explained that there were more humans there.

222

'Stand back! Get away from this wall!' The thick walls crumbled like breadcrumbs at his feet.

Connor and Bromie kept their distance as Obi moved to the next cell. They approached the first uncovered cell and watched as more half-starved people clambered out, dazed and disorientated. They were much older than the younger children on the level above them but had the same wild look in their eyes, as if they'd been in the cells forever. They walked humped over and it was obvious why – the ceilings of the cells were low, making it impossible to stand up straight.

Some of the people couldn't have been older than thirty years but already their hair was grey and balding. Their faces were sunken as if they were old beyond their years, holding expressions of uncertainty and relief.

Bromie had taken charge of the corbee and a portal soon manifested near him. Bewildered faces stared at the portal as if it were a threatening enemy. Gasps of disbelief and fear erupted from the collected group of freed prisoners, ranging in age from thirty to eighty years.

This time Arbtu sent linguistic star-spirits through the portal to help. These star-spirits were able to communicate to everyone by speaking different languages. Some of the people had been there so long that they couldn't communicate no matter how hard they tried.

'I don't believe it,' Bromie whispered. 'These people have been here so long they have forgotten how to talk.'

Obi, Bromie and Connor assisted where they could by helping people out of the cells and over the rubble. Now the linguistic star-spirits had arrived, things were happening more quickly. They'd already begun grouping certain people together and leading them through the portal.

The star-spirits sent to help were a tall race of gentle people. The females had beautiful, long flowing white hair and wore long light-blue dresses. They looked oddly out of place in the gloomy corridor. Connor imagined them more suitable in a place of worship. The men wore plain trousers and long baggy tops, draping past their waists. But the most amazing thing was the aura of light they possessed protruding an inch from their bodies. They held a certain presence of strength and appeared no more threatening than teddy bears.

'They're Palamores,' Bromie explained, smiling towards them and giving them a wave. 'Very sweet people, I might add.'

Obi came to join them. 'I don't see Lidena anywhere,' he smiled.

'Lidena?' quizzed Connor.

'Lidena is soon to be Bromie's bride,' said Obi.

'You're marrying a Pala... a Pala...'

'Palamore,' helped Bromie, grinning happily.

At that moment a single figure came through the portal. A beautiful woman was standing close to the shimmering gateway, with an anxious look in her eyes. Her white hair flowed gently in a slight breeze coming from the portal. She seemed more beautiful than any other Palamore Connor had seen. She looked straight towards Connor and her face lit up in a smile. He didn't know where to look when she began running towards him. But when she called out Bromie's name, he realised his mistake.

'Bromie!' she cried, running towards him with her arms outstretched.

Bromie rushed forward, grabbing hold of her tightly before lifting her into the air by her waist and swinging her round. Lidena's face was shining with happiness.

'Dakwin told me you were here,' she breathed happily. 'I've been worried about you. Can't you come home yet?'

'Soon,' Bromie replied, stroking her hair away from her face to kiss her forehead. 'We'll soon be finished here. I'll find you as soon as we get back.'

'Okay my love. Please be careful.' Lidena turned her head, aware that they were being watched. She smiled to the others. 'Look after him for me. I need him in one piece if we are to be married.'

'Lidena, I would like you to meet Connor,' Bromie promptly made the introduction, pulling her to his young friend. 'He's the one the Starstone has chosen.'

Lidena moved closer to Connor, walking as gracefully as if she were travelling on air. She reached her soft hand forward to shake Connor's hand. He raised his hand awkwardly, standing flustered in her presence.

Lidena smiled. Her voice had a dreamlike quality. When she spoke, Connor felt he'd been transported to another place as his attention was fixed solely on her. Even her eyes had the power to grab his attention as they searched his mind with deep intent. She was so beautiful and intelligent it was clear why Bromie loved her.

'I'm pleased to meet you, Connor. Well, I must say you're causing quite a stir at the AAA. Everyone is talking about you. There are so many star-spirits relying on you at this present time. You are their only hope of defeating Definastine. It doesn't seem fair and you doubt yourself from time to time. But you must understand the Starstone has chosen you for unknown qualities you do not know exist within you. Yet I can see them clearly. You are indeed a true leader. It seems strange one so young as you should be chosen but the Starstone has chosen wisely. Believe in yourself and never doubt your newly found abilities.'

Connor wasn't aware of his surroundings until he heard Obi laugh. His laughter seemed to break the spell.

'So she has you under her charm as well,' he chuckled.

As she turned her attention back to Bromie, Connor watched as the two of them conversed together. Only when they began walking back towards the portal did he feel able to breathe properly.

'Don't worry. She has that effect on a lot of people,' he grinned. 'She's what you would call the queen of her people.'

'A queen,' Connor whispered. 'How come she's marrying Bromie then? Doesn't she have to marry a prince or a king or something?'

Obi shook his head. 'She doesn't have to but when they met, they fell in love straightaway. It was a coincidence Bromie is a prince too.'

'Bromie is a prince?' Connor gasped.

'So am I,' smiled Obi. 'You're mixing with royalty now. We'll take you back home with us one day when it is safe so you can see our home. You'll love it.'

Connor hadn't realised this and it shouldn't have mattered, but somehow the thought of mixing with royal people made him feel inadequate.

Suddenly an elderly man, chuckling madly, emerged from another cell and was waving his arms about threateningly. A couple of Palamores were finding it difficult to help him without being hit. He had silvery white hair and a long beard. His eyes were clear blue with no pupils. It was obvious he was blind. As he passed Connor, he suddenly stopped and turned his head. Frowning, he rested his hand on Connor's arm. Once he had made contact he began nodding his head excitedly, muttering in a language of his own. Connor covered his hand with his own for a moment. When the old man eventually let go, he walked off, singing badly out of tune – but singing none the less. They watched as a Palamore guided him gently towards the doorway to the AAA.

It was very tempting for Connor to rush forward and jump into the gateway to a place of safety but knowing his friends still needed rescuing prevented him getting too close to it. He had to rescue them first.

Obi began looking puzzled. 'I don't see any signs of Sparkie or Tookar as yet.'

'They've got to be here,' said Connor. 'De-ma told us they were here.'

Obi walked to the end of the corridor. Connor followed. Here they discovered two cells on either side, which had been previously overlooked.

'Just keep clear of the wall!' Obi shouted. 'We'll have you out in no time.'

To Connor's surprise, Obi released some small, round, fluffy pink creatures. They all appeared to be heads without bodies, or were they bodies without heads? It wasn't clear what they were. Being gentle and looking rather cute beneath their pink matted fur they soon captivated Connor. They were the size of footballs with hands and feet hidden beneath their thick unkempt fur. Huge eyes that sparkled golden were watching Connor with interest. Nervously at first, Connor stroked several of them at once, but realising they wouldn't hurt him his confidence increased.

Squeaking in a bizarre language, which increasingly became irritating to the human ear, they bounced off in the direction of the portal. There were several gasps of delight from the Palamores who cuddled them and took them through to the AAA.

'We call them Pinklepoppos,' explained Obi. 'They're as gentle as rabbits.'

In the last cell on the opposite side of the corridor, Obi finally discovered Tookar and Sparkie.

'Over here, Connor!' Obi shouted.

'Sparkie! Tookar!' Connor cried.

Tookar came out first, shaking his head. 'Thank goodness you came in time. Those creatures took Sparkie away and when he was brought back an hour ago he was unconscious and he hasn't woken up since. I don't know what they've done to him, but he needs help quickly.'

'Don't worry. We'll get him to the AAA as quickly as we can.' Obi ducked down to fit into the small, cramped cell, appearing seconds later cradling Sparkie in his massive arms. Holding him securely Obi took gigantic strides towards the portal. Throughout this time Sparkie lay unconscious with his head rocking from side to side.

Tookar's head was slightly swollen and bruised. He hugged Connor affectionately. 'I'm so glad to see you alive. I knew if De-ma helped you, you would be all right. He did help you, didn't he?'

Connor nodded slowly as memories of De-ma came to the forefront of his mind.

'He said he would,' Tookar smiled. 'I wonder where he is now. If we see him again, we must help him leave this wretched place. He's different to the other rock dwellers, did you notice?'

Connor nodded again and smiled. 'He doesn't need rescuing anymore. He died a short time ago.'

'Died?' Tookar's joyful expression dropped. 'What happened?'

'He was punished for helping me. It was awful, Tookar. They tortured him. You should have seen him. He looked terrible. When I tried to heal him, it was too late. But I saw him – I saw him leave his body and disappear into a strange, peaceful light. Do you want to know the strangest thing? He smiled and waved to me as he floated upwards to the light. It was weird. He was dead and yet he looked happy.'

'You saw him going home,' Tookar smiled sadly.

'That was what Obi said. Back to the place where we all started. The land of the spirit, he said.'

'It's true,' Tookar replied sadly. 'It doesn't make it any easier to accept though, does it? When a life has been taken against the will of another individual, when murder has been committed it is a terrible crime. No one deserves to die that way. We all have the right to live a full life to progress as much as we can before our timely death arrives to claim us and take us back to the land of the spirit. People who have been murdered never get the chance to reach their full potential and level of learning.'

'But I'm a murderer,' Connor told him. 'I've killed an Armatripe already. Was I meant to let him live?'

'The Armatripes kill many innocent people. They must be stopped. They are evil and will continue to harm others. Killing those creatures will help many other people live freely without fear. There is no other way. Light *must* defeat the darkness. You don't go around killing innocent people that have caused you no harm, do you?'

Connor shook his head and turned his attention back to the Palamores standing near the portal. Many had already returned back to the AAA, since the rescue operation was now completed. The remaining few were talking briefly to Bromie and Obi before disappearing through the portal – leaving the five of them behind.

Bromie was saying his goodbyes to Lidena. Before she left she waved to Connor, but not before he saw her pass a small package to Bromie. Then the portal closed behind her.

Bromie was looking increasingly troubled after talking to

Lidena. He glanced several times at Connor and looked away quickly. This was a most unsettling experience for Connor. He sensed something was wrong and didn't like it for one moment.

Connor turned to Tookar and gasped in disbelief. For where Tookar had been standing was now a huge grey wolf.

'Don't look so shocked,' said the wolf in Tookar's voice. 'Being a wolf helps me deal with headaches. My hearing is greatly enhanced as well. I'll change back if it bothers you.'

'No, it's all right,' said Connor, trying to familiarise himself with his friend's new form and trying not to worry about what Bromie had been saying.

Tookar remained faithfully close to Connor, padding noiselessly up the corridor. His dark brown eyes stared ahead, his ears twitching.

'We've only got Kia to rescue now,' said Obi. 'De-ma said she was on level five, another two levels below this one. Apparently there's a trap waiting for us down there. Can you remember what De-ma told us?'

He looked towards Connor and then to Bromie.

It was Connor who spoke, recalling every word De-ma had said. 'He told us to be careful of Sheena. He told us not to look into her eyes.'

'Well remembered, Connor,' said Obi. 'I have no idea who Sheena is. I do not know what she looks like or anything about her at all. I imagine her looking like a woman but she may be in the form of a grotesque beast. Just be careful to avoid any direct eye contact with her.'

They followed Obi down another narrow flight of steps, not knowing what to expect. In Connor's mind he held the strong mental thought of his stone attack just in case they were ambushed.

CHAPTER TWENTY-TWO

Sheena

The stillness in the air soon became unbearably tense. Connor was fidgeting with Tookar's fur, running his fingers through the soft mane in a subconscious way to relieve his tension, ignoring the raised hackles on Tookar's neck, standing prominent like a wire brush. A low growl rumbled deep in Tookar's throat like rumbling thunder. The atmosphere became quiet, like the calm before a storm. Everyone felt it. Obi consulted the map.

'Do you see this large chamber?' He pointed to a room at the bottom of the stairs. 'I believe this is where they are keeping Kia. That's where we're heading.'

With a quick press of the yellow button, the map immediately vanished. Obi placed it back inside his pocket. Further down the steep spiralling stairwell, Obi stopped no less than eight times before proceeding again. Connor was feeling apprehensive. He hadn't seen Obi look so hesitant before. Something was troubling him. He seemed to be straining his ears to hear something beyond the silence surrounding them, yet there was nothing. Still they plodded on. Eventually as they neared the end of the stairs to level five, Obi paused again but this time he wasn't happy about moving onward.

'Keep your wits about you,' he whispered. 'Prepare for battle.'

Connor thought this was a bit drastic. He hadn't heard anything yet. It might have seemed foolish to think this way but he had never been in a situation like this before. He had no idea what to expect. To make matters worse, Tookar refused to proceed down the steps.

'They're waiting,' he growled. 'They're trying to trap us.'

This confirmed Connor's darkest thoughts, but he didn't expect this feeling to lead to a tremendous banging and crashing both above and below them on the stairs.

Obi growled and pulled out his magnificent sword to face the surge of bodies rushing up the stairs like a small tidal wave, in flimsy coats of armour.

'Here they come!' he yelled.

Bromie swivelled on his heel to deal with the torrent of bodies charging towards him. In seconds the rock dwellers came into view holding glistening daggers in their hands. Their noses were wobbling in fury and their expressions fierce. Thus the battle began.

Two accomplished giants with massive swords were keeping the enemy at bay. Although Obi had grumbled several times about the stairwell being too narrow, he was at this point pleased that it was.

Connor remained rigid next to Tookar between Bromie and Obi. He wanted to help by using his powers to turn the rock dwellers into stone, but it was too risky because neither Obi nor Bromie remained still enough for long. Occasionally Bromie and Obi staggered backward knocking into Connor but they moved quickly forward before harming him.

It was obvious the rock dwellers had been monitoring them all this time and had guessed they would try to save Kia. They had used Kia like bait, to draw them closer. The bodies continued to storm the small party.

The deafening sounds of metal crashing against metal made Connor cringe. With ear-piercing screams the rock dwellers were stabbed and killed as the sword cut through them like butter. Whatever calculated plan the rock dwellers had, it didn't seem to be working. The two giants were easily overpowering them. They never stood a chance.

'You little maggots, I'll get every one of you!' Obi bellowed loudly, his voice echoing down the stairwell.

More rock dwellers replaced their dead comrades but were struck down by one of the mighty swords in seconds. Bromie was fighting upwards in a more difficult position, but he dodged and dived out of the reach of his shorter-armed opponents. His success was due to a lengthy sword and long muscular arms. Although the rock dwellers were dressed in preparation for a battle they only had feeble looking daggers which did nothing more than scratch an itch for Bromie.

Eventually the remaining rock dwellers fled and the clanking battle ended. Although the stairwell was full of dead bodies, they quickly shrivelled up and vanished.

'That was a good fight, brother,' Bromie praised, replacing his sword.

'Saves us from getting bored,' Obi replied.

'Did you notice their blank eyes?' Tookar asked.

'Yep.' Obi stopped what he was doing. His expression gave nothing away but the tone of his voice had spoken volumes. 'They were under a spell of some kind.'

Connor went cold and shivery. If those rock dwellers had been hypnotised, maybe the person responsible for that was the same person they were about to encounter down on level five – Sheena. He gulped loudly and prayed he was wrong.

They met no further obstacles on their way, except a massive block of stone that barred the entrance to the large room.

'Do they seriously think this will keep us out?' Obi laughed sarcastically.

Connor rested his hand on Tookar's neck and was surprised to see him suddenly vanish.

'What the –?' He glanced round quickly and jumped when a small voice whispered in his ear.

'I've turned myself invisible for a while. I might be able to help better like this until we know what we're facing.'

Obi wasted no time knocking down the door. It crumbled to dust after five massive blows.

'Connor, where's Tookar?' Bromie asked urgently.

'He's invisible,' Connor explained.

Bromie nodded, looking relieved, then followed his brother who had crawled through the gap. Connor followed reluctantly, not wanting to be left behind.

The room they entered was massive. Blazing candles burned on decorative candleholders embedded in the rock walls. A huge silver object sat across the room in the gloom and a crumpled figure was sprawled next to the spaceship. There didn't seem to be anyone else inside the room. Connor recognised the figure at once and his instinct was to run across the room towards Kia but Obi held him back.

'Careful,' warned Obi, searching the room for any sign of danger. 'De-ma warned us of a trap, remember.'

Instead, it was Bromie who moved slowly forward. Each stride was shortened as he walked towards Kia. Suddenly he crashed into something and staggered backwards, managing not to fall. An invisible barrier was preventing him from getting any closer to Kia, holding him at bay like a caged animal. He thumped hard at the invisible wall, feeling it quiver gently under his hammering fists.

'It's some kind of defence,' he growled in annoyance. Kia was so close but out of reach for him.

'Keep back!' Obi raised his sword and brought it down hard on the transparent barrier, but to everyone's horror the sword snapped clean in half. For a short time Obi stood dumbfounded. His sword lay broken by his feet. He couldn't understand it. In the past he'd slashed through the strongest rock and metals – nothing had withstood his sword. 'It must be some kind of magic, it has to be.'

'What is it?' asked Connor, in a timid voice.

'It's an invisible force field,' Bromie answered, running his hand across the smooth cool surface. 'Feel it. It won't harm you.'

Connor was about to reach out when a bizarre thing happened. Beyond the invisible barrier a loud cackle of laughter broke out, filling the chamber they were in. It sounded cruel and cold. Connor jumped nervously.

In manifesting spirals of mist, a ghostly figure, eight feet tall, appeared out of thin air and was floating inches above the ground. As the mist thickened, the figure became more solid. They could see a woman wearing a long black dress and a long cloak, which trailed along the ground behind her. She was facing them with cold eyes, lined with thick black eyeliner, like an ancient Egyptian replica.

She reminded Connor of Lidena, but she certainly wasn't a Palamore. She was different in many ways, including her height.

Her face was oval, her chin slightly pointed, with high angular cheekbones and mesmerising eyes. They penetrated into Connor's mind whilst searching for his weakness. He could almost feel her glance invade his thoughts, pulling the loose cobwebs aside as if her very fingers had entered his head. Without realising, Connor was soon lost, staring into the black pools of her eyes. He briefly wondered who this beautiful woman was. And soon he stopped thinking altogether.

Long wavy, black hair flowed down to her waist and fluttered gently from a breeze blowing around her. No words needed to be said. This woman was beautiful, more beautiful than anyone Connor had ever seen before. He stood mesmerised by her, as were Obi and Bromie, all staring helplessly. Connor had surrendered to her soft voice, which was in truth nothing of the sort but a spell or charm had affected his reality and what he saw and heard was a lie. It was an illusion.

Tookar, on the other hand, had kept his wits about him. Her voice wasn't disguised to him at all. It sounded nasty, hard and shrill with as much warmth as a frozen pond. When he saw Connor standing like a frozen duck he knew he had to do something.

'Connor!' Tookar urged, quietly whispering into his ears. 'Don't look at her. You must look away before it's too late!'

But Connor had no intention of looking away. Tookar's words made little sense. Something grabbed his face on both sides, squashing it as if his head was stuck in a lift and forcefully twisting it to the point where his eyes had to break off all contact. He stood breathing heavily, panting for breath, released from the spell. How could he have been so stupid? He could have kicked himself for behaving so irrationally. But it all made sense. The woman in front of him was Sheena. He now knew what De-ma meant about her powers to hold a person under her spell.

What had the woman done to him to make him so mindless of everything, including Kia who could be lying there dead? Sheena couldn't be trusted. But neither could he now. If he were meant to be under her spell, he'd still have to act like he was, until he could think of a plan to outwit this woman before him. Somehow, she had fooled them by powers of enchantment and thanks to Tookar he had escaped.

'Now, whatever you do, don't look at her!' Tookar warned him. 'She's working for Definastine and we can't afford to become his prisoners. For now just pretend you are under her spell. Look a couple of inches down from her eyes. That should help.'

'Hello child,' she said, tilting her head on to one side, looking straight at Connor. He turned to face her, but this time avoided complete eye contact. He was looking at the gap between her eyes to make it more convincing. It was difficult but he willed himself to do it. 'So you must be the child everyone is talking about. I understand you have the Starstone?'

'Nod your head,' Tookar urged quietly.

Connor nodded.

'Excellent,' she drawled. 'There's much I could do with the Starstone. I could become more mighty than Definastine, you know. By all accounts I don't see why he couldn't be my servant. I could control him. You must know by now he wants the Starstone for his own purpose. He wants to control everyone inside the universe. I, on the other hand, will be happy controlling a planet of my own, similar to this one.'

Connor listened intently. This was a turn-up for the book – Sheena was thinking of betraying Definastine. He watched her reaching her long index finger to her mouth to tap her lips while thinking deeply.

'I've been wondering about this dilemma for some time now. Definastine isn't here and it would be so tempting to disappear with the Starstone. Just think of what my name would be – Sheena the Sorcerer – doesn't it sound delightful? And with this vehicle behind me, I could take the girl and be off in another galaxy a million miles away. Yes, the girl will be useful for my plan to succeed. She will be my pilot. Everything has gone right so far, I only need the Starstone.'

She waved her hands in a large circular motion and floated forward through the invisible barrier, which had now disappeared.

Connor sensed a movement behind Sheena but refused to look away from her face. He had to pretend he was still hypnotised. He'd caught a glimpse of the tiara on her head when she had briefly looked away. It had a black stone shining in its centre.

'Connor!' Kia's voice called out. She was struggling to get up from the ground. Sheena spun round fast to see Kia finally standing up. She was taken by surprise.

'Oh, I see the little pixie has woken up, you must want me to put you back to sleep,' the woman said coldly, pointing her finger towards her but shrieked when Kia vanished.

'Anyone who picks a fight with my friends, picks a fight with me!' Kia's voice rang out. 'Wake up, Connor!'

'Fair enough.' Sheena temporarily ignored Connor and floated upward in the air looking all around her. 'I was going to use you but now your stupidity will be your death.'

Connor heard a snigger beside him but refused to look, he kept his eyes staring straight ahead, blank and emotionless like Obi. When did Kia learn to turn herself invisible? It didn't make sense.

'Connor!' Kia's voice spoke out once more.

'They can't hear you, dear,' Sheena smiled smugly, her eyes carefully looking around the room. 'No matter how hard you try to wake them, you will fail. I know it must be hard for you but they love me and will do anything for me!' A heartless laugh erupted from her red lips. Connor shuddered.

'They don't!' Kia screamed. 'They're under your spell!'

Connor knew if he were to help at all, he'd have to come up with a plan double quick.

'Who are you?' Kia asked hotly, almost spitting her words out. 'What do you want with us?'

'Ah, my dear, so impatient – but no, you're right of course, how rude of me not to introduce myself. My name is Sheena and I have been personally chosen by Definastine to represent him and all that he stands for, including his quest to find the Starstone,' she smirked. 'Only I don't think I want to play his little game any longer. I want what I deserve. Finders keepers after all.'

'Now why doesn't that surprise me, you... bog trotter,' Kia murmured.

'What!' Sheena snapped her lips tightly together. Her cruel smile disappeared in an instant.

'Where I come from we call a creature that dwells all day in the mud eating nothing but slimy insects – a bog trotter,' Kia's voice sounded from everywhere at once. Connor had to stop himself from laughing when he saw the redness on Sheena's face. 'Someone like you!'

Connor bit his tongue to control himself. He hoped Kia knew what she was doing. She was playing with fire at the moment and he didn't want to see her fingers get burnt. He grew worried. Kia had no chance fighting Sheena alone. But she wasn't alone. Tookar was somewhere. But where exactly Connor didn't know.

'Anyway my dear, I've had enough amusement with you, you must die now!' said Sheena peevishly. She raised her hands into the air, screamed hysterically and shook her head till it looked as if it would fall off her body. Lightning crackled from her fingertips spilling into the room until a silvery spider web was revealed. Her head turned in every direction. Whatever she had hoped to see wasn't there.

Connor felt the voltage rip through his body only to discover it was nothing but his own adrenaline. The lightning was loud and ferocious like a hungry lion ready to pounce on its prey. He quivered feebly, becoming quickly annoyed at his own weakness.

Sheena ignored Connor, much to his relief. 'Where are you?' she hissed, almost spitting, but received no reply. She grunted indignantly and snapped her fingers. Slowly the web of light came back towards her and formed itself into a big ball of blinding light.

'Daya Pickaro!' she uttered.

Slowly the ball of light began changing its shape, twisting and contorting into a hideous monster made entirely from light. It grew four times the size of Obi, with fangs and a mouth that would swallow a human in the blink of an eye.

'I want you to find the invisible girl,' she ordered. 'She's round here somewhere. Sniff her out!'

The beast roared in acknowledgement and began searching the room. Its thick long tail narrowly missed whipping Connor and his friends as it passed them. For something made entirely from light it moved heavily, with every step vibrating up through Connor's legs, making him quiver. Shuffling on two massive legs, it swung its arms with amazing grace for a beast that size. But Connor knew without a doubt that if the beast were to slam its fist down hard on him, he'd disappear into the ground. Equipped with huge claws and massive fangs, it wasn't a beast to pick a fight with.

After a thorough search and failing to find the girl, the beast returned to its master.

'Well?' Sheena snarled. 'She's here somewhere. I know it!'

The beast roared and shook its head adamantly.

'Aaaahhh!' Sheena snapped her fingers and the beast disappeared immediately.

Much to her annoyance Kia spoke close to her. 'So, he couldn't find me? And I'm not leaving without my friends.'

'Oh, but I think you'll find you will and very easily,' smiled Sheena slyly, reminding Connor of a cat ready to eat its prey after it has finished playing with it. Her long index finger, appearing much longer due to her extended black fingernail, pointed to Obi. 'Give yourself up or I'll kill this ugly giant.'

'No!' Kia shouted.

'You sound worried, my dear,' Sheena smirked.

'Should I be?' Kia replied as calmly as she could. 'Perhaps we could come to another agreement.'

'Certainly, my dear, just give yourself up and I'll let your friends live,' she began quietly, but with a steadily increasing tone she began screaming madly. 'For when I have the Starstone, I shall dominate the entire Universe and mind control the star-spirits everywhere so they succumb to me. Ha-Ha!'

Sheena straightened her posture once more and smoothed down her hair.

'Never!' Kia suddenly appeared in mid-air and flew towards Sheena, who was busily yawning. Sheena raised two hands up at

Kia as she flew through the air. Black smoke shot out at her and sent her reeling backward on to the far wall, where she fell on to the ground and lay unconscious.

Connor's heart jumped – was Kia going to be all right? He wanted to go to his friend but his feet refused to move. He could feel himself sweating. Something was going to have to be done before someone else got hurt – but what? And where was Tookar?

It was at that darkest moment when the comforting voice of the Starstone communicated directly to him. Words, inside Connor's mind, told him what to do.

Take her tiara and crush the black stone. This will release her from Definastine's grasp. Help set her free. If you break the stone, all power will be broken. I can help you but your thought is the deed.

Connor studied her tiara. The black stone was the size of a pea in the very centre of it. His thought was the deed. How was he going to plan this? What must he do? Was Sheena under Definastine's power, acting out his will? Why did she want to work against him now? More questions confused him as he thought of the best plan of action. He couldn't think straight. He breathed in deeply and tried to relax.

Ignoring Obi, Sheena turned her attention back to Connor.

'Well, my little darling, come closer to me,' she purred beckoning Connor with her hand. 'Come, let me study you.'

Connor moved closer to her. He could see her black painted lips and a floating beaded necklace levitating an inch above her shoulders.

Gracefully landing on the ground she stepped closer. This was his chance. As she moved close to him, Connor decided to take her tiara, just pull it free from her hair before she could react.

One… two… three… his hand moved quickly towards her head but to his surprise two tentacles reached out from two of the pearls in her necklace and held him firmly in their grasp.

'Ahh!' he cried out in pain as they tightened their grip around him.

'What!' Sheena screeched. 'How did you do that? How could you resist me?'

Connor imagined her tiara floating off her head and exploding in the air. His hands could do nothing but to his surprise, it happened exactly as he imagined it. While she was preoccupied with Connor, she failed to notice the tiara rise up from her head.

When she noticed Connor staring upward with his jaw hanging loosely, she looked up too.

'No!' she screamed. 'No!'

She flew into the air trying to grasp it but it flew faster than she could fly. Kia had suddenly woken up, reached out and caught it, holding it tightly in her hands.

'Looking for something?' she managed to say with a smile.

As she held the tiara, to everyone's surprise the black stone exploded into fragments so small they became invisible to the human eye.

'NO!' Sheena screamed, falling to the floor. 'NOOO!'

Obi and Bromie slumped to the ground the same time as Sheena fell, groaning and clutching their heads. They were released from the spell and very confused. Slowly they stood scratching their heads, desperately trying to figure out what had happened.

Connor rushed over to Kia and hugged her tight.

'We did it!' he grinned. 'We destroyed her.'

But to his surprise Kia closed her eyes and transformed into Tookar.

'Get off me,' he grinned. 'I really fooled you, didn't I? It was me all along.'

Connor opened his mouth wide in astonishment. 'Where's Kia then?'

'When Sheena was busy talking to you, I hid Kia safely behind the spaceship. Then I went back and pretended to be her. That beast couldn't find me because he was told to find an invisible girl and I had transformed myself into an invisible man. He went right past me.'

They rushed behind the spaceship and saw Kia stretching and yawning. Her body was covered in bruises but apart from that she seemed okay.

'Where am I?' she asked rubbing her bruises. 'What happened to me? I can't remember a thing.'

Connor grinned and hugged her. 'I'll tell you later. I think it would be a good idea if we got you out of here.'

'My ship!' she cried turning around to see her ship. 'I've found my ship. Or did it find me?'

'What's being going on?' Obi asked, drunkenly.

'Sheena wooed you,' Tookar grinned. 'She fluttered her eyelids and you started drooling.'

'I didn't!'

'You did!' Tookar replied. 'You need serious training when you go back to the AAA. You need to be taught not to fall in love so easily, especially with one as evil as her.'

Tookar turned and looked down to where Sheena lay unconscious.

'What happened to her?' Bromie asked. 'Is she dead?'

'I don't think so. I destroyed the black stone in her tiara,' Connor explained. 'It was controlling her.'

'How did you know that?' said Obi, wrinkling his head in puzzlement.

'The Starstone told me,' Connor replied, looking somewhat embarrassed. Hearing voices inside your head wasn't really a good way to prove your sanity.

'Huh?' quizzed Tookar.

'Well, I heard a voice inside my head. It was as clear as hearing you speak. It told me Definastine was controlling Sheena and if I should destroy the stone, she would be released from his power.'

Everyone began talking and chatting about their own experiences, explaining to Kia about the lost children and rescuing them. There was so much to be said in the little time they had. Kia was keen to leave and go back home. After a few minutes comparing stories, their conversations stopped abruptly when a golden light began to shine in the room.

'What's that?' Kia whispered, stepping back.

Everyone shrugged and watched in awe as the light lifted Sheena up into the air. She appeared to be resting in invisible hands as she turned gently in mid-air. Still unconscious she moved peacefully, like a swan on a lake. To everyone's amazement she began to change.

Her black hair was gradually replaced with golden locks. Her face filled out and radiated warmth. Her eyes opened wide, revealing golden pupils, and her lips became as bright as oranges. Her black gown sparkled with golden stars, eventually spreading until all the blackness had disappeared. She was lowered to the ground once more and collapsed on her knees. With her back hunched over her legs she didn't want to look up. She was utterly distraught and depleted. She held her face in her hands and began sobbing sorrowfully.

Kia looked the most surprised of all. She stepped forward slowly. Tookar tried to stop her but Kia shrugged him off. 'You poor thing,' she murmured, lowering herself to the floor so she was sitting next to her. 'You must be feeling terrible.'

She placed her arms around the woman and sat close to her, comforting her as best as she could. Eventually Sheena looked up at everyone with tears flowing freely from her eyes.

'I've been rescued from a terrible fate. How can I ever thank you all enough, especially when I almost killed you. Definastine has killed my people. He slaughtered my friends and family. I am alone now.'

'No, you're not,' Kia announced, fluttering her wings gently.

'Yes I am, dear child. I watched my entire race explode years ago – right in front of my eyes.'

'You're a Tria, aren't you?' Kia asked.

'Yes… but how… how did you know?' Sheena wiped her tears from her eyes and looked directly at Kia.

'There's a Tria on our planet called the High Priestess Serena Iona,' Kia explained. 'She thought she was alone too.'

Sheena's face lit up. 'I know her well. But how could she have survived? I watched helplessly as Definastine destroyed our planet.'

'She survived because she was travelling at the time,' Kia told her. 'She's made a life on our planet now but unfortunately she has become very ill.'

Sheena's face clouded over. 'It's because of me. When one of us turns away from the light it upsets the natural energy we all share.

Serena Iona must have been under tremendous stress because of me.'

'She knew you existed,' Kia explained. 'Well, not you exactly. But she knew another Tria must have survived for her to feel so ill. I came here looking for you – and my ship of course.'

'When Definastine tried to control me at first he found he couldn't, for some reason he found me very powerful. Now I can see why. Since he thought I was the only one, it would have been easier to dominate me. But because Serena Iona was still alive she was subconsciously helping me fight against him. But he proved too strong and soon I found myself under his control. Poor Serena Iona was fighting against the darkness I found myself in. She has been sick and unwell because of me. I can't wait to see her again. She'll be all right now.'

'So what now?' asked Connor.

'It's time to go home!' Kia smiled at Sheena. 'And you're coming with me.'

CHAPTER TWENTY-THREE

The Family Pet

Together they pushed the Hyas Transporter to the surface of Dramian. Tookar had managed to get the lift working once more by shape-shifting into a bird and flying up to where the rock dwellers had sabotaged the lever. Once the obstruction was removed the lift was working again, making their job a lot easier.

The cool outside air on their cheeks was a welcome relief. Connor removed his handkerchief and breathed in deeply. Sheena came over to speak to him.

'Do you know how strong you are?'

Connor gave her a nervous look and shrugged.

'You were able to resist my power. Not many people can do that. Do you realise your powers are stronger than Definastine's will ever be? It gladdens me to know the Starstone is in safe hands. Definastine will have a battle on his hands trying to defeat you. But I don't think you realise the true extent of your gift, you must learn to control your powers and use them wisely.'

'He sure will,' Kia grinned, walking towards them. 'You're a hero, Connor.'

'I only wish there were something I could do for you, for saving my life and delivering me from the cruel grip of Definastine. I was weak and Definastine eventually controlled me but not any more. When I see Selina Iona again, the two of us will fight him together.'

Bromie approached the small group. Connor sensed he was preoccupied with something.

'It's time to move out,' he said.

'Are you all right?' Connor asked quietly, following Kia and Sheena to their spaceship.

Bromie placed his hand on his shoulder. 'Yes, I'm fine.'

'I know something's wrong,' said Connor

'I'll explain to you later. Let's say our goodbyes first.'

They walked over to the rest of the group who were already saying their farewells.

'How far away do you have to travel, Kia?' Obi was asking her.

'Through several different galaxies. Don't worry, I know all the dimensional gateways to make it back safe. My ship has a map of all the galaxies. My brother and parents will be so anxious about me. I can't wait to see them again. Thanks for your help. My family owe you a great deal.'

'Does it frighten you travelling about by yourself?' Connor asked, positively sure it would scare him silly.

'No!' she laughed, flicking back her head of multicoloured hair. 'I've been space travelling throughout this universe all my life. It'll be fun to have Sheena as a companion to go home with me, the journey can be a little long and boring when you're on your own.'

'How old are you?' Connor queried.

'That's a very rude question to ask a lady,' Sheena smiled.

'Oh, I didn't mean to be rude!' Connor blurted out. Everyone laughed.

'If you must know, I'm several hundred years old according to your time but that's still very young on my planet,' she said smiling.

'You're having me on! Really?' Connor was amazed.

'No!' she answered him. 'It was a joke. I'm a few thousand years old really.'

'What?' he gasped. She didn't look any older than he did.

'You look good for your age,' Obi replied.

'Why, thank you,' she grinned. 'Anyway, we must move on. We're sitting ducks for Definastine if we delay any longer – you'd better leave too,' Kia warned everyone. 'Thank you all for everything you've done for me. I will never forget you.'

Kia hugged everyone affectionately, including Connor.

'I'm going to miss you. I only wish my brother could have had the chance to get to know you. Don't forget to carry that flower around with you. You never know, it might save your life one day.'

Kia placed her hand on her ship and a door magically appeared. 'No one can open it apart from me, not even Sheena,' she grinned. 'Bye everyone, I'm going to miss you!'

She entered her oval-shaped spaceship, which looked oddly like a bullet. Sheena followed her, waving her long arms delicately.

'Good luck!' Connor shouted as the door sealed shut behind them. At that moment something felt missing inside. He was losing a friend he'd probably never see again. It wasn't as if she was moving house to another part of England, after all.

With a quiet hum the silver spaceship rose up from the surface of Dramian, turned around and zoomed off into space. It didn't have any spectacular lights as it blended with the night sky, disappearing from view.

'Where did they go?' Connor gasped, searching the skies.

'Back home, my boy – back home,' Tookar smiled and slapped him on his back. 'Which is where we're now heading.'

'Come. It's our turn to go now,' Obi announced, lifting out a pen-shaped object from his hand. 'This is what is known as a bridge. It'll connect us straightaway to the AAA.'

'Why don't we go through that portal doorway like the lost children did?' questioned Connor.

'Because they went straight to the segregation unit, to have their identities checked and then they will have to go to hospital for a check up. When we use the bridge you'll be coming back with me to my quarters at the AAA. You'll be able to rest there without people harassing you for your autograph.'

'Oh, that won't happen will it?' replied Connor.

'You wanna bet?'

He watched Obi twist the tip of the bridge and suddenly a blue doorway appeared in front of them. 'Come on, let's go!'

'But what about Jeremy?' asked Connor. 'Has he been found?'

'A person is only found when they want to be,' Obi replied gently.

So the four of them disappeared off the face of Dramian, unaware that someone had been watching them – a figure slouched behind the stronghold walls, watching and listening to every word as he rubbed his hands excitedly. He muttered something under his breath before throwing some dust on the ground where a temporary portal appeared taking him directly to Definastine's castle.

Back at the AAA establishment, Connor was feeling strange. He'd just walked through the blue portal door into a chasm of blackness, where he discovered a blue path leading straight towards a purple door. It was scary. It had been a short walk but when they came to the purple light he walked right through it and found himself in a strange room.

'What happens if you step off the path?' Connor asked.

'I don't know, it's never happened to anyone I know,' Obi replied. 'This is my room, please make yourself at home, Connor.'

The room looked homely enough and was full of surprises. It seemed Obi had a remote control for everything. Connor slumped himself down on the leather sofa, feeling emotionally exhausted and drained. A massive five-foot television screen appeared as the walls parted opposite where Connor sat.

He sank down on the sofa and tucked his legs beneath him in order to get comfortable. He could hear the others talking, close to him, but their voices sounded far away as if they were in the next room. Connor closed his eyes briefly, not wanting to sleep in case he missed something.

'I'll be off now.' He heard Tookar saying. 'Thanks for the rescue. Keep an eye on Connor for me. I'll be back in the morning to see how he's doing. I'm off to check on Sparkie now. He was in a right state when I last saw him.'

'Okay, Tookar, we'll see you soon. Give Sparkie our regards and don't forget to take a rest too.'

Connor heard the door slide open and close again. That was the last thing he remembered before falling asleep and missing anything else that might have happened.

It was several hours later when Connor eventually woke up.

There wasn't a window in the room but the television was still on, though much quieter than he remembered it from last night. Someone had draped a blanket over his body and placed a pillow under his head, as he lay sprawled out on the sofa, with one leg hanging down to the floor.

He groaned as he stretched, and then gave a yawn. He saw Bromie sleeping on another chair. He opened one eye as he heard Connor stir.

'So, the hero has decided to wake up after all,' he grinned, stretching.

'What's the time?' Connor asked, feeling his stomach rumble.

'Ten o'clock on Saturday morning,' Bromie replied. 'Are you feeling hungry?'

Connor nodded. 'Definitely. Where's Obi?'

'He was feeling upset about his sword breaking so he's gone to get another one. He should be back later.'

'Bromie,' said Connor, 'you were going to tell me why you were upset yesterday. Is it a good time to talk?'

'Yes,' he replied. 'It concerns you.'

'What is it? What's wrong?'

He pulled out a shrouded letter from his pocket and handed it to Connor.

'Who's it from?' he asked.

'Read it and you'll see.' Bromie pulled out a parcel and placed it on the table. It moved as if in protest.

'What's that?' Connor asked. 'It just moved didn't it?'

'Yes,' Bromie smiled, 'read the letter, it should explain everything to you.'

Connor sat cross-legged on the sofa and looked at the letter curiously. He opened the envelope carefully, pulling out a piece of blue tinted paper. Holding it in both hands he watched as the letters on it unscrambled themselves into readable words. Although he'd seen a shrouded letter before it still astounded him.

The letter read:

Dear Connor,

Lidena was kind enough to pass on this letter and gift we wanted you to have. Be brave Connor. We're so sorry we can't be there with you now, but times are hard and unpredictable. Your father and I have been sent on an urgent mission to save a planet at war with Definastine. We have been asked to help them fight, so we have taken the best fighters to help defend their planet. We love you so much.

We were thrilled to hear the lost children had been found at last. Well done son, always do your best and don't be afraid. The Starstone will not let you down.

We will meet soon, and that's a promise,

Loving you always
Mum and Dad

P.S. We have sent you another family member. His name is Hank and although he tends to talk too much, he's very loyal to his owners. Try not to upset him as he may turn himself invisible and sulk (and don't leave him alone with food, he will eat you out of house and home in a couple of hours).

'Was this why you were upset?' asked Connor.

Bromie nodded. 'I know how much you have wanted to meet your parents after all this time.'

'It's okay,' said Connor, feeling surprisingly calm about the news. 'I've waited a long time to meet them. I think I can wait a bit longer.'

Bromie cheered up in an instant. 'Really? Well, that's good.'

'Do you know what's inside the parcel?'

'I've got a good idea. Most people have one in this place.'

'Do they?' quizzed Connor. 'It's a family pet apparently. It talks and turns itself invisible.'

'I think it will appreciate being unwrapped at last. It must be hungry. While you do that I'll go and rustle up something for you both to eat.'

Connor couldn't wait to find out what his parents had given him. He clutched the parcel and felt something moving and stirring inside. He wanted to drop it but curiosity made him hold on to it tightly. What was hiding inside the parcel?

He tore at the wrapping.

'Ahhh!' screamed Connor.

'Ahhh!' screamed an unrecognisable hairball.

On his lap sat a ginger and white striped, unrecognisable ball of fluff. Its mouth was opened wide with four rows of thin razor sharp teeth jutting out. Its eyes widened in shock and surprise mirroring Connor's expression, or vice versa. It seemed a long time they both remained rigid in the same position screaming their heads off without taking in any deep breaths.

'What's happened,' Bromie rushed back into the room.

'There's a – there's a – thing on my legs,' Connor stuttered.

'A thing!' the thing replied indignantly. 'I am *not* a thing! I am a frump called Hank.'

'It really does talk!' Connor exclaimed.

'So do you!' it squawked back at him. 'I've got no time for this lark. Are you Connor?'

Connor nodded stiffly.

'I am your entrusted guardian,' Hank replied proudly, lifting his little head in the air. 'I'm here to guard you. Your parents sent me to help you keep out of trouble.'

'Well I'm in plenty of that,' he said, scratching his head. 'Trouble seems to have a way of following me around.'

'Connor has never seen a frump before,' said Bromie. 'You'd better explain more about yourself.' He left them alone to continue with the food preparations.

'Your parents saved me from a nasty situation a few years ago. I was rescued from another galaxy. My owner enjoyed playing football with me!' Hank informed him sadly.

'But that isn't a bad thing. Boys at my school enjoy playing football with their dads,' Connor butted in.

'It is when you become the football. My owner had six legs and frequently enjoyed kicking me from one foot to another.'

Connor gasped. 'You poor thing.'

'I'm not a thing,' Hank reminded him.

'Oh yeah… sorry.'

Connor was delighted with his present. He couldn't help staring at him. Hank's eyes were the size of two golf balls, with small brown pupils. His mouth had temporarily disappeared beneath his fur, a huge contrast to the previous piranha imitation. Since Hank had calmed down he now resembled a guinea pig, being the same size and looking just as cuddly. Without warning Hank sat back on his bottom and folded his arms.

'Don't think about it cowboy!' growled Hank.

'Don't think about what?' asked Connor, looking somewhat confused to say the least.

'You're looking at me as if you want to eat me!' said Hank restlessly.

Connor started laughing.

'Your stomach is rumbling and you won't stop staring at me,' snapped Hank.

'I'm just amazed, that's all,' said Connor, still laughing.

'Oh, but talking about food – I love the stuff. Is there any going spare?' Hank asked bluntly.

Bromie came back with a tray of peanut butter sandwiches, crisps and fruit. Hank dived in straightaway. Bromie picked him up by his small tail so he dangled in the air, kicking his legs madly.

'What happened to table manners?' Bromie asked.

'When you're as hungry as I am, you'd forget too! Don't forget that I've been stuffed in a box for an entire night!' groaned Hank. 'Now put me down!'

'Only if you sit over there and don't move. I'll bring the food to you,' Bromie ordered.

Muttering under his breath, Hank went reluctantly to the chair and waited impatiently for a full plate of food. When it finally arrived, he ate it in seconds, including the plate. Bromie shook his head.

'You'd come in useful at school dinner times. I haven't been often but I hate the stuff they give us, it's always rubbery and cold but I bet you'd gobble it up, including the squashy green peas they insist on putting on every plate.'

Connor could tell Hank was excited at the prospect of going to school. He watched Hank jump off his chair and on to his lap, pinching a crisp on his way. He climbed up to Connor's shoulder and curled up, falling asleep immediately. Connor couldn't understand why he'd screamed at Hank before, because from where he was sitting Hank looked as cute as a little teddy bear.

A short time later they were joined by Tookar and Sparkie who looked much better than when Connor had last seen him. Bromie offered them some peanuts.

'His pride has taken a fall but apart from that he's okay,' Tookar informed them.

'I'll have you know there's nothing wrong with me that a wholesome pie couldn't fix. I only regret not saying goodbye to that lovely girl Kia,' said Sparkie.

'You weren't really up to saying goodbyes though, were you,' Tookar smiled. 'If I'd only known a pie would have woken you up, I'd have fed you one immediately.'

'Blah!' Sparkie grumbled.

The doorbell rang and everyone looked towards the door. Bromie pressed a button and a picture of Marion, K and Deana standing outside the room, showed on the television set. He pressed another button for the doors to open wide.

'Marion!' Tookar embraced her with a reassuring hug.

'My dear Tookar!' she said, kissing his cheek.

At that moment something was bleeping in Tookar's pocket. 'Excuse me, but I must take this call.' He walked quickly into another room.

Turning to Sparkie, Marion noticed his fragile state. 'Sparkie, whatever has happened to you? What's been going on around here?'

'It's a long story, and before you say anything, I've officially retired. How are you feeling?'

'A lot better, thank you,' she smiled walking over to Connor. 'And how are you?'

'I'm okay,' he replied.

K looked tired. 'It was a horrible night, until Sparkie informed us of Dad's plan to rescue my brother Daven. I didn't even know I had a brother. It's amazing. Except we haven't heard a word from him. And none of the children brought here was Daven. So at the moment Dad and Daven are still missing. I tell you what, it's made me realise not to take my friends for granted and not waste the precious time we have. I only wish Dad and Daven were here to witness me asking this wonderful woman for her hand in marriage.' He knelt down on one knee and grasped hold of Deana's hand. 'Deana, will you please marry me?'

Deana tightened her lips as tears came to her eyes. She nodded her head. 'Yes, K, I'll marry you!'

'Yippee!' K said, picking her up and spinning her round.

'Urgh!' grumbled Hank. 'Can't stand this mushy, lovey, dovey stuff!'

Ignoring Hank, Marion smiled and stood up to give Deana a hug. 'I'll be glad to have you in the family. I can't think of anyone better that K should settle down with. You've been with us and supported us through our darkest day and now, just as Jeremy would have wanted, you've lighted a candle in our lives.'

Tookar arrived looking much happier.

'I've just received some news concerning Jeremy,' Tookar announced. 'One of our men came across him by accident on Dramian. Jeremy had told him how he'd disguised himself as a child and was taken prisoner by the atropertries. He was brought to Dramian through the portal gateway. Once he'd made it to the other side, Jeremy transformed himself into a monster and killed the little devils. Since then, he has turned himself into an insect and is currently surveying the area. Apparently he heard news that a young boy with amazing abilities was being kept alive, especially for Definastine's use. This boy was different from the others. He was able to turn into different creatures.'

'Daven!' Marion cried out.

'It seems very likely,' smiled Tookar. 'But as this child isn't kept with the other children, Jeremy is trying to find out where he is.

He passed on a message to you as well. He wanted to say sorry for the pain he put you through. He only wished he could've made things right by bringing Daven home earlier to ease your pain.'

'He'll find him,' Marion beamed, her eyes misting with tears. 'My Jeremy will find Daven and we'll be a happy family again soon.'

There was much happiness in the room and as Marion sat back down next to Connor, she said, 'I understand your parents have been called away.' Connor nodded. 'Well, you'll be looking for somewhere else to live now since your entrusted guardians are receiving treatment here. I was wondering... would you like to come and live with me? I could certainly do with your company and all.'

'I wouldn't think you'd want me. I'm a liability now, what with the Starstone and everything. Bad luck follows me around like a bad smell. And it's not just me, it's Hank too!'

Marion chuckled. 'We've all suffered from bad smells from time to time and I don't think this little guy will be too much of a problem. But think seriously about it, Connor. I mean it. I'd love you to come back home with me.'

Before she could get all her words out, Connor threw his arms around her. 'I'd love to come and live with you. I really would. I can't believe you're asking me.'

'You'll be doing me a favour too,' she chuckled, nodding towards K and Deana. 'Can't imagine K wanting to live with me much longer, can you?'

Connor was laughing and shaking his head.

'Besides, you'll be able to keep me company while Jeremy is trying to find Daven. I only hope nothing awful has happened to him. Do you like apple pies?'

'Yes,' smiled Connor.

'Good, because I make the best ones in town.'

Marion stood up from the chair and said to K, 'I'm ready to go home, dear, will you take me back?'

'But mum, you know we can't go back home,' K said, looking concerned.

'Oh, I know that,' she said. 'While you were getting a drink earlier with Deana, someone came and told me our new home is ready and waiting for us, somewhere in a place called Hampton.'

'I didn't realise anyone had told you,' said K. 'Do you feel all right about it?'

'Look son, I've been living with an alien husband for thirty-six years, who went missing yesterday. It's him I miss, not the bricks and mortar. I would have left that cottage years ago if I had my way. Anyway they've taken all our belongings to our new home. All I want to do is get settled in now.'

'It looks as if it's time to say goodbye,' whispered Bromie. He pulled out the ointment from his pocket and handed it to Connor. 'Take this. You never know when you might need it. Perhaps I'll be seeing you soon, perhaps I won't. But don't forget me, will you.'

Connor gratefully took the ointment and placed it in his pocket where he suddenly felt the necklace Tookar had passed on to him from his parents. How strange it was to have forgotten all about it until now. It was a communication device to make contact with his parents. He vowed to try and speak to them as soon as possible.

'Thanks Bromie,' said Connor, 'for everything. I don't know what I would have done if you hadn't shown up on Dramian when you did.'

'It was a pleasure,' Bromie said, ruffling Connor's hair affectionately. 'Take care of yourself. You might as well arrive at your new home by using my bridge. I could dial up the co-ordinates right away. You'd be there in seconds.'

'That's lovely of you Bromie,' Marion smiled. 'After a hectic night here, I could do with getting home quickly.'

'Before we go, I was wondering if I could see my sister, Jenny,' Connor asked, looking hopeful.

Deana almost choked. 'Your sister Jenny? Jenny who?'

K was laughing and Hank was squeaking loudly.

'Who's Jenny?' said Hank, glancing at Deana and making a face.

'He asked the consulting mirror who his sister was,' Tookar explained, smirking gently. 'Tell them what you saw, Connor.'

'It showed me a room, where Deana, K, Marion and Jenny were. As soon as I saw Jenny's blonde hair, I knew she was my sister. She looks like the photograph I have of her.'

Deana was shaking her head, looking highly amused. 'And the mirror told you it was her?'

'Yes,' said Connor, but then frowned slightly. 'Well, not exactly,' he confessed, remembering how he'd specifically asked the mirror to focus on Jenny without using the word 'sister'.

Tookar placed his hand on his shoulder. 'Ask the mirror again, Connor. Ask to see your sister's face in the mirror.'

Connor rolled up the sleeve of his jumper, revealing the small, watch sized mirror.

'It's beautiful,' Deana gasped, glancing down and looking at it closely. Hank jumped on to Connor's shoulder for a closer look, his little claws digging gently into his skin.

'Ouch!' said Connor, frowning at Hank. 'Please show me the face of my sister.' Connor proudly lifted up his wrist for everyone to see. Deana was standing so close to it, all he could see was the reflection of her face. 'You're standing too close,' he said, moving backwards from her.

Deana giggled nervously and glanced at K, who was looking highly amused.

Her face was still looking up at him from his wrist. He tapped it several times.

'Please show me the face of my sister,' he repeated, but again Deana's face smiled back at him. 'It's not working,' said Connor feeling disappointed. 'Do you think it's broken?'

Marion, who was standing furthest away from the group, stepped forward. 'Someone put him out of his misery, *please,*' she said.

As the words died on her lips, he glanced at Deana and then towards the small image on the face of the consulting mirror. It was as if time itself had come to a standstill. Her face shape, her freckles, even her eyes were undoubtedly the same as the photographs he'd seen of her when she was younger. That was why the young girl in the picture looked familiar. But how could he have been so stupid as not to have made the connection until now? Her hair colour was different, but that was it really. Everything else looked the same.

When he'd first met Deana, he'd felt incredibly relaxed in her company. He felt as if he'd known her all his life. And now as she stood before him, he realised why he'd felt that way. She was his sister.

His body began tingling, filling with warmth. Her mouth was open as if to speak but no words needed to be said. An unspoken truth had been finally realised and brought to light. No present on earth could ever be better than discovering his sister was Deana. She had proven on more than one occasion that she was prepared to lay down her life for him. He thought she was just doing her job, protecting him. But it was more than that. She'd been there from the beginning to keep an eye on him, because she loved him.

They stood watching one another; each occupied with their own thoughts. Connor looked at his sister. Her eyes had misted over with tears of happiness. Connor welcomed her arms sweeping round his body, holding him tighter than ever before.

Kissing his head, Deana whispered, 'You silly sausage. Fancy thinking Jenny was your sister. Don't worry about anything. I'll always be here for you... always.'

Feeling safe and secure, Connor closed his eyes. If there was anything better in the world than having someone truly care for you, he was unaware of it.

The room came alive with cheering. Connor, grinning broadly, finally had hopes of a better life and this time with his sister. There would be no more demands from his aunt and uncle, no more demeaning tasks. Connor quickly buried the dangers he'd encountered, only yesterday, in the back of his mind. All thoughts of Definastine were temporarily filed away. But as Deana cuddled him affectionately, it was harder than he thought to ignore the niggling doubts that clawed away inside his body, constantly reminding him that dangerous times were far from over.